Also by Megan Bowen

<u>The Ravenwood Series</u>

Ghosted

Left on Read

Like Home

MEGAN BOWEN

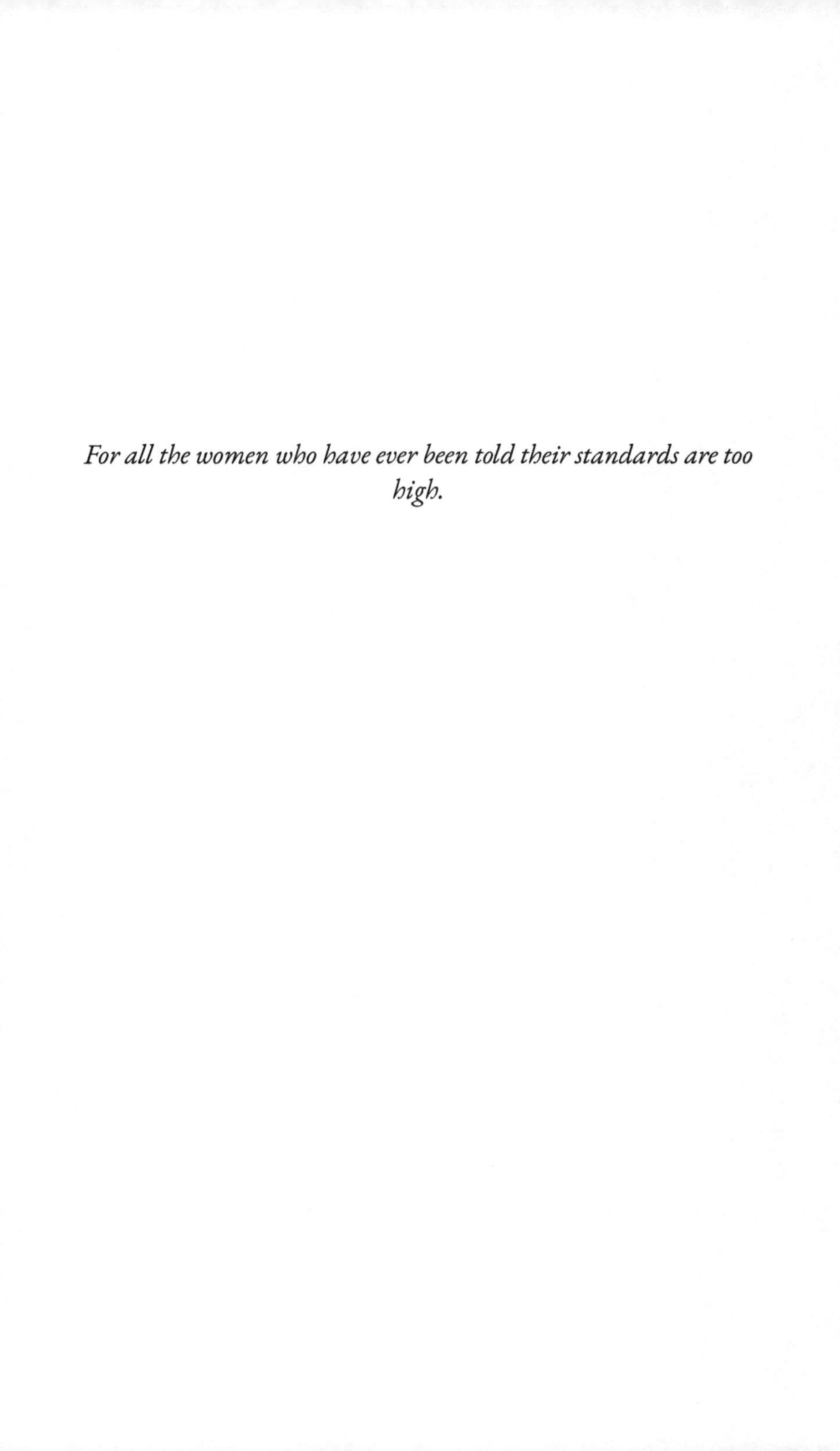

For all the women who have ever been told their standards are too high.

Author's Note

While Like Home has a guaranteed happily ever after, it does deal with themes that some readers may find difficult to read about. These themes include: Death of a parent (not on page), injured pet, sick child, explicit sexual content, explicit language, alcoholism, and separation of parents.

Like Home is the story of a plus-sized woman finding love. However, you will find very little mention of her body other than necessary descriptors. There are a couple of instances where her size negatively comes into play, but for the most part, her body is not a plot point. She does not go on a journey of self-love over her size, there are no descriptions of dieting, and it is not a point of contention for her romantic relationships. Her being plus-sized is simply a part of her. I was very intentional in the way I chose to write about it.

Like Home also deals with the intricacies of co-parenting and navigating new relationship dynamics with an ex who also happens to be the parent of your child. It was important to me (as a mother and as a child of divorce myself) to portray a co-parenting relationship in which the child (almost—looking at you, Jared) ALWAYS comes first. Summer and Jared can be toxic, but they always ensure that Emma doesn't feel that toxicity.

This book is for everyone, but it is especially for the girls who have never been a size two and who want to read a romance where the heroine looks like them. For the girls who want to read about a plus-sized lead without the book being *about* her size.

Despite the content warnings, Like Home is a relatively light-hearted read that aims to make you swoon and your heart swell. However, if any of the listed content warnings make you question your ability to read beyond this note, do what is best for you, always.

CHAPTER 1

Summer

I pull open the now empty drawer and contemplate what to fill it with. It's been seven years since I've had a dresser all to myself. The space now feels like a luxury. *Can I have a separate drawer for socks and one for underwear?* The thought pathetically excites me. It's been too long since I was able to single-handedly make decisions for my own space.

"Summer?" A gruff voice that I'm all too familiar with pulls me out of my underwear reverie. I snap the drawer shut with a hollow *thunk*. I take a second to look around the room and realize that despite a few empty drawers, the room still looks remarkably unchanged. The same sage green comforter, the same large window that lets in just a little too much light in the morning, the same mismatched furniture, pieced together over years of looking for good deals. It feels like the room should look completely different.

"Yeah, did you need any help?" I ask Jared, my very recent ex. It's been awkward while we transition out of the life we built together and into the new one. It feels a little like a new pair of shoes that need to be broken in. The heel chafes a bit, but you know if you walk around in them for a while they'll eventually fit the way they're supposed to.

"Nah, me and Duncan got the last of the stuff," he replies. I nod, giving him a tight smile. His best friend, Duncan, has always been a sore spot for us, and it seems fitting that he would be here to witness this final end.

"Okay." He sighs, running his hand through his short, dirty blonde hair. I used to thread my fingers through those same strands, and the act of him doing that reminds me of sharing first kisses in the halls of Lakeland High.

The memories make me wish that it could be different. That it didn't end this way. I wish we had gotten our happily ever after. Although, that wishing is kind of what got us into this mess.

"Okay. Well, I'm going to go say goodbye to Emma. Will you walk me out?" he asks. I nod and we leave our — *my* room.

"Daddy!" Our six-year-old daughter, Emma squeals as we get to her room down the hall. I lean a shoulder against the door jam as Jared walks in to hug her tightly. He pulls her onto his lap and sits on her twin bed, brushing aside the princess curtains that frame it. She curls into his chest, biting a tiny, pink-painted fingernail. "So, you're really leaving?"

"Yes, Em. Remember, Mom and I just talked to you about this? Daddy is moving into an apartment in town where you'll come to stay every other week. This week, you'll be with Mommy, and next week you'll stay with me," Jared says, brushing her long, strawberry-blonde curls out of her face.

She sticks out her bottom lip, a trick she learned could get her near anything from her dad, "I won't see you until next week?" That pouty lip starts to wobble with unshed tears. It hurts to see her hurting, but she'll have to get used to this. I know these first months will be hard, but I hope eventually it becomes second nature.

He looks down to see tears rolling down her cheeks. "Oh,

sweetie." He brushes them away with his thumbs. "I'm sure I can come by and see you a couple of times this week." He looks to me for assurance. I nod and step away, wanting to give them a moment alone.

I head to the kitchen and pour myself another cup of coffee in my favorite mug decorated with little painted suns. After dosing it with creamer and giving it a good stir, I take a sip, looking out the bay window of our breakfast nook. I'm only twenty-five, but in this moment I feel ancient. I guess that's what happens when you have a child so young; you're forced into a much older mindset, sooner than you're ready for. I feel like I've already lived a full life-time between having Emma who just started Kindergarten the previous fall and choosing to end my first and only relationship.

I take a seat at the small round table nestled near the curve of the bay window. This little bench that borders the table along the window has always been my happy place. I have multiple, thriving plants that hang in front of the large window and built-in book-shelves stuffed to the brim with books for myself and Emma along the sides. I turn to look out the window where Duncan is outside in his truck scrolling on his phone. I look away quickly when I see him shift in his seat before we can make eye contact. Duncan's dislike for me runs deep and I've never understood why.

All three of us have known each other since high school. Duncan and Jared were best friends, even then. When I joined their Spanish group project senior year and Jared took an interest in me, Duncan seemed to resent the time we spent together. Maybe he felt I was taking away his best friend, or maybe he didn't think I was worthy of him. Either way, he never moved past his dislike for me. It actually got worse when I got pregnant soon after graduation.

* * *

"I still can't believe you got her pregnant, man. You could do so much better than an overweight chick with daddy issues." My heart drops and I nearly drop my glass along with it. I hear Duncan's voice clearly through Jared's speakers on his gaming computer in the living room. It makes me stumble because even though they look very different, Jared and Duncan sound remarkably alike, especially when filtered through a speaker.

I have one hand on the doorknob of our bedroom and the other drops to my rounded belly. I'm currently eight months pregnant, and when I'm not working, I spend most of my time resting. I never thought this level of exhaustion was possible. I've pulled two all-nighters in a row to study for finals and still never felt this run down.

"Bro shut up. Like you can do any better," Jared retorts over the clicking of his keyboard. They're playing some sort of online multi-player like usual. The dulcet tones of rapid gunfire explode in the silence. I know that Duncan is Jared's best friend, but I can't believe that Jared wouldn't defend me. I feel the telltale burn in my sinuses before a tear rolls down my cheek. I quickly swipe it away, debating whether I should keep listening. It feels like an invasion of privacy, but I can't pull myself away.

"You know she's just baby-trapping you. She knows you're way out of her league and made sure you could never leave," Duncan sneers.

Just like that, he hits on my biggest insecurity. Jared was popular in high school. He wasn't much of a sports guy, but everyone liked him. Girls fell all over him and the guys wanted to be friends with him. He had that boy-next-door look and an easy charm that attracted everyone. He was muscled and tan from working on his grandpa's farm on the weekends and during the long summers between school.

I, on the other hand, was a debate nerd with a small group of friends. While I've never been shy, I also never had people climbing over themselves to be my friend – or boyfriend for that matter. I was a size 14 by the time I was fourteen, and as my curves matured, my size continued to tick up. With the extra height puberty gave me, my belly flattened out a bit, but I was still plus-sized.

"Duncan. Enough," Jared's voice suddenly has a rough edge.

"What, can she hear me?" Duncan's voice lowers enough that I have to press my ear to the cheap wood of the door to hear them.

"Nah, she's sleeping, but you shouldn't talk about her like that. I love her and she's going to be the mother of my child." Too little, too late, I think.

"Whatever, J. One day you'll realize what a mistake you're making."

* * *

I shake my head, dispersing the bad memory before it has a chance to grow claws. I never told Jared that I overheard their conversation, choosing instead to bury it. I didn't want the conflict when we would be having a baby so soon. Moving on wasn't hard to do, especially because Emma was born just three weeks later via c-section. The conversation got lost in the newborn fog and postpartum recovery.

I never forgot it though. With my insistence, Duncan didn't spend much time around me after that. From what little I've gathered of Duncan's past over the years, I know his parents were pretty awful and he doesn't seem to have anyone but Jared in his corner these days. I have empathy for the guy, but I don't want someone like that around my daughter.

Jared walks in scrubbing his five o'clock shadow, looking older than he is. "She's playing with her Legos now." He looks like he wants to sit across from me on one of the stools, but chooses instead to lean against the small island of the kitchen.

"Okay, good. Did it take you long to calm her down?"

He shakes his head. "I told her I would call her every night before bed and I'd try to come by and see her at least once this week. I hope that's okay with you." He grabs his canvas jacket from the bench and slides it over his shoulders.

"Yeah, that's fine. You know I don't want you out of her life. That's not the reason for all this," I gesture outside to Duncan's truck loaded with the last of Jared's boxes.

"No, I know. It's because I can't be your perfect romantic hero." He gives me a wry smile, but it doesn't reach his eyes.

"I never asked you to be perfect. I just wanted you to show me you cared. That you loved me, that you thought about me, even when I wasn't directly in front of you." I sit up a little straighter, the frustration a steel rod in my spine.

"I did my best, but it was never enough for you." His arms uncross and he grips the island at his back so hard, his tanned knuckles turn white.

"What part of never setting a date for the wedding, never doing anything for my birthday or our anniversaries, and never taking me out says you 'did your best?'" This is an old, tired argument, but we bait each other into it regardless.

His brow creases in anger even though I see a flicker of what might be remorse in his dark eyes. "I've apologized a million times for those things! Sorry I was working my ass off to make sure Emma was taken care of. I didn't have time for those things."

I roll my eyes. "I was working, too! I still never forgot to celebrate your birthday. I still tried to do things that interest you. Hell, I even tried to fix our sex life." I whisper the last comment, not wanting Emma to hear. "The point is, we both have a lot going on. We've both been stressed, but for the last five years, I'm the only one who's been putting in any effort." The anger deflates as quickly as it surged. I am tired of this argument. I take a deep breath and rake my fingers through my long auburn hair.

"I know," he says quietly, "I really am sorry. I never wanted to hurt you." He looks down at his feet, a line etched between his brows. His hands relax from their grip on the tiled counter and he shakes them out.

"I know," I echo his words, peering into my half-empty coffee cup. I sigh and change gears to something we can agree on, "Look, just call my phone every night at eight. I'll hand it over so you can talk to Emma. I don't want this to affect her any more than it has to. We have to work together for her."

He gratefully takes my opening to switch subjects, "On Wednesday, I'll bring her by to show her the new place and we can have dinner. I'll just pick her up from school and have her home by seven. Does that work for you?"

I nod, a small smile on my lips. Despite everything, I am so thankful to be co-parenting with him. He puts Emma above all else. We both want her to be happy. It's such a switch from what I had growing up. I know firsthand how much separation can mess a kid up. I'm determined to make sure pick-ups and drop-offs don't include shattered kitchenware and threats spit between angry lips. I won't repeat the cycle.

He looks around the kitchen one last time, his jaw working. I wonder if he's taking stock of everything he's improved in here. The utensil drawer with its replaced track, the new hosing for the dishwasher, the replaced faucet.

Even though he's technically just moving into his apartment today, he's been sleeping in the guest room for the last month. He's also been out as often as possible, either working more overtime or out with Duncan. This hasn't felt like his home in a while, but today makes it more final.

I stand, ready to get this over with. "Okay, well, call me if you need anything. Maybe some decorating help so your apartment doesn't look like a total bachelor pad for Emma's sake."

He rolls his eyes with a smile. "Will do. I'll call at eight tonight. See you later?" He starts to head for the front door.

"Sounds good," I say, going to the door behind him. I watch him jump into the passenger seat of the truck. I wave goodbye as he closes the door, the midday sun glinting off the window and hiding him from view. I blow out a breath and lean against the door, yanking the sleeves of my shirt down to cover my hands from the early spring chill. I feel proud that I'm not repeating my parents' mistakes, but nervous all the same. *Now my new life begins.*

CHAPTER 2

Summer

My first week as a solo parent flies by. Between work and the daily school, gymnastics, dinner, and bedtime routine, I am so exhausted that I fall asleep the second my head hits the pillow. I don't even have time to escape into my romance books. Being a single parent has rocked me in ways I wasn't prepared for. Jared may have made for a shitty partner, but he has always been a good dad. We split the parenting duties in a well-coordinated dance that we perfected over the years. I hate to admit it, but doing this without him is hard.

It's Friday night, Emma is in bed, and I finally have a chance to sink into the couch with a book. I toss my checkered throw blanket over my lap and crack open my new billionaire romance. Sipping on my glass of wine, I get through almost half of the story before my eyes are too heavy to continue. It's almost midnight by the time Gabi tells Lucas that she won't be coming with him on their "business trip" to Europe, and I realize I need to get to bed.

I rinse my wine glass in the sink before going down the hall. On the way, I peek into Emma's room to make sure she's still sleeping. It's a habit I think I'll have until she moves out. I move on to my bedroom and set my book on my nightstand. I can never be too careful with where I keep my most spicy books now that Emma is advancing beyond the beginning stages of learning to read.

As I change into comfy pajamas and brush my teeth in the harsh overhead light of the bathroom, I contemplate the book I'm reading. Lucas is a big fan of grand gestures. Giant bouquets dropped off on Gabi's doorstep, buying her the expensive coat she was eyeing when they went shopping for his assistant together, a loosely disguised business trip to Europe, just because she said she'd never been.

My heart swoons at the thoughtfulness of it all. It breaks a little too. I never expected Jared to do anything like that, but I just wanted him to show he cared about me. I wanted him to shoot me a text when he was at work to tell me he loved me, maybe pick up my favorite candy when he was at the convenience store, or take me out on a date every once in a while.

When Emma was a baby and I was at home with her, I started reading to pass the time, and I quickly discovered romance was my favorite genre. They were easy to read, sweet, ended happily, and provided a reprieve from the daily grind of motherhood.

At first, I would roll my eyes as the hero went above and beyond for his love interest, thinking that no man would do such things. Once men had you, I reasoned, they grew content and stopped trying. I thought I was okay with that. I thought I was in the know like the rest of the women before me who had settled for what their partner was willing to give. But the more I read, the more I started to realize that I deserved passion and to feel valued. While I never expected Jared to pull the same stunts as the men in my books, I wanted more than just the promise of love on the tip of his tongue while his eyes looked past me.

I started bringing it up to him. I wanted him to show me that he loved me. He insisted that his words should be enough. He shouldn't have to prove himself.

Over the last few years, it's been a constant back and forth. I would try to encourage Jared to do things with me. I offered everything from going on a date to finding video games we could play together. He would go along with it for a week or two. I'd think things were getting better. Then, he'd fall back into his old routine, playing video games with Duncan every night after Emma went to bed, forgetting to kiss me goodbye in the mornings, being too tired for sex. And so the cycle would continue.

At some point, he started to pay attention to what I was reading and that's when the arguments really took off.

*   *   *

"Love Me Like You Hate Me. Summer, what is this?" He bursts into our bedroom and holds up one of my latest romance purchases like it's covered in filth. I feel my cheeks redden as I snap my eyes up from my aimless scrolling.

"It's a book, Jared. You know I like to read."

"Yeah, but it's so trashy! I skimmed through it and I can't believe you read this junk." He scrunches his nose and tosses the book on the bed towards me. "Is this why you've been all over me lately?" He's going for teasing, but the disapproval is rolling off him in toxic waves.

I turn even more red, wishing the bed would open up and swallow me whole. I try to think of a way to explain myself, finally saying "It's not just the sex that draws me to them, you know. It's the romance of it. Not all of the books I read have so much sex in them. Most of them are really sweet, and the focus is on falling in love. They both do everything they can to be together and prove that they love each other."

"What, our life isn't good enough? Our sex life isn't good enough? Do you have to read about fake couples to be happy? You read all the time, every day. Any spare moment. Are you really trying to escape our life that bad?" He sits on the corner of the bed and faces me, his arms crossed over his chest.

I look down and pick at the pills on our comforter. "It's not that our life is bad, it's just that... I don't know Jared. We're only twenty-one for fuck's sake and we already act like an old married couple. When's the last time we had sex or even went on a date?"I finally look up to meet his eyes, hoping he sees that I'm not trying to hurt him.

"We have Emma! It's not like we can go out every night with a two-year-old running around," he argues.

"I'm not asking for every night but even just once a month would be nice. We could have your mom watch her for us and we could go out for dinner or a movie."

"We can do that. Why is it my fault that we don't?" he retorts.

I sigh. "It's not just your fault. We both should be doing more. But you can't play video games every single night when we could be spending time together and expect that I'm going to be happy with that. I wouldn't mind if it was a few nights a week, but I feel like you don't even want to spend time with me." I feel tears well up in my eyes and my nose burns. I just want to feel wanted.

He comes to sit beside me and wraps an arm around me, squeezing me to his side. "I do want to spend time with you. I'm sorry. I'll make more of an effort. I just got caught up in the new game with Duncan lately. Why don't I call my mom tomorrow and ask if she can watch Emma for us on Friday night? We can go get dinner and *a movie." He kisses my temple and continues, "But, Summer, you can't compare me to those guys in your books. They aren't real. I doubt there's a single guy alive who acts the way they do. You know I love you. You shouldn't need some big gesture to tell you that."*

I nod because at least we'll be going out on a date this week. Maybe things will get better. Maybe he's right and I need to let this go.

* * *

They did get better. For a week or two, Jared would text me that he loved me out of the blue, bring me home flowers, and we went on a date ending in mild-mannered sex that only left one of us satisfied. Then, once he felt he had done enough, he was back to his old routine. Wash, rinse, repeat.

I get into bed, turning off the bedside lamp as I do. As I stare at the ceiling, dappled with silvery light from the full moon, I wonder if I've made a mistake. Maybe Jared was right. Maybe no one will ever love me the way I want to be loved. Maybe I should have just been happy with what he offered. I roll over and try to banish the thought.

* * *

Late Sunday morning, Jared comes by to get Emma. I spent the morning helping her pack her sparkly gymnastics bag with all the necessities for a week spent with her dad. I know he got her the basics so she wouldn't have to cart her entire life back and forth, but a week's worth of clothes, toys, gymnastics gear, and her favorite teddy have the bag stuffed to the brim. I had to have Emma sit on it just so I could zip it shut.

Jared slings the bag over his shoulder and carries it out to his truck. I pull Emma in for a hug and kiss the top of her head. I look up and blink to diffuse the tears that are threatening to spill. This will be the longest I've ever been away from my daughter. I never wanted her to go through this. I never wanted to have to be without her. "Mommy, why are your eyes shiny?" Emma looks up at me, concern marring her little brows.

"I'm just sad because I'm going to miss you, sweet girl. You're going to have such a good time with your dad though, okay? Don't worry about me. I'll be just fine." I squeeze her for emphasis.

"Are you sure? Maybe Daddy and I can stay here with you so

you won't be lonely." She pouts, trying the same tactic that she uses with her dad.

I let loose a wet laugh. "No, Emma. There's no need for that. Your dad has his own place and this is mine. You're so lucky because you get both!"

"Why can't we all have the same house anymore?"

"Because, baby girl. Daddy and I have decided that this is what's best for our family. You'll see. It's going to be even better than before." I stroke my hand down her long, tangled ponytail.

"If you say so." She sighs, giving me one last squeeze before she lets go. "Are you going to call me every night like Daddy does?"

We've already been over this, but I can tell she needs the extra reassurance. Anything I can do to make her more comfortable with this, I will. Even repeating myself a thousand times. "Of course! Eight on the dot. You and I will have dinner on Wednesday too." I help her into her daisy printed jacket and zip the front up. She can do it herself, but I feel a desperate need to make her feel taken care of.

"Okay, bye Mommy. I love you." Her chin trembles and it takes everything in me not to demand she stay with me. Not to throw my hands up and give in, welcoming Jared back. I roll my head to the side, popping the tension from my neck. I want to be the example for my daughter. I want to show her that it's okay to have standards for how you want to be treated. It's okay to walk away if they aren't met.

I smile and say, "I love you too, baby girl. I'll talk to you tonight."

She heads to Jared's truck where he's waiting to help her into her booster seat. I follow her out so I can say hello and goodbye to Jared. We've been doing a really good job of being civil and even friendly the last week. I don't want to be the one to ruin it. "Hey, Jared." I lean against the bed of the truck and shove my hands in the pockets of my sweats.

"Hey, Sunshine," he says with a boyish grin. The likes of which made me swoon as a teen. I roll my eyes at the old nickname. He knows I hate nicknames between couples. Anything more than "babe" or "honey" makes me wrinkle my nose. Ask me how I feel when I read my romance books.

"Jare-bear," I retort in a syrupy-sweet voice. His laugh booms from him in a way I haven't heard in a long time. I laugh too. There's an ease between us now that hasn't been there in years. When there's no pretense of a relationship, we get on well. I feel the thing that had been winding tighter in my stomach loosen. *This* is what I want for Emma. Amicable, friendly parents. We can do this. *I* can do this.

"I'll talk to you tonight, Sunshine," he says in farewell, shooting me a wink before touching my shoulder. He rounds the hood to the driver's side and I take a few steps back.

"Talk then," I say with a wave as I head back up the driveway to my little home. It's in a nice neighborhood on the outskirts of town. Definitely one of the smaller homes, but it works well for Emma and me. It worked well for my mom and me also when it was just the two of us.

My heart aches a little at the thought of my mom and the way I'm inadvertently following in her footsteps. I was so dead set against separation for years because I was scared just the act of it would turn Jared and I into my parents.

The melancholy grows as I realize I'll be alone for more than a day or two for the first time in my life. I went straight from living with my mom to living with Jared and Emma. I've never really been alone. I can't say I love the prospect.

* * *

It's late and I'm reading on the couch again to distract myself from the loneliness when I feel a drip of something cold on the top of my head. I look up in confusion. As I'm staring up at the

15

old water stain on the ceiling trying to figure out if I imagined the sensation of something on my head, another fat droplet hits me square in the eye. "Ah!" I exclaim, standing quickly and wiping at my eye.

"I swear, if I get pink eye I'm going to kill Jared," I grumble to myself while I scurry to the kitchen to grab a large bowl. I push the couch out of the way and place the bowl directly under where the drip almost took my eye out.

Tonight is the first time it's rained in a while, and of course, it's supposed to pour for the next few days. The last time we had a storm like this, it leaked in the same spot. Jared told me he would fix it and since it hasn't rained since then, I thought he had. California isn't exactly known for its rain, so it's been a while since our last storm.

I look at the clock and see that it's just about eight, so I pull out my phone to give him a call. "Hello," he answers after a couple of rings. I can hear Emma splashing in the tub in the background.

"Hey, Jared. I know I'm calling a bit early, but I needed to talk to you before I talk to Emma."

"Oh, sure," he says with trepidation, "What's up?" The sounds of Emma's splashing dims as he moves away from the tub.

"Well, the roof is leaking again. Same spot."

"Shit."

"Yeah. So, listen, did you ever try to fix it?" I ask.

"I meant to look at it sooner. Sorry. With us– with everything going on, I just forgot. Hold on, I was going to call a local contractor to take a look. My coworker, Ben, gave me this guy's card after he and his wife redid their bathroom. I think it's still in my wallet. I'll take a picture of it and send it to you." Rustling invades the quiet as he pulls out his wallet and shuffles through the contents. Within a minute my phone vibrates with the picture.

"Okay, thanks. Don't worry about it. If I get pink eye though, you're footing the bill."

"Pink eye?" he asks, confused.

"Never mind," I laugh, "Listen, is Emma done with her bath yet? I'll say goodnight if she is."

"Yeah, she's just getting out now. I'll let you FaceTime her while she finishes getting ready." He video chats me and I spend the next fifteen minutes chatting with my daughter as she brushes her teeth and gets comfy in bed. Despite the motion sickness that comes along with a six year old handling a phone, my heart aches so hard, I have to rub the spot to ease it.

CHAPTER 3

Summer

The next morning I get ready for work, putting on slacks that compliment my curves, nipping in at the waist and flowing over my lower belly. It wasn't a point of contention for me until I had my c-section. After that, it never looked the same and became one of my biggest insecurities. I pair the slacks with a top with an asymmetrical neckline and my favorite heels for work. I check myself in the mirror one last time, making sure everything is in place and that I didn't forget to put mascara on like I've been known to do.

Before leaving for work, I dump out the half-full bowl of water and replace it under the drip. I really hope that someone will be able to come out soon and fix the leak. I shudder to think of the mold moisture like that could grow. I vow to give them a call on my lunch break. I grab my bag, coat, and umbrella before going through the door to the garage.

Despite the rain, it's a quick drive to First Bank of Lakeland. One of the biggest perks of living in a small town is that it only takes a maximum of fifteen minutes to get anywhere. I push through the door, hook my umbrella on the stand that's older

18

than me, and go to greet the only coworker here before me today, Sherry.

Sherry has been a teller at FBL for nearly thirty years. The job satisfies her nosy tendencies because you learn a lot about people when you're in charge of their money. We're usually the first to know who got fired, who's getting divorced, and if someone is moving or making a big purchase. If you pay attention (like Sherry), you can put all the pieces together to form the picture of someone's life. She's the one who trained me when I first got hired right after graduation. I wave to her before I set my things in the break room and head to my station.

"Hey, doll!" She gives me a quick, pearly white smile and turns to her computer where she's pulled up a game of solitaire, smacking soundly on the ever-present gum in her mouth. She used to be a smoker, but the oral fixation never went away, so she always smells like classic Hubba Bubba mixed with Chanel No. 5.

I turn on my computer and get my station set up for the day. Being a bank teller isn't a glamorous job, but it's one I enjoy. I love the routine and the fact that I get to chat with different people all day.

Mark and Rachel, my coworker and boss, burst through the door and we all work on getting the bank ready to open by nine. I switch out our promotional posters hanging in the large front windows and finally manage to take down the Easter decorations that have been hanging around for too long. I stuff them into the decorations bin in the storage closet and mourn the empty look of the bank. Even though the Easter decorations were a little tacky in the way they always are in corporate environments, they provided a break from the boring but practical beige color scheme. Soon, Mark flips the sign to 'open' and the first customers wander in.

By twelve, I'm just about ready to take my lunch when I hear the door jingle cheerily to herald the arrival of a customer. I paste a bright smile on my face and use my best customer service voice before even looking up from the loan application I'm going over.

"Hi! Welcome to First Bank, what can I do for you?" My smile falters as I finally look up to see the most gorgeous man I have ever seen in this small town walking towards me. I blink and renew the smile that slipped, not wanting to obviously ogle the man.

The first things I notice are his striking green eyes that peer out from under a ball cap pulled low over his brow, and his dark brown hair trying to escape the confines of his hat. The next things I notice are his broad shoulders, narrow waist, and big hands. I try my best not to swoon. I'm a hand girl, what can I say? "You're new," I blurt out. It's a small town, so I'm pretty sure I would have seen him around and I definitely would have remembered him.

I'm silently thanking God that Sherry is on her break and that it's her turn to grab food for everyone before the weekly meeting. She would be incorrigible around this man.

His answering laugh is low and smoky and delicious. He says, "You can say that. I grew up around here but moved away freshman year of high school. I just got back into town." He approaches my station and leans forward just a bit, resting his hip on the counter. I inhale and smell a whiff of something warm and spicy that makes me want to lean in closer.

I right myself when I realize I'm leaning over the counter like a plant starved for sun. "I've lived here my whole life. Never got to see much outside of Lakeland, but I can't complain. It's a good place to live. What brings you back?" *Be normal,* I command myself.

"Work, actually. I'm a contractor and found a job working under Davidson Construction here in town. I was sort of traveling around, doing odd jobs here and there, and wanted to settle down somewhere. My sister is also close by in Springview, so I figured Lakeland was a good place to set down some roots. It's got the perfect small-town feel. I missed it."

I tilt my head, the name of the company sounding familiar, and ask, "Davidson Construction?" He nods and I pull out my phone to look at the picture Jared sent me last night. Sure enough, that's the name of the business he gave me. "I was actually just about to call you guys on my break. I have a leaky roof issue that I was hoping to get fixed soon."

His brow creases with concern. "Is it bad?" He leans in like I'm holding a secret hostage behind my teeth and he wants to find out what it is.

"Not terrible, but I'm having to use a bowl to make sure it doesn't ruin my furniture or floor. I'm more worried about it getting worse. It's an older house and not much work has been done since it was built." He nods and opens his own phone, tapping around on the screen for a while.

"I have an opening at three today. Does that work?" he asks after a minute of silence. *Oh.* I blink.

"You're going to come check it out? Not Dan?" Dan is the head contractor and business owner, and whose card I have a picture of.

"Yeah, Dan has a full schedule today, but I'm free." He seems to go a little red under the shade of his hat. "Unless... Unless you want to wait for Dan. He might have something later in the week. I get that I'm new, so you might be more comfortable with him since you know him." He scratches his bearded cheek.

"No!" I exclaim. Then, more calmly I say, "I mean, no. I don't know him either. A, uh, friend gave me the number, so I'm not loyal to anyone in particular. I'll have to leave work a bit early, but it shouldn't be a problem." I smile in a way that I hope reads more reassuring and less serial killer.

He smiles warmly in reply, showing off straight white teeth. "Great. Can I have your number and address? I'll need it to bill the job." I rattle off both as he inputs them into his phone. He glances up at me and seems to look directly at my chest which quickly flushes red. I hear him mumble, "Summer," and realize he was looking at my name tag. I suddenly feel ridiculous for assuming he was looking at me with anything more than professional curiosity.

"My name is Ryan by the way." He sticks his hand out with a grin.

I grip his large, warm hand in mine and give it a solid shake. "Summer," I offer, even though he just wrote it down. He's still smiling at me, holding my hand in his for a beat longer than normal when I gently tug it away. "So what brought you in today? Aside from getting a new customer," I joke.

"Right, I definitely didn't just come in here to meet the pretty bank teller." He looks at me and winks. Before my brain has a chance to process that information and reboot, he says, "I actually came in to open an account. I wanted to set up a direct deposit with work as well."

I carefully sidestep the 'pretty bank teller' comment because I'm sure he flirts with anything with legs. He's the most handsome man I've ever met, but that doesn't mean I'm going to fall at his feet over a single compliment. I have at least one morsel of self respect currently fighting for dominance.

"Okay, let me get that started for you, Ryan." After a few clicks on my computer, I print out the forms for him and show him where to sign.

"Thanks so much. I'll see you at three?" He backs up, rolling the papers before shoving them in the back pocket of his worn jeans.

"Yes, see you then. Thank you for doing this on such short notice," I say, happy that this is one more thing I'm getting ticked off my list.

"No problem. It's supposed to rain the rest of the week, so we should probably get it looked at sooner rather than later." He gives me a wave while opening the door, letting in the heady scent of Petrichor. "Bye, Summer."

CHAPTER 4

Ryan

I step out into the rain, leaving the shelter of First Bank of Lakeland behind. My heart is still thudding irregularly from meeting Summer. I thank whoever is listening that her roof is leaking, giving me an excuse to see her again.

Even though I spent a good chunk of my childhood in this town, I don't think we've ever met. There are a few grade schools and middle schools that all filter into the same high school, but since we left at the very beginning of freshman year, I doubt I ever got the chance to bump into her. I feel certain I would have remembered her.

Driving through Lakeland brings back so many memories. I've only been in town for a week and most of that time was spent unpacking and getting my house livable. Frequent Target runs with my sister, Layla, to get all the essentials marked the days I had free before I started work last Thursday.

After having her son, Hudson, a few years back, she'll take any excuse to get out of the house. I appreciate her readiness to help me make my place a little more homey because without her it would have been the stereotypical single man's house. Not a picture frame or throw pillow in sight. She even convinced me to buy a blanket for the couch and a floor lamp to use instead of the overhead lighting.

On my way back to work, I pass my old karate studio where I spent every Thursday in sixth grade learning how to kick the shit out of other kids. I snort at the memory of accidentally kicking my friend, Luke in the mouth and knocking his already loose tooth out. Safe to say that was the end of my karate career. Maybe one day I'll have a little Ryan who will be better at karate than me.

One of my main reasons for moving to a small town like Lakeland and ending my nomad days is to finally feel settled. I miss having a sense of community and solid friends. I miss real relationships and putting forth actual effort because I know I'll see them for longer than just a month or two.

I had a good time moving from place to place and it satisfied my desire to see more of the world and meet new people. When my then-girlfriend, Lydia, went to complete a master's degree abroad, I figured I might as well take the time to do some exploring myself.

I always thought that when she was done, she would come back to me and we would make a home together somewhere. Didn't exactly work out that way. As I pass through the small town of Lakeland though, I'm sort of glad it didn't. Lydia was never one for pastoral backdrops and felt more comfortable being dwarfed by skyscrapers, so we never would have ended up somewhere like this. This place is idyllic and quiet. The mountainous backdrop doesn't hurt either.

Once I get back to the office, I do the last of the administrative work I need to get done for the day. Really, I'm just puttering around until I can leave for Summer's place. Being that I just got started here, it probably isn't the best idea that I moved a new client of mine to tomorrow to make room for her in my schedule, but I couldn't resist.

I try to justify it to myself: a leaking roof is more of an immediate concern than new overhead lighting for Mr. and Mrs.

Webber. I know that Dan won't actually care. When he hired me, he knew that I had been working independently for the last few years, so he promised to be mostly hands-off as long as I got things done.

It finally hits 2:45 and I can't wait any longer. I grab some of the tools and materials I think I'll need for the job and head out into the rain again, pulling the hood of my sweater up to shield my face from the storm.

After putting Summer's address into my navigation app, I hit the road. While driving to her house, I realize she lives fairly close to me. I could walk from my house to hers in ten minutes or less. I choose to ignore how happy that makes me when I park my truck. I need to remain professional. She didn't seem to enjoy the compliment I gave her at the bank. For all I know, she's married with a bunch of kids. Didn't see a ring though. I grunt in annoyance at myself before hopping out of the truck and into the cold rain.

While I grab my tools, she swings into the driveway in an older, red Honda Civic that looks like its heyday was sometime in the late nineties. She waves through her window and pulls into the garage. I shut the tool bag and can't help but stare as she gets out of her car. It feels like she gets out in slow motion; her heeled foot slinking out and the rest of her shapely body following it in a serpentine motion.

She bumps the car door closed with a plump hip and for some reason, I find the move mouth-watering. "Come on in! You're getting soaked," she calls from inside the garage. I hustle towards her because she's right. I'm drenched. I was standing there in the rain drooling over her like an idiot, and now I'm paying the price. She kicks off her shoes just outside the door that leads inside and I step into my boot covers. We walk into her kitchen and I set my tool kit on the small island countertop.

I take a second to look at my surroundings. The kitchen is definitely an original build, probably early 2000's judging by the worn tile countertops and the honey-colored cabinets. The kitchen is a bright white, and the bay window to the left lets in a lot of natural light. She has plants and books taking up all the real estate on the window ledge. I can just picture her curled up on the built-in bench in that breakfast nook with a cup of coffee and a book. It's a cozy space.

"Sorry, I hope I'm not dripping on your floors," I say sheepishly as I realize my hair and tool kit are, in fact, soaked and forming a steadily growing puddle on the linoleum floor. It's raining so hard it soaked through my hat.

"Well, I doubt you could do much more damage than that damn leak." She points a finger toward her living room where furniture is pushed around in odd places.

She opens a drawer and pulls out a kitchen towel before handing it to me with a smile. "Here you go," she says, motioning to my dripping face.

Damn, but she really is pretty. She has bright hazel eyes that are offset by her fiery hair and a constellation of cinnamon-colored freckles dot her face and chest. Without permitting them, my eyes trail down her body as I towel off. She's curvy in a way that almost feels sinful. I flit my eyes away, not wanting to creep on her in her own home. The last thing I want to do is make her uncomfortable.

I follow her into her living room, squinting up at the ceiling where a wet spot is forming inside a larger, dried stain. Her dark green couch is askew, her rug is rolled up and pushed aside, and the bowl catching the water sits in the middle of the floor.

My eyes catch on what looks like a family portrait on the wall next to the TV. "Is that your husband and daughter?" I ask, pointing to the framed picture hung on the wall. In it, I recognize a slightly younger Summer with an adorable pigtailed toddler on her lap. Behind them, a hand on Summer's shoulder is a blonde man who looks about Summer's age. He's smiling down at them adoringly. Lucky man. I try not to let the kernel of disappointment sprout.

"Oh, um. No?" I hear the question in her response.

I shouldn't pry into a client's life, but I can't help myself. I'm intrigued. "No? Is he your brother or something?"

"God, no!" She goes a little green and continues, "He's my ex and that's our daughter. Sorry. It's a pretty new breakup, and I'm still adjusting." She gives me a tight-lipped smile that shows me how uncomfortable she is with this conversation.

"Oh, got it. Sorry, didn't mean to pry. Cute kid." I want to throttle myself for making her uncomfortable again. "Do you have an attic access?" I quickly change the subject so I don't make it worse.

Not married, a devious voice whispers in my mind. *Not exactly available either,* I whisper back. It sounds like she just got out of a relationship. One serious enough to result in a child. She's probably not interested in anything but getting her leak fixed right now. *Why don't you find out?* I roll my eyes at myself as I follow Summer down a hallway lined with doors. She shows me the attic access and I head back to my truck to grab my ladder.

I quickly find the leak, head out to the roof to do the repair, and am finished in thirty minutes or less. I'm toweling off my hair again when I pause. This will be the last time I get to talk to her unless I have urgent banking needs or her house springs another leak. Her ceiling *could* probably use a fresh coat of paint. Maybe she has other repairs. I don't typically take such small jobs, but it's worth it to see her again. Reassured by my new plan, I finish drying off and head back to the living room.

Summer has changed into some cozy sweats and a thermal shirt that hugs her every curve. My mouth runs dry. "Fixed it?" she asks, popping up from the couch where she was curled up. She flips over the book she was reading so the cover rests face down on her coffee table. The corner of my lips twitch. My sister used to do that when she was embarrassed about what she was reading. Judging by Summer's cheeks turning a pretty pink, I'd say she was reading something *interesting*.

"Yeah, you're all good. I'd like to come back in a few days or so to check on it and make sure it holds up."

She gives me a relieved smile. "Okay, great. Thank you so much. How much do I owe you?"

For some reason, the thought of her paying rubs me wrong, "On the house. Don't worry about it. If it's a bigger issue when I come back, you can pay me then. You also might want me to paint your ceiling," I gesture up to the brown spot, made a deeper, uglier shade by the fresh water.

"Are you sure? I can't not pay you." She crosses her arms defiantly.

I hold up my hands, "I'm sure. It doesn't feel right to charge you for less than thirty minutes of work." I can be stubborn too.

"Is your new boss going to be okay with that?"

"I'll handle Dan. For the most part, we do our own billing. It shouldn't be a problem. The rain is supposed to stop by Friday, so can I come by Saturday morning? That way I can take a look at your attic once it's dry to make sure I don't see any mold forming."

"Yeah, that works for me. Can I offer you anything to drink before you go?" She moves towards the kitchen. It's always telling when someone offers me a drink or whatever while I'm working. I've had my fill of customers who act like I'm an inconvenience even though they're literally paying me to fix or install something for them. Kind people like Summer stick out.

"A bottle of water would be great, thanks," I say.

"Sure," she replies. I try not to stare as she squats down in her pantry to grab me a bottle. "Here you go." She hands it to me with a small smile. I chug it, realizing I haven't drunk anything since lunch. Thinking about her got me so derailed afterward.

A bead of water trickles from my mouth. When she shifts on her feet, I side-eye her watching it trail down my neck before disappearing under the collar of my black t-shirt. I try not to smile. I fail. She clears her throat, the hungry look gone from her eyes. "Thirsty?" she asks.

"Mmm," I respond nonchalantly as I recap the empty bottle and place it in a basket on the counter labeled 'recycle.' Thirsty in many ways it would seem. "So, I'll see you Saturday. Call me if you see it leaking again before then." I hand her one of my new cards with the Davidson Construction logo on the top and my information underneath. I need to get out of here before I do something inappropriate, like ask her what she was reading that had her so embarrassed before I walked in a few minutes ago.

CHAPTER 5

Summer

I close the door behind him and fan myself despite the cool temperature outside. *God he's hot,* I can't help but think. I know a crush on him would be useless right now. I have way too much going on and from the sound of it, he does as well.

I sigh and return to my newest book boyfriend, Raj. Tall, dark, handsome, and, most importantly, fictional. Raj won't be breaking my heart any time soon. I blush just thinking about the scene I was reading when Ryan came down the hallway. Raj was just about to have a *very* interesting meal. I snicker at myself before avidly returning to the scene, getting lost in a romance that isn't my own.

I'm so immersed in the book that when I get a text from Stephanie, my best friend, it completely startles me.

STEPH

Hey girl! How was the first solo night?

It was alright. Weird, and I miss Emma already, but I did it.

Proud of you. Do you want some company tomorrow night? We can binge Gilmore Girls.

It's not even Fall yet! You can't watch GG any other time of year.

Yeah, but it's your comfort show. You're sad, so screw the rules. It'll make you happy. I'll bring wine and chocolate.

Say less. Come over at 6? We can do dinner too.

Perf!

I set my phone down, smiling because Steph always knows how to cheer me up. She's been by my side since we were ten years old. Her family moved to Lakeland from Washington the summer before 5th grade. She and I got seated next to each other in Mrs. Alvarez's class, and after she complimented my fuzzy pencil case, we've been inseparable ever since. Not even a teen pregnancy got between us. I'm thankful for her. Aside from Emma, she's the only family I have left around here.

After work the next day, I make a stop at the local supermarket to grab some essentials for my *Gilmore Girls* marathon with Steph. Namely, junk food to eat in keeping with Rory and Lorelei. I grab pastries, popcorn, candy, and ice cream before browsing the fresh produce aisle. I decide to make a good salad for lunch tomorrow because I know my stomach will be protesting all the sweets if I don't.

I'm prodding the heirloom tomatoes when I hear, "Mommy!" I look over my shoulder and see Emma bounding toward me, the heels of her rain boots making loud *clip-clops* against the concrete floor.

"Emma!" I reply with the same level of enthusiasm. I set my grocery basket down and bend to scoop her up. Her little legs go around my middle and I hug her tight. I breathe in her scent - apple shampoo, sweet-scented lotion, and sweat from the school day. "Hi, baby girl. How was your day? Where's Dad?"

"Daddy is getting us chicken for dinner tonight. I saw you and he told me I could say hi."

She looks down– a maneuver I know means she's fibbing, but before I can ask, I see a harried-looking Jared appear from one of the aisles. His head is whipping around frantically. "Jared!" I call, waving him over. Relief washes his face clear of the stress that had been there moments before.

"Oh, thank God." He makes his way to us and scolds, "Emma Marie Forrester! You scared me half to death. No running off without telling me where you're going!" He bends over, hands to his knees, and blows out a breath. Emma hides in my neck.

I gently pull her back and look at her contrite face. "Emma, you lied to me and said your dad knew you were with me. That is not okay. Next time, you tell the adult you're with where you're going. It's not safe for you to run off."

"Sorry, Mommy. Sorry, Daddy. I just got real excited when I saw you. I wasn't running off 'cause I was coming to you, Mommy," she explains, tears welling in her eyes. She has always been a crier when she gets in trouble.

"Yes. But, Emma, I didn't know you were with Mommy. We both have to know where you are. It helps keep you safe," Jared says gently, his tone much more calm than before.

"I'm sorry!" She cries, fat tears rolling down her cheeks. On instinct, Jared and I both hug her. She's sandwiched between the two of us, Jared's arms around Emma and me while I'm supporting her weight. Over Jared's shoulder, I notice Ryan pushing a half-full shopping cart and looking at the watermelons.

I meet his eye and he gives me a wave and a small smile that looks nothing like the wide grin he gave me yesterday.

I pull my eyes away from him and disentangle myself from the hug, setting Emma back on her feet. I squat down to her height, cupping her soft cheeks in my hands. "It's okay, Emma. Now you know what to do if something like this ever happens again, right? You tell the adult you're with where you're going. Always," I emphasize. She nods and sniffles. I glance back to where Ryan was standing and find an older woman in his place.

"Alright, Emma, come on, let's go get our rotisserie chicken for dinner." Jared puts a hand on her shoulder. I nod at him before pulling Emma in for a quick hug and kiss on her cheek. They head off through the sparse crowd in the direction of the deli. I feel a pang of longing when I watch them walk away. It still doesn't feel real that I have to go days without seeing my daughter in person.

I do my best to shake off the sadness, pick up my basket, and rush to grab the rest of what I need. I don't want to be late and leave Steph hanging outside my house. I set my basket on the belt of the checkout line and put down the divider before grabbing an extra bag of spicy chips off the rack for Stephanie.

A velvety voice made rough with gravel says behind me, "Your daughter is adorable. How old is she?"

I turn to find Ryan behind me in line, unloading his groceries on the belt. "Thank you. She's six," I say, perusing the gum and candy above the belt to avoid meeting his eye. I don't know how to talk to him when we aren't working. Those other situations have a script. I know what I'm supposed to say, how I'm supposed to behave. When he's just choosing to talk to me like this, I'm an actor thrust on stage who forgot her lines and what she's supposed to do with her hands. To busy mine, I grab a pack of gum to gift Sherry. It's always better to be on her good side and small gifts are a worthy sacrifice.

"So, was that the ex?" he asks casually, his eyes on the groceries he's lining up on the belt. I note that he's purchasing my favorite snack, sea salt kettle chips, and am strangely pleased that we have something in common.

"Yeah, that's Jared," I say while we both step forward in line when the customer ahead loads her bags and heads out.

"Hi, how are you?" I greet Anthony, the cashier. He has the sort of face where you can't tell his age. Around the holidays when the store gets busier, he could be in his sixties, but tonight when he can work at a leisurely pace, he might be just past his prime.

"Hey, Summer. Can't complain," he replies. He's been working here since I was a kid, so he feels a little like an honorary uncle with how often I see him and the fact that he's watched me grow up. "What's this I hear about you and Jared?" I roll my eyes. Cashiers are just as nosy as bank tellers.

"We broke up. It's fairly new, but we're doing okay," I decide to reply. Even though I hate the way everyone feels entitled to your business in Lakeland, I'd rather be the one telling the story so an accurate retelling is at least possible if not probable.

"I'm sorry to hear that. You two made a good couple. High school sweethearts and all that. Cute kid too," he continues, scanning my items with the sort of rote efficiency that working the same job for a long time gives you. This news will be all over town by the end of the week. People have already noticed that I haven't been wearing my engagement ring for the last six months. I've had more than a few comments from customers asking if I was getting it cleaned or if it had gotten lost.

I make a noncommittal noise, because really? What do you say to someone rooting for a relationship that's been over for years even if it just became official? "Uh, thanks, Anthony." I pay the total and grab the two grocery bags before heading towards the door.

"Summer, wait up!" Ryan calls. I pause just inside the door, feeling my face flame as Anthony's eyes go back and forth between

Ryan and myself, an eyebrow raised. *Great, another thing to add to the rumors. 'Hot guy harassing local, newly single mother.'*

After paying for his groceries he pushes his cart towards me. "You can throw your bags in here," he says, pointing to his cart. I place them inside with a questioning look. "I want to walk you out. It's starting to get dark," he explains. I turn my eyes to the darkening sky outside and realize he's right. Even though Lakeland is a relatively safe town, it's still smart to be careful.

I smile and say, "Thanks. My car is right over there," I gesture to my red Honda on the far side of the parking lot. I pull my hood up to keep the rain off my face and we start heading towards my car. Luckily, the rain has slowed to a drizzle, so we aren't getting completely soaked.

"You really had to park way over there when it was starting to get dark? There's hardly even lights over there, Summer! That's not safe," he says, playfully exasperated with me.

"I'm a grown woman, Ryan. The parking lot was packed when I got here." I reply, hoping he can somehow hear my massive eye roll. "Why are you so concerned about me anyway?" We reach my car and I pop the trunk.

"I'm not." He sighs, lifting his hat to scratch through his dark waves before plopping it back on backward, "I mean, I'm not concerned about you. I just want you to be safe."

I tilt my head and say, "That's the same thing."

"I'd do the same for any woman," he counters, batting my hands out of the way so he can grab my bags and place them in the trunk, "It's par for the course when you grow up with a little sister who likes to get into trouble." The comment stings even though it shouldn't. A small part of me hoped he was interested in me.

"And do you flirt with every woman too?" The question is out before I can stop myself. I meant it to be playful, but when it leaves my lips it comes off accusatory. I mentally facepalm, *real smooth, Summer.*

"What? No. That's not who I am at all." He shakes his head, closing my trunk.

"So, you don't frequently throw compliments at every woman you meet?" I ask skeptically.

"Only pretty bank tellers," he says with a grin while I roll my eyes, fighting my own smile. A part of me thinks that he could just be teasing me. The kind that happens between friends and nothing more. He searches my face and continues, "Seriously, Summer. I don't flirt with every woman I meet. I just can't seem to help myself with you."

"Well, thanks," I say, blushing. "Not for the flirting, for walking me to my car," I blurt. *Now would be a great time for one of those alien abductions to happen to me,* I think while my face flames a yet undiscovered shade of red.

I walk quickly towards my driver's side door and pop it open. Before I can make my escape, his large hand holds the door, caging me in. My breath catches as he bends at the waist, and his face is suddenly much closer. I look into his eyes and am momentarily mesmerized by the startlingly green color and thick, sooty lashes.

"You're welcome. For both," he says, those eyes twinkling with mirth. The spearmint on his breath fills my lungs, and for a crazed moment, I want to lean in and taste it for myself. "I'll see you Saturday?" He leans back, giving me room and I feel my sanity return. *Did I really almost kiss him? Am I insane?*

"Yeah, Saturday," I reply, trying to regain control of myself. I peel my eyes away from him and start my car. He shuts my door before stepping back. He moves himself and the cart to the side, waving to me as I pull out. I wave back, a ball of excitement tightening in my stomach. *Saturday.*

CHAPTER 6

Ryan

I load up my groceries in my truck and hustle home. As much as I want to replay the way Summer looked up at me from her car, seeming like she might lean in and kiss me, I can't. I shouldn't.

My sister, Layla, and her family are coming for dinner, and I was supposed to have it started by now. Her and her husband, Todd, are very specific about Hudson's bedtime. I can't blame them because I've seen the little monster he turns into when he gets tired.

As I rush to unload the groceries in my kitchen, I leave out the ingredients to make carbonara and a salad. Pasta is always a guarantee for my nephew to eat, and I'd rather not sit through a chicken nuggets standoff. Just as I'm slicing up the pancetta, my front door opens, and my sister pokes her head through. "Hey!" she says, stepping the rest of the way inside. She sheds her damp outer layers in the entryway, hanging up her raincoat and setting her shoes by the door.

"Hey, Lay. Where's Todd and Hudson?" I ask, washing my hands at the sink.

"They'll be inside in a second. Hudson decided to take off his shoes in the car, but is demanding he walks by himself to the front door. So, Todd's in the middle of some pretty intense negotiations." She hip-checks me out of the way and starts washing her hands.

"I thought we don't negotiate with terrorists?" I ask jokingly.

"Yeah well, when you live with one–" she says, cutting herself off with a laugh. "At least I have a good negotiating partner." She heads to the stove and stirs around the pancetta I have browning, and I take a moment to look her over.

Layla used to struggle with depression pretty heavily in her teens and it got scary there for a bit. After a lot of therapy and a little medication, she vastly improved, but the worry is hard to shake. She has her thick, dark hair pulled back in a ponytail, so I can see her side profile. Other than looking a little tired from chasing her three-year-old around all day, she looks good. Happy. I breathe out a small sigh of relief that I don't see any of the empty, vacant look she used to wear.

We're a little less than two years apart, so it's not like I'm all that much older than her, but I still feel the urge to protect her and make sure she's okay. It wouldn't matter if I was only a minute older, the big brother in me is woven into my DNA. "You can stop assessing me now Dr. Ryan," she says with an eye roll that takes me back to middle school.

We used to race to be the first in our shared bathroom in the morning, forcing the other to sit in bladder-bursting agony. She gave me that eye roll every day (she always beat me to the bathroom) when I told her that I was *literally* going to die from a bladder explosion.

"You have something on your face," I lie, coming up beside her so I can toss the pasta noodles into the boiling pot. Her hands immediately come up to feel her face and I snort a laugh.

"God, you're annoying," she says, walking to the fridge to pull out ingredients for the salad dressing. This is a meal we're very accustomed to making together. Our dad is half Italian, so carbonara and salad was a weekly meal growing up. We both learned our love of cooking from him.

We bicker good-naturedly over who exactly is the most annoying now versus when we were growing up. Eventually, Todd and Hudson burst through the door. "Mama, I got my shoes on all by myself," Hudson declares proudly before plopping unceremoniously on the floor and yanking said shoes off. Todd looks at us and gives a little shake of his head, eyes wide and white like the victim of a warzone, contrasting with the deep black of his skin. I hide my smile by turning back to the stove where dinner is almost done cooking.

* * *

We're watching from the couch as Hudson runs laps around the living room and uses Todd's broad back as a springboard after dinner. Over the cacophony of a three-year-old hyped up on carbs, Layla turns to me and asks, "So, how are you settling in? How's work?"

"Work is good. It's a little weird to know that I'll be in one place indefinitely, but nice too. I also ran into Luke. Remember him?" When she nods, I go on, "Anyway, he and I got to talking and we're going to grab dinner this week and catch up."

"Aw, look at you making real friends for once," Lay teases, punching my shoulder.

"I know, I'm excited for it," I say truthfully.

"I'm glad you're finally sticking around in one place," she says, watching her son's impromptu dance routine. "I worry about you. I know you wanted to sow your wild oats or whatever, but you've always liked structure and routine. That's why it surprised me so much that you stayed on the move for so long."

"It's my job to do the worrying," I say, trying to divert from this topic of conversation. She gives me another epic eye roll, and stares me down so I reluctantly say, "I know. After Lydia, I just didn't feel right about settling anywhere. I needed to do some soul-searching or something."

Layla mock gasps, "You *have* a soul?" Now it's my turn to roll my eyes. "Sorry, go on. Soul searching, et cetera."

"Right. So, you know the plan was always to get married and find a place to settle down, but obviously, that didn't work. So, when I was left without the ten-year plan we had, I just needed to– I don't know –" I struggle to find the words to describe how empty and betrayed I felt. How directionless.

"Find yourself?" Layla supplies.

"I guess," I say with a shrug. "I needed to figure out who I was as an individual and not just part of a couple. I had joined my life so completely with hers that I needed to take time to figure out what *I* wanted. I mean, we were together for years and had planned to have a future together. Everything became 'we' and her wants became my own," I finish with a shrug. While that isn't a bad thing, I can recognize that I completely eclipsed my needs with hers to make sure she was happy. It was a hard lesson to learn that even if I put myself dead last, it didn't mean the relationship would be a forever thing.

"And what *do* you want?" she asks. I almost laugh at the serious turn of our conversation while poor Todd is now being forced to spin Hudson around and around while the little terror cackles wildly. Layla is unbothered, so I take a second to seriously consider her question.

"Well, I was sick of traveling and living out of a suitcase." I pause to think. "I guess I just want to have a community again. I spent the last few years being selfish and now I want to have people to take into consideration. I want good friends. I eventually want to settle down with someone."

Layla claps giddily at that. "Ooh, do you want me to set you up with one of my friends? I promise I won't get mad at you this time." We both laugh at the shared memory of when I took one of her friends to prom. She was (rightfully) furious, but teenage hormones can't be reasoned with.

I shake my head. "Not yet. I want to try to meet someone organically first."

She snorts, "What like in the produce aisle? Get with the times, old man. Now we rely on the internet to find us dates." She waggles her phone in my face.

I push her shoulder, "I'm only twenty-eight. I'm not *that* old."

"I think it's about time we get your last will and testament in order. You're just about over the hill," she says, reaching over and scrunching my forehead to create wrinkles.

I pin her hands in one of mine to stop the assault when Todd says from across the room, "Is this what we have to look forward to when we eventually give Hudson a sibling?" That stops us and we both laugh while I release her hands.

"Yeah, sorry to tell you," I say. I forget sometimes that Todd is an only child. He always studies us with equal parts confusion, fear, and amusement when we're together.

"Maybe just the one then," he replies, chuckling.

Layla levels him with a playful glare and says, "Nope. You knew what you signed up for when you married me. We need at *least* two more." Todd mock shivers and we all watch Hudson zoom his toy cars around the floor.

"So, how do you plan on finding someone to date, then?" Todd asks eventually.

I shrug and say, "I'm hoping it just happens, you know. Maybe a client or something." I can't stop the image of a certain curvy redhead from entering my mind. Plush lips, glossy and pink, less than a foot away from mine.

Layla must see the glazed look in my eyes because she says, "Do you have someone in mind?"

"No," I reply too quickly, and immediately recognize my mistake when Layla's green eyes light in triumph.

"Oh my god, who is it?" she pesters.

"No one!"

"Tell me!" she exclaims.

I decide to give in because I know from experience that otherwise she won't stop. "Ugh, fine. It's not going to go anywhere, but one of my new clients is really pretty." *Stunning. Sexy. Drop-dead.*

"Why isn't it going anywhere?" Todd asks. "I don't think you've ever had trouble in that department," he continues matter-of-factly. Layla scrunches her nose in mild disgust which makes Todd laugh.

I chuckle too, because any chance to make Layla mildly uncomfortable I'll take. It's my brotherly duty. "Well, no," I admit, "But from the looks of it, she's just out of a relationship and isn't really on the market."

Layla peers at me thoughtfully, "You know, they say that a woman emotionally leaves a relationship way before it actually ends on paper. If she's the one ending it anyway." She shrugs. Todd looks at her, a mild panic drawing his thick brows together. Layla's eyes soften and she says to him, "Don't worry. I'm still firmly planted with you." I want to be disgusted because she's my sister, but I can't feel anything but happy that she's found her person.

While they make googly eyes at each other, I take the opportunity to get on the ground and play cars with my nephew. He's a huge reason I moved closer to my sister. We take turns smashing our cars together.

Hudson lets out a huge, jaw-cracking yawn and that's the signal for Layla and Todd to get everything together and head home for bedtime. When I close the door after they leave in a flurry of chaos, I can't help but be a little sad at how quiet and empty my house feels without family to fill it.

CHAPTER 7

Summer

I have Gilmore Girls paused on the TV and I'm just pouring out the freshly popped bag of popcorn into a serving bowl when the doorbell rings. "It's open!" I call, snagging the bowl of popcorn and two wine glasses so I can deposit them in front of the TV. My door opens and Steph steps through, her bag of goodies haphazardly thrown over her arm. She takes off her shoes and launches herself at me.

"Hey, girl! How are you?" Steph steps back, still holding my shoulders and takes me in. She looks almost the same as she did in high school. The same curly hair that falls just past her shoulders, the same light brown, flawless skin, and the same big smile pointed at me without reservation.

"I'm alive," I deadpan, pulling her down on the couch with me. She drops her bag of snacks on the coffee table and tucks herself under the throw blanket with me.

"No seriously, Summer. Are you doing okay?"

"I mean, no? I don't know. Everything still feels weird. Jared and I officially broke up, like, a month ago before he moved out, but it feels like we broke up years ago. The last few years, we stayed together for Emma's sake and it honestly felt mostly like co-parenting under the same roof than being in a relationship. So, I'm freshly single, but I'm mourning the fact that Emma won't live with both her parents anymore, rather than the relationship itself," I pick at a string on the throw blanket over my lap.

She nods. She's heard all of this before. "I get that. You guys have been having a hard time for a while. It's admirable that you kept trying for Emma, even though Jared never treated you right."

"It's not like he abused me though, Steph. Things were fine. Not passionate, but fine. I keep wondering if I made a mistake. Not because I'm madly in love with him, but because I don't want Emma to struggle like I did growing up. Living out of a duffel bag your whole childhood and never feeling settled is really hard." I feel horribly selfish for choosing to break up Emma's happy life. For choosing to make her live an iteration of what I went through growing up.

"Two things. One, just because he wasn't abusive doesn't mean it was a good relationship. You haven't been happy for a long time and you deserve to be." I open my mouth to interrupt, but she talks over me, "Second, Emma will not struggle the way you did. I don't like Jared for you, but he is a good father. You're a great mom and you both want what's best for her. Yes, she may have to go back and forth, but both places will feel like home, and you and Jared will actually work together to make her feel safe and loved. It's not the same thing you grew up with." She places a warm, perfectly manicured hand on my shoulder.

Growing up, my parents split up before I was even born. My parents hated each other, so the drop-off and pick-up process was always chaos and usually ended in a screaming match that left me wanting to run away. To be in any life that wasn't my own. My dad was in and out through most of my childhood until middle school. Then, he finally moved elsewhere and I stopped seeing him completely. My dad hated my mom so much that he didn't even come to her funeral. I haven't so much as seen a postcard from him in over a decade.

I know that Steph is right. Jared and I would never do that to Emma. "You're right about Emma for sure. We both love her more than life."

"What, I'm not wrong about you and Jared? You want to get back with him or something?" She looks at me like I sprouted a second nose.

"No, it's not that. It's just... I feel like Jared is the best I'll ever get. I know he wasn't great to me, but can I really expect anyone to treat me better?" I gesture vaguely over myself.

Her eyes slit and she glares at me. "You stop that bullshit right now Summer. You are freaking stunning and yes, you should expect any man worthy of your time to treat you like you hung the moon. You are the kindest person I know, you're gorgeous, and you're hilarious once you open up to people. You're the whole package, babe. It sucks for Jared that he didn't see how good he had it. I think as soon as he realizes you're actually gone and this isn't temporary, he'll regret every single moment he took you for granted."

I pull her in for an awkward seated hug. "Thanks, Steph. I needed to hear that." She's always known just what to say to make me feel better. If it weren't for her, I probably never would have left Jared. She never pushed me one way or another, but talking it out with her made me realize I wanted more. That I deserved more.

Her lips curve into a smile that makes me think, *uh-oh.* "Speaking of men and you moving on... What's this I hear about a gorgeous man hitting on you in the supermarket?"

I pull away from her hug. "What? Who told you that?" I ask.

She smacks my shoulder. "So there is a gorgeous man hitting on you?"

"No! I mean, yes, Ryan is arguably gorgeous, but no he wasn't hitting on me," I fumble, cracking open the bottle of wine and pouring us each a glass.

"Are you sure? No offense Summer, but you can be pretty dense when it comes to guys being into you. Who is he anyway?" She grabs her glass and takes a sip, waggling her eyebrows.

"He's just my contractor. He fixed the ceiling leak," I wave a hand to the offending stain, "He's new in town and popped into the bank yesterday to open an account. We got to talking and I realized he was a contractor. He had time in his schedule, so he came and fixed it. We bumped into each other at the supermarket, and he walked me to my car because it was getting dark. That's the big story," I take a sip, "How do you know about him?"

"Anthony. I must have come in just after you. He was talking all about how you and Jared broke up, and he was speculating on whether or not you cheated with the new guy." She laughs, "I obviously knew that wasn't true. You aren't a cheater."

"That nosy man! We literally had a two-second conversation and now everyone is going to think the worst." I pinch the bridge of my nose in frustration.

"So. Ryan, huh?" She smirks at me over the rim of her wine glass.

"There's nothing there, Steph," I sigh, "He is way, way out of my league."

She smacks my arm again. "The moon, Summer. You hung it."

"Okay, alright. That doesn't change the fact that he's definitely not into me." I look away from her and down into the swirling liquid in my glass like I can divine answers from it.

"Again, you aren't the best at reading flirty cues despite all those romances you read. I mean, he walked you to your car, right? That's overprotective and caveman-like."

I look at her and make sure she can see my eye roll. "He has a little sister. It was a nice gesture towards woman-kind. Not anything special for me. He told me so." I won't mention the 'pretty bank teller' comment because I know she'll blow it way out of proportion and insist I carry his beautiful babies.

She scrunches her nose and says, "Fine. Let's watch Rory and Lorelei order a bunch of food and then not eat it."

I press play and hand her a Twix, her favorite. "We'll eat it for them."

CHAPTER 8
Summer

On Wednesday after work, I head to Jared's new apartment. Today will be the first time I've seen it other than the few pictures he showed me when he first signed his lease. I pull into an open spot in front of the small apartment complex, rain pounding steadily on the windshield. I sit for a moment and close my eyes, listening to the staccato beat against the metal and glass of my car. The sound of the rain has always been steadying for me. I hear my phone ping with a new message. I open my eyes and unlock the screen.

RYAN:

How's your ceiling holding up? It's coming down pretty hard today.

No bowls have been necessary so far.

Good. I wouldn't mind the excuse to see you again, though.

Ah, yes. The old leaky roof wingman. Sorry to say he's failed you this time.

Damn. Last time I count on him for anything.

I suck my lips in to squash my giddy smile and exit out of my messages app. I need to get Emma soon so we can enjoy dinner without having to rush.

Jared was lucky enough to find an apartment complex that only has one story - no one above or below him to gripe about normal kid noises. Before moving into my house, we had an apartment with a downstairs neighbor who would beat the ceiling with a broom every time Emma dared toddle too loudly.

This complex only has five, single-story units and he got the one on the corner with only one neighbor. I knock on the door and have to wait just a handful of moments before Emma throws it open excitedly. "Hi, Mommy! Come on, I wanna show you my new room." She grabs my hand and tugs me inside, pausing impatiently for me to take off my shoes.

While I toe off my ankle boots, I take a brief glance around, noting that while sparsely decorated, the apartment itself has potential. The walls are a dull beige to match the equally dull beige carpet but that's nothing a good rug and some artwork can't fix. I mentally check myself, *Not your job anymore, Summer.* Once my shoes are off, Emma pulls me through the living room and down a short hallway with three doors, one to the left and two to the right. As she's opening the last door on the right, I ask, "Where's your Dad?"

"Right here," he emerges from the door next to hers, steam billowing out after him. He's wearing a white undershirt and low-slung grey sweats, his typical after-work attire. As a foreman at the local lumber mill, he spends his days in uncomfortable hard hats, steel-toed boots, and thick utility pants. When he comes home, he likes to be comfortable. The familiar scent of his body wash and hair products assaults me, and a wave of unwanted nostalgia rolls over me. If I didn't know any better, I'd think he timed his shower on purpose. He knows a freshly showered man is my Kryptonite. They just smell so *good* and the wet, dripping hair really does something for me.

I avert my gaze and swear I see him suppress a smile. As casually as I can manage, I say, "Hey, Jared." I turn to Emma gesturing at the door in front of us, "So, this is your room?"

She gives me an excited nod and pulls me inside. My heart squeezes as I realize her room is the most decorated in the apartment. She has a pink heart-shaped rug in the center, fairy lights strung along the wall behind her bed, and an oak bookshelf and dresser combo that I recognize from his parents' house. She proudly points to the purple tufted bedspread that swallows the twin-sized bed whole, "This is what Daddy and I picked out last week. Isn't it so pretty, Mommy?" She plops on the bed.

"It sure is, Em. It's a little big though isn't it?" The bedspread looks like it's meant for a queen-sized bed rather than her twin.

"She insisted on this one even though I told her it wouldn't fit," Jared laughs as he enters the room behind us.

"Better for forts!" Emma says, a little hand gesturing to the bookcase and bean bag chair where I'm presuming she makes her forts.

"Can't argue with that," I say, sitting next to her. "So, where do you want to get dinner? We can go to Jack's here in town, or we can go get lasagna at Little Ravenna's. What are you up for?"

"Lasagna! Lasagna! Lasagna!" she chants, standing from the bed to twirl in a circle. I laugh because I had a feeling that would be her choice.

"Okay, Garfield. Let's get out of here, then. It's a thirty-minute drive to Ravenna's and we want to get you home in time for bed." I stand and touch her shoulder.

"Make sure you grab your raincoat, Emma," Jared says, moving aside so she can dart past him. He turns his whiskey barrel eyes on me. They sweep down my body lazily before he meets my eyes, "See you when you get back." He produces a key from the pocket of his sweats, "I figured you should have the spare. Feel free to let yourself in." He hands me the key, his fingers lingering against mine as I grab it. I try to brush aside the implication in his tone.

I slide past him, throwing a "Thanks," over my shoulder. I cannot handle flirty Jared right now. I blow out a breath before pasting a smile on my face. "Hey, Em. Ready?"

"Yup," she pops the p and comes toward me. "Bye, Daddy!" she calls over her shoulder. I lock the door behind us and lead her to the car, both of us hustling to stay as dry as possible.

* * *

On the ride back to Jared's after dinner, Emma and I are singing along to a pop station on the radio when she says, "Mommy?"

I flit my eyes to hers in the rearview mirror, "Yeah, hun?" I turn the music down so I can hear her better. She's twining her small fingers together and picking at the chipped, sparkly pink polish on them.

"Are you and Daddy ever gonna get back together?"

The question is a gut punch, even though she's asked it a few times over the last month. It never gets easier. "I don't think so, Emma," I say gently.

"Daddy says 'maybe' when I ask him," she states, a hopeful lift entering her voice.

I hold back a sigh of frustration and keep my eyes on the dark, rain-slicked road ahead, "'I don't think so' and 'maybe' are kind of the same thing, Em." My warm and fuzzy feelings over Jared decorating Emma's room evaporate.

"'Maybe' sounds better."

"I know, Em. I'm telling you now, though, that it is very unlikely that your father and I will be back together any time soon." I hate being the one to disappoint her, but I can't have her dealing with false hope.

"Why not?" she asks quietly.

"No one knows for sure what the future holds, but right now, at this moment, I don't think we'll ever be back together."

"So, maybe?" she asks, hopefully. I laugh rather than answering her, because if I open my mouth I'll say something hurtful about her dad and she doesn't need to hear that.

When we get to Jared's apartment, I help Emma out of her booster seat and we plod through the wet grass to the front door, the cold rain doing nothing to diffuse my fury. We swore we would do our best to be on the same page and not confuse her or give her false hope. I get the door open and usher Emma inside.

Jared is, predictably, playing a game on his computer. He's wearing his gaming headset, so he doesn't hear us. "Go ahead and start getting ready for bed, Emma. Brush and floss." I nudge her towards the bathroom.

"Can you both tuck me in like we used to?"

"Sure, sweetie. Give us ten minutes." Because his desk is facing the wall, Jared doesn't even see Emma go past him. I roll my eyes and approach him, pulling down his headset when I get to him.

"Ah! What the hell?" He swivels around, panic widening his eyes, "Jesus, Summer. You scared the hell out of me," he mutters, turning around again, and getting straight back into the game, fingers flying over the keys.

I rein in my annoyance with a deep breath in through my nose and out through my mouth. I want a civil conversation, and that won't happen if I don't check my anger. This is just too reminiscent of the last seven years - me wanting to have a conversation or spend time together, and then him deciding that he'd rather do anything else (but would mostly rather play video games). "Jared."

"Give me a second, okay? I can't pause it. You know this. We've been over it a thousand times." Rapid fire clicking ensues while I contemplate pulling the plug on the whole system. I feel my anger rising like a swift tide and work to keep it toned down.

"Listen," I tell the one ear he's graciously left out from under the headset, "I really need to talk to you and we only have, like, ten minutes until Emma is ready for bed. I told her I'd tuck her in with you."

To my surprise, he sighs, presses a button on his headphones, and says, "Sorry guys, duty calls. I'll be back on in thirty." Then, he exits the game and swivels to me. "What's up?"

"On the way home, Emma asked me if I thought you and I would get back together," I say, gauging his reaction.

He laughs, his foot that he had crossed over the other coming up to nudge me on the thigh, "She's been asking that at least once a week, so what? It's a normal question for a kid in her situation."

"I know that, Jared. *I* told her that I didn't think we would be getting back together. Do you know what she told me you said?" He gestures at me to go on. "She said that you told her 'maybe.' You can't go giving her false hope like that. You and I have talked about this. When she asks those questions, we're on the same page. No wishy-washy language, or deviating from what we talked about. This is already so confusing for her, I don't want to make it worse." I sit on the nearby couch, crossing my arms and legs.

He moves to sit on the worn coffee table in front of me, "Okay, but it is a 'maybe.'"

"It's not. I'm done, Jared. We've been done for way longer than just the last month. We just finally made it official."

"Well, what if I'm not done?" He rests his hands on the outside of my thighs, his palms ghosting up and down the soft fabric of my pants.

My heart jumps at the contact. An old, sad part of me is desperate for affection that he never willingly gave. I take a steadying breath. "This," I gently remove his hands, "might have worked a year ago, but I'm not a dog begging for treats anymore. You'll be affectionate with me for a week, and then you stop. We go back to the way things were and it repeats. I can't anymore. I need you to understand that."

"Is this because of Supermarket Guy?" he asks, leaning back out of my personal space and removing his hands.

"Oh my god. I'm truly going to murder Anthony. I don't care if he sends me a gift basket for Christmas every year," I throw my hands up in exasperation, "Ryan, 'Supermarket Guy,' is just the contractor I hired to fix the leak. We bumped into each other after I saw you and Emma and he walked me out because it was getting dark."

"I would have walked you out if you wanted me to," he says, arms crossing defensively.

"No, you wouldn't have. You haven't walked me to my car since probably our first anniversary, Jared." I shake my head because he always chooses a random detail to focus on in an argument rather than trying to fix what's actually wrong.

He has nothing to say to that, so instead he switches tactics, "Any guys you date you have to run by me."

I release an incredulous, "Excuse me?" I sit up a little straighter, my brows shooting toward my hairline.

He clears his throat uncrossing and recrossing his arms, "Well, I don't want random guys around Emma."

I work to keep my voice down, "You know damn well I would never bring 'random guys,'" I use air quotes around the offending language, "Around Emma. If and when I date, that is my business-" he tries to interrupt, but I hold up a silencing hand, "-If it gets serious enough that I would want Emma to meet him, I would of course introduce you to him first. I expect the same courtesy from you for any woman you date. But I won't be running any and every guy who might show interest in me by you."

He deflates, "Fine. Okay." He waits for a beat and then, "So, Supermarket Guy is showing interest?"

I roll my eyes, "One man does something nice for me and suddenly the whole town thinks he's down on one knee."

"Well, that is kind of what happened with us, remember? I started carrying your books to class for you after two months of trying to get you to talk to me about anything that wasn't school-related. When you let me, that's how I knew you were into me. You don't let anyone in. You never accept any help. When you do, that means you care, whether that's friendship or something else."

The bathroom door opens and I stand. "I guess. Doesn't mean anything is going on though." *When did he get so observant?* He's right, of course. I struggle to let anyone in because I'm so afraid of the pain of losing them. I don't accept help because one of the earliest lessons I learned is that you can only truly count on yourself.

Before I forget, I take Jared's key out of my pocket and set it on the coffee table. I don't want any part of what keeping it would insinuate.

"I'm ready for bed!" Emma calls down the hallway.

"We good?" Jared asks as we head towards her room. I give his shoulder a squeeze and nod.

* * *

After I leave Jared's, I rush back to my car and get on the road. The rain is coming down so hard, I have my windshield wipers on the highest setting and they still hardly clear my vision.

As I make it to the outskirts of town where my neighborhood is, I see a white lump in the middle of the road. Just as I'm about to swerve around it, the lump moves and I see a head turn toward the headlights of my car.

"Oh shit, dog!" Thankfully, I manage to swerve around it. I pull to the side of the road, turn on my hazards, and get out of my car, the rain instantly drenching me. I cautiously approach the large dog and put a hand out to show I'm not a threat. Its tail gives a feeble thump and I approach quicker, seeing that it's friendly. "Hey, pup, why are you out in the middle of the road?"

The poor thing whines and as I get closer, I see that their back leg is twisted at an odd angle. My stomach heaves and it takes everything in me to keep my lasagna down. I avert my gaze from the leg and look the rest of the dog over, quickly noticing that she's a *she* and appears to be otherwise uninjured apart from some scrapes making her white fur rust-colored in some spots.

"Oh no, you poor thing!" Tears slip down my cheeks and burn my throat. I've never been able to hold it together when I see an animal in pain. I gently pet her head, and she licks my palm, eliciting another sob from my throat. I quickly get myself as composed as I can, and try to lift her but stop when the struggling makes her let out a yelp of pain.

"Okay, pup, we're going to figure this out." I pull off my raincoat and drape it over her so she warms up a little. I shield my phone with my upper body and when I press the button to wake my phone, nothing happens. "Oh, come on. My phone is seriously dead?" *Why does this shit always happen to me?* I put the useless hunk of glass and metal back in my pocket and go back to stroking the dog's head, hoping a better idea comes to me soon because we're both freezing.

CHAPTER 9

Ryan

I tap my thumbs on my steering wheel to the beat of the song coming through the radio. I'm headed home after helping Luke install a new ceiling fan. He's pretty handy, but isn't a fan of electricity. I snort a laugh at the memory of the panicked look in his eyes when I asked him to flip the light switch to make sure the wiring was connected properly. Luckily it was, and I was able to head home soon after.

I'm on the last stretch of road before I reach my neighborhood when I notice a car with hazard lights blinking in the distance. I squint through the rain streaking my windshield as I slow down, realizing there's something in the middle of the road. My brows draw together in concern, and I hope everything is alright. I pull to the side of the road behind the car because I want to make sure they're okay and see if they need help.

I hop out of my truck, grab my flashlight from my tool kit and shine it on the pile in the road. It can't be... "Summer?" I ask, rushing closer. She looks up at me, squinting in the light and I realize she's kneeling over a huge white dog. She has her jacket slung over it and she's gently petting the dog's head. She's completely soaked through, her top and slacks clinging to her body.

"Ryan?" she asks through chattering teeth.

"It's me. What happened? Are you alright?" I can't help the panicked way I'm looking her over, searching for any sign of injury.

"F-fine. Just cold. This poor girl was in the middle of the road. It looks like someone hit her and then drove off." She pauses to collect herself and then continues, "I almost r-ran her down again, but was able to stop. I was trying to lift her so I can take her to the vet, b-but when I tried it hurt her. I'm not strong enough to lift her without jerking her around and I don't know how badly she's injured."

"Okay, let me help. Just give me a second. I'll be right back," I say, already jogging back to my truck. I grab one of my sturdy work jackets from the backseat and hustle over to them. I drape the jacket over Summer's shoulders and bend down to let the dog sniff my hand. She licks it and I give her a head pat. "Does she have a name tag?"

"No, just a collar. She's got to be someone's pet because she's really sweet and looks well taken care of otherwise. Thanks for the jacket by the way." She turns her hazel eyes to me, mascara running down her cheeks from the rain, tears, or both.

"You have to be cold. You're drenched," I say gruffly, unreasonably annoyed that she put herself in harm's way. She even gave the dog her jacket. I admire the selflessness, but damn if the caveman part of my brain isn't frustrated that she didn't put herself first.

"Well, *my* leg isn't broken," she huffs, "Come on, let's get her up and into my car. I want to get her to the vet ASAP." She stands and quickly pushes her arms through the sleeves of the jacket.

"My truck. There's more room in the back seat and you can sit with her to keep her calm." She nods and I gently scoop the dog up in my arms, jacket and all. She whines and I soothe her as best I can. "It's okay, sweet pup. We're going to get you taken care of." Summer jogs ahead of me to my truck and opens the back door. I slide the dog in, careful of her twisted back leg. She rests her head on the seat and my heart breaks a little. The poor thing is shivering just like Summer.

"She must be exhausted," Summer says, looking in on her. She starts to round the truck to hop in by the dog's head.

"Hold on," I say. She gives me a questioning look. "Get in your car, I'll follow you home and then we'll take my truck to the vet. I don't want you leaving your car out here."

"But-"

I hold out a hand to stop her, "Your house is literally five minutes away. She's not bleeding out. We'll be able to do both. Stop arguing and get in your car." She glares at me for a second, before stomping to her car. *I don't think she likes being told what to do.* Despite the circumstances, I laugh a little. I jump behind the wheel and crank the heat up.

I follow her home, being cautious to stop gently and go as slowly as I can around corners so I don't jostle the dog. I'm buzzing with adrenaline and misplaced frustration. Logically, I know that what Summer did was brave and selfless, and something to be admired. But my brain keeps replaying the image of her shivering in the middle of a dark road, drenched with rain, where anything could have happened to her. I pull to a gentle stop in front of her house. Summer is waiting on her front porch for me. As soon as she sees my truck, she runs to it, getting in the back seat and placing the dog's head on her lap.

"Why didn't you call someone?" I ask tersely. My heart is still pounding with the last dregs of adrenaline at finding her in the middle of the road alone.

"My phone died. I didn't want to leave her there, but I didn't know what else to do."

"So you were just waiting for someone to come along and stop at-" I check my dashboard clock, "Nine at night?" I shake my head. I admire her willingness to help, but the woman has no self-preservation instincts.

"I guess I was. What was the other option? Leave her to get run over again?" she asks heatedly.

"No, I guess not." I sigh and shake off the last of the tension, "Sorry, you just scared the shit out of me. When I stopped and saw that you were in the middle of the road, I thought something had happened to you."

"Thanks for stopping," she says quietly. I wave away her thanks because only an asshole would have driven around them without stopping. I follow Google's navigation instructions to the vet. I peek at Summer and the dog in the rearview mirror and I can hardly take the sight of her gently stroking the dog's head and murmuring softly to her. Her eyes are still tearing up, but she keeps petting the dog, making sure she feels as safe as she can with two strangers. *I'm in trouble,* I think, rubbing my suddenly aching chest.

CHAPTER 10

Summer

We pull up to the vet's office, and Ryan rushes in to get help while I stay with the dog. I continue petting her head and telling her how brave she is. Ryan's comment still stings. *"Why didn't you call someone?"* He clearly didn't feel like dealing with this. I can't exactly blame him, but I'm thankful he helped me anyway. I wrap the thick jacket tighter around myself, feeling like a TV dinner in need of thawing.

Ryan pops out of the building, guiding two women in navy scrubs over to the truck. He opens the door and one of the women looks at me. "Hi. I'm Dr. Barnes. I'm going to take a quick look and make sure there are no obvious spinal or neck injuries before we risk moving her again. Thank you so much for bringing her here. Most people, unfortunately, would have left her on the road. Ryan told me the whole story."

She expertly runs her hands over the dog's back and feels gently around her neck. "Okay, good news, I don't feel any spinal or neck injuries. It doesn't mean she's out of the woods yet, but that's a good sign. Ryan, I'm going to have you lift her and we'll head inside." She looks to the other woman in scrubs next to her, "Jules, help him keep the leg from catching on anything."

We make it into an exam room, the bright lights overhead blinding after being in the dark for so long. The poor dog starts to tremble and pant even harder when she realizes where she is. Before doing anything else, they check her for an identification chip. Luckily, she has one and they find the owner's information.

Jules, the vet tech, sticks her head in the exam room. "So, her owner is on the way over now. Apparently, Coconut here doesn't like storms and ran out the front door a few hours ago." Jules places a hand on Coconut's side. "She's been looking for her ever since. Anyway, we'll take good care of Coconut. You guys are free to go."

I ask, "Can we wait with her until she gets here? She's comfortable with me and I don't want to leave her all alone." Jules smiles at me and nods, administering what she says is pain medicine.

"I'll leave you guys here for a bit. Dr. Barnes is prepping for surgery. We'll have to x-ray first, but she's pretty certain she'll need to operate on the leg." Jules exits the room and I lean on the large silver exam table, rubbing Coconut behind the ears. Luckily, that pain medicine seemed to work fast and she's already relaxing, seeming to melt into a white fluffy heap on the table.

Ryan stands next to me and tentatively wraps an arm around my shoulder. The heat radiating off him makes me remember how cold I am. My teeth start to chatter, and I lean into him, just for the warmth *obviously*. He rubs his hand up and down my arm. After a beat he says, "Sorry for snapping at you earlier. I was just worried and it came out angry."

I smile a little and look up at him. "It's okay. I get it. Stopping and helping a random woman and dog probably wasn't part of your plans for the night."

"It's not that at all. I'm glad I was the one who found you. Besides, you're anything but random. Not anymore. This experience bonds us for life," he says teasingly, squeezing me into his side and then letting his arm drop from my shoulders. I immediately miss the reassuring weight of it. He scratches Coconut's head and asks, "You're really great with dogs. Why don't you have one?"

"I love dogs, but Jared kind of hates them. I guess he had a bad experience with one as a kid. He vetoed any attempt I made to get one using Emma as an excuse. Horrible excuse, by the way, Emma loves dogs too." I shrug. "Maybe I'll get one eventually now that I don't live with him anymore. Emma would be ecstatic." I smile at the thought. She's been asking for a dog since she learned how to talk. She would always point at every dog we passed on the street, gasp, and say excitedly, "Dog?!" She eventually became more eloquent and persuasive, but it's tiny Emma that sticks in my brain.

"Who doesn't like dogs?" Ryan asks incredulously. "I had a dog the whole time I was growing up. It was the best. I'm sure Emma will love it if you decide to get one."

I'm about to reply when the door opens. "Coco! Oh, my sweet little lady. You poor thing!" An older woman rushes into the room. She was obviously out in the rain, gray hair plastered to her face and head. Ryan and I move to the side to give her space in the small room. She bursts into tears while gently stroking Coconut's body, her other hand hovering over the mangled leg. "M-my God. Look at you." She sniffs and looks towards us. "Thank you so much. I don't know what I would do without her." I hand her a tissue from the box off the counter with a small smile.

"Thank her," Ryan says, squeezing me to his side again, "She's the one who found her and stopped to help. I was just the muscle to carry her in." I shake my head a little at how he downplays his own role.

The woman hugs me and whispers a tight 'thank you' in my ear. I hug her back and say, "Of course. I couldn't just leave her there." Afterward, I pet Coconut again and say goodbye to her, getting another tail thump in farewell.

In the truck on the way home, I sit up front and Ryan blasts the heat. I pull down the visor, flip open the mirror, and groan at my appearance. I look like a ghost from a horror movie with the black smeared around my eyes and trailing down my pale, freckled cheeks. My cheeks and lips are bloodless with the cold. I try in vain to scrub the mascara from my face, but only end up smearing it worse. Ryan snorts a laugh and I glare at him. "You pull off the drowned rat look well," he teases.

"From pretty bank teller to drowned rat. Oh, how the mighty have fallen," I quip, flipping the mirror and visor back up. Despite the heat, my teeth haven't stopped chattering, and Ryan shoots me a concerned look. Even my bones feel cold. He reaches over and grips my cold hands in his warm one, lending me his heat again.

We pull up to my house and sit in his truck for a bit, processing the last hour. I finally feel at least partially dethawed, and my brain feels like it's powering back on. I suddenly don't know how to feel about the hand holding and side hugs. Were they just a gentlemanly way to share warmth, or did they mean more? How am I even supposed to know without asking? God, I miss high school right now and how black and white things felt back then. Being an adult is weird and confusing and no one tells you anything straight out. Maybe I'll just be a hermit from now on.

Eventually, he turns off the ignition. "Let me walk you to your door," he says. I'm too tired and too cold to argue, so I just unclip my seatbelt and take his offered hand when he rounds the truck to my side. We hustle to my door and after unlocking it, I go to open it. His hand stops mine and he says, "That was really brave and really selfless what you did tonight, Summer. You probably saved that dog's life." He brushes an errant strand of wet hair behind my ear.

"You helped a lot," I say, looking him in his eyes so he can read my sincerity.

"Maybe," he concedes, "But you found her, stayed with her in the pouring rain in the middle of the street, protected her, and made her feel safe. Look at you, you're freezing, soaking wet and you didn't complain once. You just kept comforting Coconut. I don't think I've ever met anyone like you." His words feel like a warm blanket and a hot cup of coffee. I want to sink into them and live there for a little bit.

I turn and hug him, wrapping my arms around his firm middle and pressing my cheek to his chest. "Thank you, Ryan," I say into his chest. His arms wrap around me, and I allow myself to indulge in the feeling of being comforted.

"You're welcome, Summer." His voice rumbles in his chest against my ear. "Now, go inside, take a hot shower to warm up, and go to sleep." I can't be sure, but I swear I feel his lips brush the top of my head before he pulls away.

"Your jacket," I say, starting to take it off.

"Keep it. I can get it later." He tugs it closed again and ushers me inside.

I turn to look at him and see a soft look in his eyes that I can't interpret. "Thank you for stopping tonight, Ryan. I couldn't have helped Coconut without you." I gently shut the door before he can respond.

CHAPTER 11

Ryan

On Friday, a few days after the dog incident, I'm sitting on my couch with a beer trying to decide what to do with myself for the night. Before I can make up my mind, I get a text from Luke.

LUKE:

Hey man. Some of the guys are going to The Taproom. You in?

I might just stay in tonight. I have a job tomorrow morning.

Oh come on, it's Friday! Just one drink and a couple rounds of pool. You can be home by 10.

Fine, but I'm in my truck heading home at 9:45.

It's a deal Grandpa. Get down here.

I'm grateful to have Luke pulling me out of the house even though it's going to be hard to peel myself off the couch. Since I haven't spent more than a few months in one place at a time in the last five years, I didn't make many friends and the ones I did make weren't lasting. The loneliness is what really motivated me to move back to Lakeland.

I change out of my athletic shorts and into a pair of jeans. I take a cursory look in the mirror, and after running wet hands through my hair to get the worst of the hat head tamed, I decide it's good enough.

* * *

I enter The Taproom and am surprised to find it crowded with what looks to be every Lakelandian under the age of forty. When Luke suggested playing pool and having a drink, I was expecting a seedy dive bar with a suspiciously stained pool table. Instead, forest green walls, gold accents, and a cigar room feel round out the place.

"Hey, Ry, over here!" Luke, who towers above everyone else, is waving to me from one of the three pool tables at the back of the bar. With him are two other guys that he introduces me to as Victor and Chris.

"Nice to meet you, man," Victor says, giving me the handshake and half hug that all men seem to know. He has tattoos crawling up his right arm and sticking out the top of his t-shirt. Chris gives me the same greeting, pushing up his thick-rimmed glasses after I accidentally knocked the corner of the frames with my shoulder.

We order another round of the house brew on tap. Chris and Luke bring the four overfilled glasses to our table and set them down on paper coasters emblazoned with The Taproom's gold and green logo. Chris and I team up against Victor and Luke for pool and we gather around the table. We play a few rounds and my side loses terribly.

I clap Chris on the shoulder, grimacing a little. "Sorry, when we were picking partners I should have warned you that I'm not very good at pool."

He laughs. "No worries. I just owe Victor a round the next time we go out."

"*They* play pool. I either watch or relieve one of them when they get bored. Don't feel bad, they've been playing against each other since Victor's dad got a pool table in the fifth grade," Luke says, guiding us to a high-top table near the bar. I give him a look and he says, "It's only nine, Gramps, you can hang for a little while longer."

"Fine, but I'm having water. I already had an extra drink," I say, sliding into the chair and catching the heel of my work boots on the footrest.

"So, does that ever get old?" Victor asks, nodding to a group of women at the bar not so subtly staring at me. If I take a guess, I'd say they're having a bachelorette party, judging from the one woman in a sparkly white, impossibly short dress and tiara.

"Sometimes," I answer honestly. At the incredulous look on his face, I go on, "The attention can be nice, sure. But, I'm not really a hook-up kind of guy. That's all most women want from me because they automatically assume that's what I want from them."

"What a problem," Chris chides, bumping his elbow into my side.

"I know, I know. I'm just more of a serious relationship person. When I was traveling around, I avoided it all for the most part because I'd be on to the next place quickly. I'm not above a hook-up here and there, but it gets old fast." The truth is, the emptiness I felt afterward wasn't worth the physical release.

"I can see that. I've been with my girl, Grace, for almost five years now, married the last two," Luke says, showing the group the lock screen on his phone where a pretty brunette smiles at the camera snuggled into his side.

"More like ten years. You two were on again, off again since Junior year until you finally got your head out of your ass and got serious about her," Victor states, taking a gulp from his beer.

"She'll never let me live down not taking her to senior prom," Luke grimaces before laughing, "In my defense, she broke up with me a month before, and at least I didn't take anyone else."

After some back and forth, the guys ribbing each other about their various relationships, current and past, Chris turns to me and asks, "So, are you with anyone?"

"Not right now. My last serious relationship ended a few years back. She went overseas for her master's degree and I stayed here. After I got my contractor's license, I decided to travel around the state a bit and stayed in one place long enough for a big job or two and then I'd move on. We tried to make the long-distance thing work for a year, but. Well. I found out she was cheating on me. I called her one day outside of our usual time and a random guy answered.

When I confronted her later, she admitted to cheating and swore she'd never do it again. I just couldn't trust her, especially since she still had to be in the U.K. for another year to finish up her program." I shrug off the discomfort of talking about Lydia. I've been over her for a long time, but the betrayal still stings.

"So, how come you haven't dated since?" Victor asks, reclining back in his chair.

"Well, since I was traveling around and never in one place for more than a few months, I never started anything serious. I wasn't willing to do the distance thing again, and I also didn't feel ready to settle anywhere. Honestly, part of my moving back here is so that I can eventually find someone and put down roots. I'm almost thirty and my younger sister, Layla, is already settled down with her husband and son." I take a drink from my water in the silence.

Eventually, Luke leans in and says, "Anyone caught your eye? I can set you up with one of Lauren's friends."

I tilt my head in a noncommittal gesture. "I've only been in town for a little less than a month now. Although, I did meet Summer." 'Meet' feels like too insignificant a word to use to describe the last week with Summer, from fixing her roof to the random run-ins, but I don't feel like going into full detail either. "She's definitely got my attention, but I'm not sure if I have hers."

"Summer Evans? Isn't she still with Jared?" Victor asks.

"Nah. She and Jared ended things pretty recently, I think. I work with him and overheard him talking about getting an apartment a while ago," Chris replies.

Victor looks at me, eyebrows raised, "You sure you want to go after someone who just got out of a relationship? You know she has a kid too, right?"

"Yeah, I know. I fixed her roof at the beginning of the week. I'm actually going over there tomorrow to make sure it held up through the rain. She had a picture of all of them in her living room." I take a sip of my water to give myself time to think over my next words. "As far as going for her, I'm not actively pursuing her. I'm just testing the waters and seeing where things go." I shrug, hoping I come off casual. I know it isn't rational how much I'm already into her, but I can't stop myself.

"So how do you like being in construction?" Chris asks. "My dad was a project manager for years before he retired. He always talks about how much he enjoyed it but I remember lots of bitching when I was growing up."

"I like it a lot. I've always enjoyed working with my hands and just couldn't picture myself behind a desk. My old man was a contractor, and when I was a teenager, I worked with him sometimes on the weekends to make a little extra money. It's nice to do different stuff every day. Don't get me wrong, it can be really frustrating too, and there's always rude customers, but overall it's good."

I don't mention it because I don't know these guys very well yet, but I feel a huge sense of pride to follow in my dad's footsteps. He is one of the most hardworking, down to earth people I know, and anything I can do to emulate him is worth doing.

When I was floundering around after high school, he was the one to bring up getting into construction. I had never been great at school and couldn't see myself sitting inside an office all day, so I started an apprenticeship with him. I wasn't the best protege at first. I always wanted to screw around and thought I could get away with it because my old man was my boss, but he set me straight pretty quickly. He made me meet him in his office one day after I ditched work and said, "Son, you are in charge of your life now. What you do with it and the choices you make are your own. That's one of the great privileges of adulthood, but it's also one of the scariest things about adulthood. You have to make the choices that are in your best interest because from now on, no one else is responsible for you. Make the choices that, in thirty years, you'll look back on and thank yourself for."

He then said much less eloquently that I needed to get my head out of my ass. He was right. I spent the next few years with my head down learning everything I could and taking any classes I needed to to round out what my father couldn't teach me. Before he retired, I felt ready to go it alone.

"So, tell me, what's with Anthony?" I ask, wanting to change the subject to something I've been wondering about. That guy was staring daggers at me when I walked Summer out.

Luke informs me that Anthony along with a woman named Sherry are the two biggest gossips in town. They frequently swap information like trading cards, in a competition with themselves over who has the juiciest piece of news. It then gets spread through town by word of mouth since they both see a lot of folks on the daily. Which explains why Mrs. Webber asked me about

Summer seemingly out of the blue when I was installing their new lights. Thankfully I gave a diplomatic answer about her leaking roof and diverted her attention.

I shake my head, a little blown away that the whole "small town gossip mill" is a real and active thing. What have I gotten myself into?

CHAPTER 12

Summer

I wake up at 7:30 on Saturday morning to the sun shining through my curtains and a text from Ryan asking if nine works for him to stop by. I shoot him a quick reply confirming the time before hopping out of bed and into the shower. I try not to think too closely about why I'm making sure every inch of me is smooth, going over my legs a few times with the razor to catch stray hairs.

I apply some product to my damp hair and leave it to air dry, preferring the natural waves to the curling iron I subject my hair to most work days. I stare at my closet, daunted by the task of picking out an outfit.

Typically, on Saturdays, I stick to sweats and an oversized t-shirt if I have nowhere to be. Since a cute contractor will be seeing me today, I want to look a little more put together but I don't want to make it obvious that he's the reason I'm putting in more effort. I just really feel the need to upgrade from "drowned rat."

I settle on a pair of light-washed mom jeans and a cropped, loose-fitting t-shirt that ends just at the high waist of the jeans. The jeans are just tight enough around the waist and butt to accentuate my figure without making me feel like a sausage stuffed into a too-small casing. After a minor debate with myself, I opt for some light makeup and leave my room before I can second-guess everything. *Jeez, Summer. He's helping you with repairs, not taking you on a date,* I chastise myself.

I head into the kitchen and make a half pot of coffee, wanting to have extra in case Ryan wants a cup. I pick up my current read, *Ghosted,* and sit down in the breakfast nook while I wait for the coffee to brew. Just as the spirit-seeing Rae and her newly deceased Tinder date run into each other for the first time since he died, the coffee pot beeps letting me know it's ready. As I pour myself a cup, I wonder if having a ghost for a boyfriend wouldn't be so bad. Kinda hot if you ask me. They have that brooding smolder automatically built in with the whole being dead thing.

I sit down, ready to pick up where I left off in my book when there's a knock at the door. I look outside through the tangle of flowers planted in my window boxes and see Ryan's silver truck parked by the curb. Ryan is my kind of guy: not only on time but a hair early. "Come on in!" I call.

I close the book, inserting my favorite bookmark that Emma made me out of construction paper and glitter glue before meeting Ryan's striking green eyes as he walks into my kitchen. The sight of him in his dark jeans and light blue shirt nearly knocks the breath out of me. He smiles, seemingly unaware of the effect he has on me, and leans against the island. "Hey, Summer. Good morning so far?"

"No complaints, but it's only nine AM. The day is young," I stand, "Want some coffee?" I'm trying to be light because our last in-person encounter got deep quickly, and I feel like I'm floundering in the aftermath. Luckily, Ryan doesn't seem to pick up on my awkwardness.

"Oh, sure." He sets his tool bag on the floor by the wall and comes to take the mug I poured. He adds some sugar and takes a sip. "So, what are you reading?"

I blush, crossing my arms. "Just a book. I read a lot to pass the time."

"Well obviously it's a book," he chuckles, "What's it about?" He leans against the counter again, mug in hand.

"You can't laugh, okay?" He nods sagely, so I hesitantly continue, "It's a romance about a girl who sees ghosts. Everyone she tells thinks she's a freak, so she eventually just stops telling people. Then, she meets a guy on Tinder that she really likes. They go on a date, he dies the next day in a freak accident, and then they meet again when he's a ghost. It's called *Ghosted* because she thought he ghosted her after their date and only realizes weeks later what happened to him. That's as far as I've gotten," I shrug, "I know it's silly, but I like to read fun books with happily ever afters. I want an escape when I read." I realize how nice it is to talk to someone about my books who genuinely seems interested. I can always talk to Steph, but I feel bad when she's my only outlet and not a huge romance reader.

To my surprise, he says, "Yeah, I get that. It's the same reason people watch TV or sports. They just want to step outside themselves and their lives for a bit. Sounds like an interesting book. I'm not much of a reader myself, but maybe you can tell me the highlights after you read it." *Is he implying he wants to see me again? Is he teasing me and I'm just not getting it?* I blink.

"You don't think it's dumb?" I ask, baldly.

"Why would I? Love is a huge part of the human experience. It's arguably the best part. What's so dumb about wanting to read about that?" His brows draw together in genuine puzzlement.

"I don't know, it can be unrealistic. No guy, no relationship looks like they do in romances," I repeat what I've heard from Jared too many times to count with a shrug. Even though I left him because I couldn't accept that, a small part of me still fears he's right. I can't help poking that old bruise to see if it still hurts.

"A dead guy and a medium might be pushing it for the sake of realism." Ryan smiles at me and I laugh. "But I don't think it's so unrealistic to be in a relationship that makes both people feel loved. My parents are like that. They met in their early twenties, fell in love hard and fast, and have lived happily ever after, I guess you could say. After my dad retired last year, they took off on an RV road trip around the U.S. I get picture updates every few days and they seem as happy as can be." He shows me his phone and scrolls through some pictures of his parents. One of them is outside their RV in the desert somewhere, another is of them posing in front of a "Welcome to Georgia" sign. They look happy, beaming at the camera from their awkward selfie angles.

"I love how happy they look, even after, what, thirty years?" I ask.

"Thirty-two if you include the year they dated before marriage," he replies, a soft smile tugging at his lips.

"That's actually one of the sweetest things I've ever seen," I state, gesturing to his phone.

"I know, isn't it sick?" he asks with a laugh. He shrugs, "I want that someday. They gave me one hell of a blueprint for happiness." He looks down at his phone, making the screen go dark before he shoves it in his pocket.

"Happily ever afters are kind of foreign to me in the real world," I say into my half-drunk mug of coffee. "My dad was a deadbeat and my parents split before I was even born. They fought like cats and dogs until the day my mom died. She passed from an aneurysm when Emma was one. She was at work and just...dropped dead. This was her house, actually." I take a second to look around the kitchen, my eyes catching on the permanent marker lines along the pantry that marked my growth and the ticks in dark blue pen that mark Emma's. "And well, you've heard about Jared and I. So, yeah, happily ever afters seem – I don't know. Unreachable for me, I guess." I clear my throat and turn my back on him, rinsing my mug in the sink.

A large, warm hand rests on my shoulder and his low voice rumbles in my ear, "I'm sorry about your mom, Summer. I can't imagine how hard that must have been trying to be there for your daughter while you were grieving." I feel my tense shoulders drop at the way he gets to the crux of the issue so easily.

I blow out a breath and turn, his hand falling away, "It was. I was only twenty when she passed, so I felt robbed. Even though the timing of Emma was rough because I just graduated high school, I'm kind of glad I had her so young. My mom got to meet her and be a grandma before she passed." I move away from him and shake my head at myself, "God, I'm sorry. I'm just trauma dumping all over you and we don't even know each other." I hide my face in my hands, wishing there was a way to suck all the words back into my lungs.

"Hey, don't do that," he says, gently removing my hands from my face. He keeps his hold on my wrists and waits until I look him in the eye, "I know we just met, but I like you, Summer. I want to know you."

"Like, as friends?" I regret the words as soon as they leave my mouth. I can't believe I just *friend-zoned* the hottest, possibly sweetest guy who has ever looked my way.

He steps back, dropping my wrists. "Yeah, friends." He scratches the back of his neck.

"So, friend, are you gonna take a look at the leak, or what? I'm not paying you to stand around my kitchen drinking my coffee," I say jokingly, trying to divert attention away from the awkwardness that suffuses the air like cheap perfume.

"You're not paying me at all," he replies drily, bending down to pick up his bag. I start to protest, but he talks over me, "Friends don't charge friends for small jobs, Summer. I'm going to go take a look in the attic again and then the roof. Be back in a bit." He heads out and I try valiantly not to stare at his tight butt in those jeans as he walks away. *Friends don't stare at each other's asses either, Summer.* I sigh.

* * *

After a half hour or so, Ryan joins me in the living room, where I'm continuing to read, *Ghosted.* "Anything good happen yet?" He asks, plopping down on the couch at the other end. His eyes snag on the solo picture of Emma that hangs in the place of the family photo that used to be on the wall. To my relief, he doesn't remark on it and slides his eyes to me instead.

"Not really. Rae is trying to figure out how Dean died. Turns out it wasn't a freak accident, but a murder," I set the book on the coffee table and turn to him.

"An unsolved murder is pretty juicy."

"*Oh.* I thought you were asking if they've figured out how to have sex yet. The answer is no by the way." I tuck my feet to the side and lean against the back of the couch.

"I think an unsolved murder is more important than ghost sex, Summer." He rolls his eyes at me.

"Mmm, I beg to differ. Maybe in a thriller, but this is a romance. The murder is just an extra plot line on top of their undying love."

"*Ba dum tss.*" He mimes hitting drums at my pun and we both laugh. "So you think they'll be able to figure it out?"

"The murder? Yeah, romance books tend to tie everything up neatly, even murder plots." I shrug a shoulder and try not to ogle the way the planes of his stomach flex under his t-shirt as he sits up straighter.

"No, the sex. How would that even work?" He seems to think over his own question, brows narrowing in a deliciously broody way.

I get hot all over at the thought. "I'll let you know when I find out," I say against my better judgment. I change the subject for my own sanity, "So. My leak. Is it bad?"

"Luckily, no. It looks like your roof wasn't draining the water out properly before I fixed it. It was clogged up in one spot, which led to your leak. I cleaned out under the tiles and added some flashing to the spot. It should improve the flow a lot and mean that you shouldn't have any more leaks."

"I don't know what any of that means, but I'll take it as a good sign that it didn't take you too long to fix." He snorts and nudges my knee with the toe of his boot. "Is there any water damage?"

"Surprisingly no, other than your stain," he points to the ceiling. "I did leave a fan running up in your attic to help dry it out. Do you want me to paint your ceiling?"

I wave away his offer. While I wouldn't mind another excuse to see him, I have a sneaking suspicion he wouldn't let me pay him. Again. "Oh, no. I can do that. I have leftover paint from a couple of years ago when I repainted all of the ceilings."

"I can help if you want," he offers with a shrug.

"I can't in good conscience let you help since you won't let me pay you." I shake my head.

"How about you take me to your favorite dinner place after?" he asks. At my raised eyebrow he says, "As friends! A nice, friendly dinner outing. I need more options. I've been eating at the same Chinese takeout place once a week since I moved in."

"China House?" I ask. He nods, so I continue, "It's good, but yeah you need to branch out." I give myself a moment to think and then say, "Okay. We'll go to Little Ravenna's afterward. Best lasagna ever according to my six-year-old. How about two weeks from now? Emma will be at her dad's again, so we won't be tripping over her Barbies and Legos while we paint."

"That sounds good to me. I love Italian food. My Grandma on my dad's side was Italian, so this place better be good or my *nonna* will roll over in her grave."

"High stakes," I say with a laugh.

"Definitely," he replies gravely. "Okay, well I have to get going. I have another job in thirty minutes. I'll see you in a couple of weeks." He stands from the couch and groans, pressing his fists into his lower back until something cracks. My mouth runs dry at the sliver of skin peeking out above the waistband of his jeans during his stretch.

"Sounds good," I manage to squeak out.

"Lock up behind me," he says, heading out the door.

I roll my eyes, getting up to do as he asks. "Do you have a safety kink?" I fight the urge to clap my hand over my mouth and feel a raging blush bloom over my chest, neck, and face. I can't believe I just asked him that.

His eyes flare as he looks over his shoulder at me from the porch. "I seem to when it comes to you," he says simply. I close the door and bite down on the smile that's trying to escape.

CHAPTER 13

Ryan

On Wednesday the following week, I'm lying in bed binge-watching my newest TV obsession and crumbing up my sheets with some salt and vinegar kettle chips. Ever since I moved here and committed to slowing down, I've actually had time to watch TV. Now I see what the hype is all about for *Game of Thrones*. My phone buzzes with a text from Summer and pulls me out of Westeros.

SUMMER:

Lol ghost sex is WILD

Oh yeah?

Ya know how ghosts can move stuff?

It went into detail?

Oh yeah. I'll let you borrow it. I just finished the book.

I told you I don't read. Describe it to me

I sit up in bed, setting my bag of chips aside, and watch the three little dots appear and disappear letting me know she's typing. I pause the show. I wonder if she'll take the bait. She does.

SUMMER:

Well, let's just say that Rae was very satisfied.

I need more details. Who did what?

Five minutes go by and she doesn't respond. *Shit,* I think, *she probably thinks I'm some pervert. I knew I shouldn't push her.* After ten minutes go by without a response I start to panic. As much as I'm attracted to Summer, I don't want to lose her friendship either. I could use good people in my life and she's one of them.

RYAN:

Sorry, didn't mean to make you uncomfortable. You obviously don't have to go into any more detail.

Mercifully, after another five minutes, she responds. I let out a breath and read her text.

SUMMER:

You didn't make me uncomfortable. I'm the one who started the conversation. Jared just brought Emma back from their day together. On Wednesdays whoever doesn't have her for the week picks her up after school and has her until bedtime. I just got her down.

I admire how well you guys seem to work together for her. I bet it means a lot to her.

I don't think she gets it yet, but she will one day. Thanks. Really trying to not be my parents.

You're doing a good job. So… back to the ghost porn

LOL it is NOT porn. For your information, we in the serious literary community call it smut.

Tomato, to-mah-to

Maybe I'll tell you about it next time we hang out. It seems like the perfect conversation to have over lasagna

I'll hold you to that.

I can't get the stupid smile off my face no matter how hard I try. It feels like it's permanently tattooed. I recline back in bed, rewind a few minutes on my TV show, and press play. I try hard not to think about Summer or her smutty book for the rest of the night. I fail miserably.

* * *

For the rest of the week, Summer and I text back and forth every day. We talk on the phone more days than not. Sometimes we talk about silly things like the best ice cream to eat after finding out your husband cheated on you (brought on by her current book). Other times, we delve into more serious topics like her fears of what the separation is doing to Emma or how lonely I was when I was moving around, and the betrayal I carried around for years. The more we talk back and forth, the more I realize I like her. Not just an infatuation, but genuinely like her as a person. I'm quickly realizing that she's someone I want in my life one way or another.

On the following Monday, I'm greeted with a text from Summer after turning my alarm off in the morning. I rub the crust out of my eyes and check it.

SUMMER:

I'm sad

What's wrong?

Shit, I didn't wake you did I? Sorry, you were the first person I thought of. I should have texted Steph.

You didn't wake me. I get up at 6:00 on work days. Now what's up?

Okay good. Emma's at her dad's again this week and it just makes me sad. Never thought I'd have to split half of my daughter's life with someone else.

I'm sorry. That has to be hard. I'm here for you if you want to talk or I can come over after work to keep you company for a bit. We can play Scrabble. I bet you'd ruin me with how much you read.

Decimate. I would decimate you.

See? It'd be fun.

Rain check? I'm going out to dinner with Steph tonight.

Yeah sure. We can add Scrabble to our list of things to do this Saturday.

Perfect. Thanks for being here Ryan. It means a lot.

Anytime.

'You're the first person I thought of.' It's been forever since I was in this position. Something inside me preens at being the first person she went to when she was in need. I've always had an innate need to be useful and reliable. It's a part of myself that I've been neglecting ever since Lydia. She took that part of me and twisted it, making it so that something I've always liked about myself became something to be ashamed of.

'I just got so bored, Ryan,' I can practically hear Lydia say. I wasn't exciting enough for her, so she cheated. Went and found that excitement with someone else. I just hope Summer doesn't get bored of me too.

CHAPTER 14

Summer

After work, I meet Steph at The Taproom for dinner. We always prefer the lighter Monday night crowd over the rowdy weekend one. The bar is divided into three: the main bar, a pool section, and a dining section. The dining section is to the right and only holds a few tables and booths. She's already seated at one of the low booths and waves me over.

She's wearing a cute black sweater dress and her hair is piled on top of her head in a stylish bun. Her red-painted lips stretch into a grin as she greets me, "Hey, girl! I already ordered drinks for us."

I plop down in the booth across from her, wishing I had packed a pair of flats to slip on after work. "My feet are killing me," I complain, reaching down to rub the back of my ankle.

"At least your legs look phenom in those shoes," she says, passing me a menu.

"Thanks," I reply with a smile. "How was work?" I ask. Steph is finishing up her second year as the speech and debate teacher at Lakeland High.

"It's alright. Kids are starting to get antsy as the year comes to a close. They're out June fifth, so by the time April rolls around they're just done, especially after Spring break. My debate club has one more competition in a few weeks, so I'm trying to get them prepped for that. What about you?"

I shrug and reply, "Same old, same old. Nothing exciting ever really happens at the bank. I think Sherry is going to retire soon though."

Steph snorts and says, "She's been saying she was going to retire since before you even worked there." She waves her hand to indicate a change of subject is in order and leans in, "So, let me live vicariously through you. You've been talking to Ryan a lot." She waggles her dark eyebrows at me suggestively. I've been keeping her updated on all things Ryan at her insistence. After the night with Coconut, she required a full, hour-long debrief on the entire encounter.

I wait as our waitress drops off our drinks, a gin and tonic for me and a dirty martini for Steph. I take a sip and hum in appreciation before I say, "Yep. We've been talking pretty much every day."

"About what? There's no way a man that pretty is also interesting, It's just not fair," she gripes.

"We talk about everything. We've talked about our exes, our families, and whatever else comes up." I shrug, not meeting her eye.

"Oh you are in *deep*," she says gleefully, clapping her hands.

I sigh and acquiesce, "I'm really starting to care for him. He's genuinely a good guy and he makes me feel seen. Even if nothing happens romantically, I still want him to be my friend. It makes me feel crazy because we've only really known each other for, like, three weeks. Also, Jared and I just broke up. I don't want to be *that* girl."

Steph raises her eyebrow at me. "*What* girl?"

I stir my drink absently with the cocktail straw, making the ice clink against the side of the glass. "You know, *that* girl. The one who can't be single, so she jumps from relationship to relationship without a breath in between." Before I can continue, our waitress stops by to take our orders.

As soon as our waitress is out of earshot, Steph says, "You are so not that girl, Summer. Even if you hopped into bed tomorrow with Ryan— which I highly encourage by the way—" I roll my eyes which she tactfully ignores, "You wouldn't be that girl. You and Jared haven't been in a true relationship for probably the last two years. Not to mention, the last six months have been completely cold. You've been co-parents more than anything. And honestly, Summer? You deserve better than that. So who cares if that comes a month after you officially broke up with Jared, or a year after?"

I take a breath. "I know you're right. I do deserve better." Damn her persuasive debate skills. "But I *am* worried that I'm getting feelings for Ryan so quickly because he's the first man to show any sort of romantic interest in me in a long time."

"That you've noticed," Steph snorts. When I glare at her she sighs and says, "That's a fair concern. You don't have to marry the man right now. Just don't get in your own way. Let things play out naturally and see what happens. I mean, you *did* friend zone him, so that's bound to slow things down." She laughs at the despair written on my face at the reminder.

"Stupid, stupid, stupid," I chant, thumping my head on the back of the booth in time with the words. Just then, our waitress returns with our food and gives me a concerned look. Steph pinches her lips together, thanking her before she bursts out laughing.

"Oh, man. You better watch out. Our waitress might be calling to get you some help," she says through her giggles.

"Eat your food," I order primly, cutting into my salmon.

"Yes, mom."

As we're finishing off our meals, I say, "So we've been talking about me a lot. What's going on with you?"

She shrugs, "Nothing much, honestly. Other than work, I've

been on a few first dates here and there, but no one I connected with. Half of them just wanted to hook up and the other half were a mix of catfishes and red flags."

"Well did you hook up with any of them? My turn to live vicariously through you. I haven't had sex in, like, a year," I lean in, sipping the last dregs of my drink.

"You're practically a virgin," she teases. She waits for a beat, and then goes on, "Yeah actually. I matched with him last week on Friday and we met up on Saturday." She takes a sip of her drink.

"Go on," I say, waving my hand. Steph gives me a scathing look before gulping her martini. "Nuh-uh. You don't get to demand details about my love life and then give me nothing in return. Especially because my romance senses are tingling and I can tell it's juicy." I bounce my shoulders at her.

"Ugh fine! So, on Saturday we met up for drinks over in Springview. He was in town for his Grandpa's funeral-"

I interject incredulously, "He was mourning his Grandpa and wanted a hookup?" I scrunch my nose.

"We all grieve in different ways, Summer." She glares at me playfully. "Anyway. He wanted a warm body to keep him company and told me so upfront. I was fine with that because it's been a while and he was hot. So, after drinks, we went to his hotel and had a very fun night."

"Was it good, or was it awkward?"

"Oh yeah, it was *good*. You know in your romance novels where the woman gets off like four times because the guy is so attentive? It was like that," she says wistfully, fiddling with the leftover olive toothpick in her drink.

"Damn. Four times?" I raise my brows and nod approvingly.

"It was actually three, but who's counting?"

"You are, clearly," I laugh. "Okay, so did you stay the night? Are you going to see him again?"

"I stayed until five the next morning. I left because I didn't want to bump into his mourning family who was staying on the same floor. We haven't spoken since, so I doubt I will. He was only in town for the funeral anyway." She shrugs a shoulder and says casually, "At least he was a good lay."

"I am green with envy. It's been too long since I had an orgasm from another person," I sigh.

"Yet another reason to pursue things with Ryan. If he looks at you the right way, I bet you'd come. He's just got that vibe about him."

"You think he's slept around a lot? I was kind of worried about that. I mean, a man that looks like that could go through a new woman every other day if he wanted. You know me, I can't do casual. I am very in need of attachment."

"I haven't met him, but from what you've told me, I don't get that sense. He would have already tried something with you rather than respecting your dumb boundaries." She laughs when I throw my drink straw at her. "What? It's true. If he was only interested in what's between your legs, he would have left by now because you've kept them firmly closed."

I think over what she said and finally reply, "That's true. Anyway, are *you* going to pursue the man of multiple orgasms?"

"Nah. I don't chase after men, they chase me." She gives me a devilish smile and I laugh. I wish I had her confidence. "Anyway, I should probably get going. I have to grade some speeches tonight and I need to prep for tomorrow." We both stand and I whimper a bit when my blistered heel protests the motion.

I shake it out and reply, "Yeah, you need to get home and do that so you actually get some sleep." We hold each other in a quick hug, and I am reminded once again how lucky I am to have a friend like her.

CHAPTER 15

Summer

Wednesday night after putting Emma to bed at Jared's, he stops me from walking out the door with a hand on my shoulder. "Hey, Summer, before you go, can we talk?"

Trepidation washes through me, but I nod and sit on the couch, tossing my bag on the coffee table. No matter what, someone asking to "talk" just presses the panic button. "What's up?" I ask, trying to sound casual.

Jared sits next to me on the couch, angling his body towards me so our knees touch. He sighs and says, "We've been trying out this separation thing for almost a month now. I just wanted to check in and see how you're feeling."

"About..." I draw out, waiting for him to fill in the blank.

"Being separated. Are you still feeling like this is the right decision?" His chocolatey eyes meet mine. I try to gather my thoughts because I want to tell him once and for all that this is done. "Because I still love you, Summer." *Oh.*

Before I can process his declaration, he's leaning in and his eyes are closing. His hand softly traces my jaw before going to tangle in my hair. He pulls me in for a gentle kiss that tastes like pancakes on a Saturday morning. Comfort and routine built from years of repetition. I feel frozen even though I know my body is responding, my lips are moving against his, and I reach up to fist his shirt either to pull him closer or push him away. Just as he's angling his head to deepen the kiss I push him back with the hand that's still got a hold of his shirt.

"Wait," I say, feeling breathless and confused. I let go, smoothing the wrinkles I made in his shirt absentmindedly. "Jared, you can't just *do that*," I say, scooting as far away from him as his small couch will allow.

He closes the space I created and grabs my hand, "Summer listen, that's what you've always wanted me to do, right? Kiss you out of the blue and *show* you how I feel. I've been thinking a lot the past month and I realized I can't do this without you. You were right to give me this wake-up call. I see it now. I'm going to do better." His face is sincere as he looks at our joined hands.

"How is this time any different than any other time you've told me that, Jared?" I search his face, indecision twisting me in knots.

"Because, this time you've actually made me see what it would be like without you. What it would be like to have our family split up."

I take a breath and rest my head back on the couch, closing my eyes. His thumb is tracing little circles on the back of my hand. His words make some kind of sense; every other time we've had this conversation, the threat of leaving wasn't real. I finally made it a reality.

* * *

I walk into the spare bedroom that Jared has made his gaming room. There's a guest bed, but it's overshadowed by his giant setup, the LED lights lining the ceiling, and the closet full of games and consoles. Jared seems to be trying out a new organization system for his games, because there's a huge pile on the bed that he's sorting through.

He finally notices me standing in the doorway. "What's up?" he asks, going back to his task as soon as the question passes his lips.

I tug the oversized t-shirt down, hoping it will cover the bottom hem of the lingerie I'm wearing. I ordered it online in the hopes that it would entice him. It's been a year since we last had sex and several months since I gave him back the engagement ring. I have a masochistic need to know if it's me that's the issue. "So, your mom has Emma for the whole afternoon right?"

"Yeah. I figured I'd sort out the games and get rid of some like you asked a while ago." He sweeps his hand over the piles on the bed.

I finger the hem of the shirt, "I think I have something better to do." I shoot for coy, looking up at him from under my lashes. I slowly raise the shirt up and overhead, revealing the black lace teddy underneath. His eyes drop to my lace encapsulated breasts and then sweep lower before tracing a path back to my face.

"I don't know, Summer. I really want to get this done before Emma is back. She always opens up all the cases and mixes up the games."

My stomach drops, my confidence deflating like the last sad balloon at a party. "Are you serious right now? You'd rather sort through your game collection than have sex with me? Jared, it's been a year." My cheeks burn in embarrassment at the rejection as I look down at the lacy lingerie. I feel exposed in the least sexy way ever.

He rolls his eyes. "No way. You're being dramatic."

"I am not," I wake up my phone and go to my cycle tracking app. "See?" I turn the phone towards him, "A year and five days, actually."

"You're tracking how often we have sex? That's kind of weird." He shakes his head at me.

"It's really not if you consider us not tracking got us pregnant with Emma," I say, folding my arms across my chest.

"Okay, so maybe it's been a year, but we've fooled around since."

I huff out a laugh, "You mean I've gotten you off. Yep, we've definitely done that."

He crosses his arms, mirroring me, "I've reciprocated."

"Like three times! And newsflash: I faked it!" I hiss the truth, vindictively hoping it will reflect my embarrassment back at him. I scoop the discarded shirt up from the floor and leave the room, wanting desperately to be more covered up.

I pull on some old sweats, the lace that felt so luxurious earlier now itching my belly under the shirt, and Jared walks in. He yanks his shirt over his head and comes toward me. "You did not fake it," he rumbles. I try to protest but he cuts me off, "And even if you did, you won't this time." He grabs my hips, pulling me flush against him. My stomach churns. He runs his nose along my neck and whispers in my ear, "I'll make you feel so good, babe."

I wrinkle my nose and push him back, "No Jared. The mood is ruined now."

"You don't have to be such a bitch about it," he says, his cheeks burning in both anger and embarrassment at my rejection. He's not used to me rejecting him. It's only ever been the other way around.

My anger burns me up. "Name calling? Really? Did I hurt your pride so much you have to turn into a stereotype? You know what, Jared? I'm done. I literally cannot do this anymore. You need to start looking for another place to live." I sit on the bed, tears leaking from my eyes.

The color drains from his face. I've thrown around the idea of taking a break before, but this is the first time I've told him to move out. "What about Emma?"

"You really think us fighting like this is good for her? It's not like this is the first time either. We've been a sinking ship for a long time." I sniffle, wiping the dripping mascara from under my eyes.

"I know it's not. Look, I'll try harder. Let's go on a date. Screw the game organization." He grabs my hand and tries to tug me with him, panic in his eyes.

"No, I'm done. I have to be. This isn't healthy for Emma and it isn't healthy for either of us. I deserve better than this."

His eyes narrow. "What, like the guys in your stupid books? Good luck finding that in the real world, Summer. I'm the best you'll ever get. Who's going to want to go all out for an insecure single mother?"

"Wow." A harsh laugh exits my lips and I look around at the room we share. All the little pieces of us. The sonogram picture with Emma's profile tucked into the mirror, the photo booth picture strips from the mall, the movie tickets from our first date, framed and placed on the dresser. I suddenly realize that there is nothing we've saved from the last three years.

He walks next to the bed and kneels down so we're eye level, saying softly, "I'm sorry. That was out of line."

I hold up a hand, cutting him off. "Too late. We've tried. I've tried so hard the last few years and you've given nothing back. Over and over again, you make me feel like shit and then give me a bit of what I ask for to keep me around. I can't anymore, Jared. Please. Go. Stay with Duncan for the night so we can both cool off. I don't want Emma to feel the tension." I wasn't going for an ultimatum earlier, but I can't take this any longer. This last rejection was the proverbial straw.

"Okay, we'll work it out tomorrow," he says, grabbing an overnight bag to throw some clothes in. I can tell from his casual posture that he thinks this is just like every other time.

"There isn't going to be anything to work out between us. I'm going to do some research tonight to figure out the best way to break it to Emma and what kind of custody schedule is best for her. You need to start looking for somewhere else to go." I feel exhausted and wrung out.

"You're serious about this aren't you?" He turns to look at me, his face drawn, bag clutched in his hand.

I nod once. "Yeah. I really am."

* * *

I open my eyes, banishing the memory of our last fight before we split up officially. "I don't know, Jared. It got bad there for a while," I hedge.

"I promise, it won't ever be like that again. Please, babe, I miss you so much. I swear I'll be a better man for you." He lifts the hand he's holding and brushes his lips against it. *This is all I've ever wanted from him,* I can't help but think.

Green eyes come to mind. Dark waves that can't be contained by a ball cap. A smile that radiates happiness. As if he can sense me wavering, he says, "And think about Emma. Wouldn't you have loved to have your parents together? No arguing, no going back and forth from house to house. Don't you want that for her?" The question is a gut punch.

"You know I do. I just– I don't know. I need to think," I say, standing up and disentangling my hand from his. My head feels muddled and my heart bruised.

"Take the time you need, but I'm not going anywhere. I'm going to keep showing up." The words sound both like a promise and vaguely like a threat. He walks me out and kisses my cheek. "I'll see you Sunday," he promises. As I walk to my car, I take a deep breath of the cool spring air hoping it will help clear my head.

CHAPTER 16

Ryan

I only heard from Summer on Wednesday morning. Usually, we text back and forth throughout the day, and sometimes we'll call each other at night. I don't think much of it because I know she's with her daughter and that one-on-one time is important for them. I choose not to bug her and decide instead to finally set up the home gym I've been buying things for.

When most of Thursday comes and goes without hearing from her, I start to wonder about her. We've talked throughout the day every day up until yesterday. I psych myself up and call her, hoping I'm not being too much.

I grab the broom from the coat closet and start sweeping the kitchen while I listen to the line ring. It's a pretty narrow alley kitchen that doesn't require much work to keep clean, but if I so much as open the fridge it feels like crumbs sprout from the linoleum floor.

Just when I think it will go to voicemail, her sweet, slightly raspy voice says, "Hello?"

I feel my face tug into a smile instantly at the sound. "Hey. How are you? We haven't talked much the last couple of days." I hope I don't sound needy, but it's true that she has me nervous. I can't help but wonder if I did something, or maybe she's realized how boring I am to keep around.

"Oh, um yeah. I'm fine," she says with a fake sense of casualness. I can hear in her voice that she is definitely *not* fine. It's got that wobbly quality it had when we were dealing with Coconut.

I lean the broom against the counter, unable to focus on sweeping. "You sure? Is everything good with Emma?" I feel a little panicky at the thought of something happening to her or Emma. I haven't met the little girl yet, but with how much Summer talks about her, I feel like I know her.

I hear her sigh. She hesitates a beat before saying, "Emma's fine. She's doing great actually. She told me today that she was able to do a back handspring unassisted for the first time at gymnastics."

"Oh wow, Summer, that's awesome!" I feel the tension release from my shoulders. I know Emma has been working on that skill for a while. Summer wouldn't be upset about that though. "So then what's up? You don't sound like yourself." I stick the broom back into the closet and lean against the counter in the silence.

"Jared kissed me last night," she blurts. I start to see red and realize I'm squeezing the edge of my countertop so hard, it's going to leave impressions in my palms. I know I don't have a claim over Summer, but the thought of another man, let alone *that* man having his mouth on her makes me want to break things. It's not the same, but flashes of Lydia and a masculine but posh, *"hullo,"* answering her phone flit through my mind. I close my eyes briefly before I process that Summer doesn't sound happy about the kiss. I start seeing red for another reason.

I force my petty jealousy aside and ask through gritted teeth, "Did he force himself on you?" *I'll kill him,* I think. *Plenty of new construction sites to hide the body.* Okay, I wouldn't actually kill him, but I might go slam his face into a wall if he forced himself on her.

"No, oh my god no, Ryan. He didn't force himself on me,"

she soothes. I release my grip on the countertops and run my hands through my hair.

Relief hits me first, brisk and sharp, and then my stomach drops, "Oh. I mean, did you want to kiss him?" I don't want to ask the question, but I promised her that we would be friends. I'm not someone who goes back on my promises, and a friend would try to see where her head is at.

"No! He kissed me and then I was so surprised I sort of kissed him back. When I pushed him off of me, he stopped," she says.

I quickly shake the mental image of Jared with his hands and mouth all over Summer. After a sigh that crackles down the line, she starts over, "He said he wanted to talk after we put Emma to bed. I thought it was going to be about Emma or something, but then he told me he still wants to be with me and that he still loves me." My head hangs and I press my lips together, not wanting to interrupt her. "Then he kissed me. It surprised me. What he said, the kiss, all of it, so I kissed him back before I realized what was happening. It's like muscle memory or something."

I take the swelling jealousy and compact it back into a nice, small box to examine later. I ask the question I really don't know if I want the answer to, "Do you want to get back with him?" Even if it kills me, I want her to be happy. If that means I have to just be her friend and watch Jared have her, then so be it. I want to be there for her any way she'll have me.

"I don't think so. We were really bad together," she sighs, "But he brought up Emma and mentioned that I've always wanted to give her the childhood I never had. Two parents under the same roof who don't fight." *The asshole is using Emma to manipulate her.* I shake my head, wishing I could show her the woman I see; the one who is worth so much more than what he can give her. Someone who deserves the world.

"Okay," I say gently, "But how do you know that you two won't fight again like you were?" I tell myself I'm asking these probing questions to help her and nothing more.

"I don't. He said that he's really going to change this time because he's finally seen what it would be like to be without me. I told him I needed to think, and he said that he would keep showing up and proving that he loves me." I hear the splashing of her sink and the clanking of dishes, and it makes me smile despite the conversation. Without even talking about it, we're on the same page. I turn on my own sink and start doing the dishes left over from dinner.

"Listen, this is obviously up to you. If you really want to try again, it sounds like he's willing," I grit my teeth before continuing, scrubbing much harder than necessary for the mostly clean dishes, "But, as your friend, I have to ask that you try to think this through logically. Think about the fact that Emma is doing well right now. You guys have been apart for a month now and she's still thriving. Is a two-parent household the ideal? Sure. But having two parents that love you, even in different homes is pretty good too."

"Trust me, I know it is. I would have killed to have that growing up. I don't love him anymore. I haven't for a long time, I think. But it's just what's comfortable, you know? Not to mention, I'm terrified I'll never do better than him. That I'll have torn apart my daughter's secure foundation for nothing." Her voice is tight like she's holding in tears. Against my will, hope beats in my chest, '*I don't love him anymore.*'

After Lydia, I'm terrified of giving everything to someone again. I wasn't okay for a long time after we broke up. I thought I was going to marry her and instead went on a multi-year soul-searching journey that landed me here. I know that I've already given Summer too much when she's still trying to figure things out. I just can't seem to help myself where she's concerned.

I hear my voice soften, "Summer, just from what you've told me about the two of you, I know you can do way better than him," *Me for instance*, "But you have to decide for yourself.

Everyone can tell you how amazing you are and that you deserve the world because you are and you do, but you have to believe it."

She sniffles and says, "Thanks, Ryan. Sorry for the drama."

"Don't apologize, okay? I'm here for you. You heard my whole sob story about my ex and told me that I deserved better. I'm just repaying the favor. You're allowed to be sad and confused right now."

"Okay. Are we still on for Saturday?" I can hear the hope in her voice and feel my own bursting in response.

"Wouldn't miss it," I say, smiling again at the thought of seeing her. It's only been two weeks since I've seen her in person, but it feels like forever. She makes me feel like a teenager with a new crush. She's all consuming.

"Two o'clock sound good? That way we can paint, change, and still get to dinner at a reasonable time." Her voice is giddy and I feel a huge smile stretch across my face in response.

"I'll be there." We hang up and I feel a newfound determination to show Summer exactly what she deserves. I want to show her that I can be someone worth taking the risk for. Worth investing in. She won't jump unless she can be sure that she has a soft place to land. I can't blame her since she has a lot more to consider, but I hope to make the jump more enticing. Friend zone be damned.

CHAPTER 17

Summer

Saturday comes in a rush of fluttering anticipation and I'm feeling more like myself again. I'm still torn because I know for a fact that I fell out of love with Jared a long time ago, but Emma having her parents together under one roof is a dream I've held on to for so long.

I also know that Ryan is right. The fact that Emma is loved and thriving despite the split makes me hope that she really will be okay in the long run. The last thing I want to do is give her the same trauma I have. As a parent, you know you'll never be able to protect your child from every hurt, but at the very least you don't want to be the thing that lands them in therapy later. I shake my head. I've been going over it and over it since Wednesday and I need to stop. I've been looking forward to today and I won't let myself ruin it.

I've thrown my hair up into a messy but hopefully cute bun and am wearing old jean cut-offs and an oversized t-shirt that says 'plant lady' in a font made up of different houseplants that Steph got me forever ago. Both are splattered in paint from the last time I did a home renovation project.

I'm just setting out the tarp in the living room when Ryan

opens the door. At this point, he knows my habit of leaving it unlocked for guests. "Hey," he greets behind me.

"Hey," I throw over my shoulder, situating the tarp so it covers the furniture as well. I turn and a smile blooms across my face when I see what he's holding. "You brought flowers." My heart pitter-patters like a puppy whose owner just got home after a long day at work.

He holds up his other hand, a grin on his handsome face. "And Scrabble." He hands me the wildflower bouquet before setting the game on my dining table.

When he walks over to me, looking like a calendar model for blue-collar jobs in his work pants and shirt that contours to his muscular frame, I pull him towards me in a hug. "Thank you. No one has ever gotten me flowers unprompted. What are these for?" I squeeze him, inhaling his delectable spicy scent. His warm hands wrap around my back, with the top one going to cradle my head at the nape of my neck. Butterflies take flight in my stomach.

"Like I said, you deserve the world, Summer." I swear I hear the unspoken words, *And I can give it to you,* but try not to read too much into it. "And I got them for you because I know you're having a hard time right now. I wanted to cheer you up."

He gives me another firm squeeze before loosening his grip. "So, painting. Is there anything you don't have that we need? I brought my usual stuff just in case," he says. As his arms drop, and we both tip our heads back to look at the ceiling, I'm already itching to touch him again.

I work to get my mind on track and off the lines of his throat as he looks up. "I don't think so. The only thing I didn't have was primer, and I ran to the hardware store yesterday to grab some."

"Oil based?"

"Yes?" I shrug, drawing out the word.

He laughs, grabbing the can of primer from the floor. "Nope. Water based. Be right back." He disappears outside. I rifle through my kitchen cabinets to find a vase for the flowers. Ryan brings a new can of primer down on the floor in the living room. "Just for future reference, if you have a water stain, you want oil based. Water based primers will let the stain bleed through while the oil ones do a better job of holding it back."

He shows me the can and points to the label where "oil based" is written. "That makes sense. I didn't really do much research," I say sheepishly. I put the flowers in a vase with water and return to the living room. I bend down with a paint key to open the can of primer over the tarp.

He grabs the roller brushes, getting them situated on the handles, "It took me years to learn all of this. It's not something you would know unless you've had to deal with it a hundred times." He shoots me a grin that could only be described as panty-melting. "What would you do without me?"

I meet his eye, and the bright green color still takes my breath away. "I honestly don't know." After a beat, I feel as though I've exposed my soft underbelly, so I add, "I mean, I'd definitely still be using that bowl to catch water and potentially getting pink eye." He laughs, but I can tell he caught the undertone. "Anyways, let's knock this out so I can decimate you at Scrabble." I'm trying my damndest to navigate us back to the familiar, friendly footing we've had the last few weeks, but his sudden flirtation is unnerving me.

We get all the painting done, but it takes longer than antici-pated because we had to go over the entire ceiling in the living room, kitchen, and down the hall. When we painted over the stain, it was a completely different color than the rest. Painting with him was a fun release I wasn't expecting. We cranked up some oldies and danced and sang along. Even though my neck hurts from looking straight up multiple hours in a row, I'd do it all again in a heartbeat. It's the most carefree I've felt in a while.

"Okay, well, I am officially sweaty and in need of a shower before we go out." He waves a hand over himself where he is, in fact, gleaming deliciously.

My mouth runs dry at the thought of him in the shower. I swallow around my suddenly dry throat and say, "Yeah me too."

We're sitting on the tarp in the center of the kitchen so we don't get paint on any of the furniture. Ryan leans in and my breath catches as the air around us hums with the static of longing. He takes his thumb and rubs it along my cheekbone like the strike of a match.

"Paint," he says simply before removing his hand, making the air breathable again.

"Even more reason to shower. Little Ravenna's is pretty casual, but not so casual that we can walk in sweaty and paint-splattered," I say. I stand, wiping my hands on the seat of my shorts.

"I'm going to head home to shower and change. I'm only a couple minutes away, so I'll be back soon," he says, standing as well. We take a quick second to clean up the tarp and paint supplies before he heads out the door. "Lock this," he says, pointing at the door on his way out.

"You know I won't when you're just coming right back," I say sweetly. I hear him grumble something that sounds like, "insufferable woman" before he waves and heads to his truck.

As soon as he's gone, I call Steph who's been on standby all day waiting for details. "Please tell me you've seen that man naked by now," she says when she picks up.

I let out a surprised laugh and say, "And hello to you too."

"Yes, hi, hello. Let's get to the point." Her impatience only makes me laugh harder. I think she's more excited about the prospect of me getting laid than I am.

"No, I have not seen him naked," I state matter-of-factly.

"Have you even kissed?"

"No. He was a perfect gentleman." She lets out a groan that lets me know just how disappointed she is. I laugh again and say, "If it helps, I think our not date is going to turn into a date. I don't know where it's going to lead, but I want to find out.

He's been flirting overtly with me all day. Even I couldn't miss it."

She squeals like a schoolgirl and says, "Yes! I knew if you spent some casual time with him you would get over your hesitation."

"I've just been so confused the last few days after Jared," I groan. She huffs in annoyance at his name, so I rush out the rest of my thought before she can interrupt, "But, honestly, I can't even describe to you how natural it feels with Ryan. He and I just click. It's never been like this for me." I go into my bathroom and turn on the shower.

"No, it hasn't. You always felt like you were indebted to Jared because you thought you were just lucky to have him. As your best friend, it is so good to hear you're figuring out that this new guy is lucky to have *you*."

"Okay, I don't want to get ahead of myself. Ryan and I haven't even talked about where this is going." I let out an agonized sound and lean my head back against the cool glass of the shower wall. "If anything, we've talked more about my rela-tionship with Jared."

"Well, that just goes to show that he's a good guy. He's trying to be there for you. Don't let that go to waste."

"I won't," I reply, determined to make that true.

"Okay, go shower and put on those thigh high boots. Your legs look incredible in them. Make it clear that this 'not date' is definitely a date."

I bite my thumbnail to stop my smile from spreading. "The thigh highs?"

"Oh yeah, make that man want to crawl to you." We both laugh and when I hang up, I get ready to make that happen.

CHAPTER 18

Ryan

After giving my close-cut beard a trim, I put on my favorite cologne and throw on a short-sleeved button-down. Summer says that Little Ravenna's is pretty casual, but I want to look nice for her. *Not a date*, the annoying voice in my head reminds me. Well, she might not think it's a date, but I'll be treating it like one.

Once I'm back at her house, I knock before trying the knob. Just as I expected, the door is unlocked. "Damn it, Summer," I mutter, entering the house. It drives me insane that she won't lock her damn door. It still smells like paint fumes, so I go around and open some windows. "Hey, I'm back!" I yell down the hall towards her bedroom.

The door at the end of the hall opens and she pops her head out, long red hair dripping wet and her shoulders bare, glistening with water droplets. A manicured hand clutches a fluffy white towel around herself as she says, "Shit. You're quick. Okay, give me another twenty and I'll be ready." She disappears behind the door again, but she leaves it cracked open. It takes everything in me not to take that as an invitation to go to her when she's still warm and damp and naked from her shower. *Fuck.* I blow out a breath and do some multiplication tables in my head like I used to when I was a teenager.

Once I calm myself, I sit on her couch and scroll through my phone. This feels very domestic: me waiting for her to get ready so we can go to dinner. After some mindless scrolling, the *click clack* of heels snap me to attention. I look up and immediately have to start multiplying in my head again.

She looks edible in tight jeans that hug her sumptuous hips and an off-the-shoulder top that she has tucked in at the front. Black thigh-high boots climb her legs and I have to try very hard not to envision her in those boots and nothing else. *Seven times eight is fifty-six. Seven times nine is sixty-three...*"Ryan?" I hear through the fog.

"Huh?" I ask, dumbstruck.

"Are you okay? You kind of disappeared there for a sec. You know, lights on, but no one 's home?" She comes into the living room and casually plops on the couch beside me. She smells sweet and clean like candy wrapped in fresh linens. Her red-toned brows pinch together over her beautiful hazel eyes. I notice that she's put on makeup as well and wonder if I'm not the only one thinking this is a date.

"Yeah, uh, yes. I just— You look beautiful." I fumble over my words and mentally kick myself. *Smooth.*

She flushes a red that rivals her hair and says quietly, "Thank you. You look really nice too." Shy Summer is maybe the cutest thing I've ever seen.

"So, are you ready to go eat?" I ask. She nods and I stand, offering my hand to pull her up. She takes it and tugs me by the hand to the garage.

"I'm driving," she says with a challenge in her voice like she already knows I'm going to argue.

"Summer, no. Let me drive us," I say, pulling her to a stop at the driver's side door before she can get in. She still hasn't let go of my hand and I'm taking full advantage.

"Nope," she says, popping the 'p.' "We agreed that I would take you out as a thank you for helping me with the leak and painting." She pokes me in the chest and I capture her hand there, wondering if she can feel my pulse pounding under her palm.

"Fine," I say, considering my next words, "But I get to drive you *and* pay next time." I gauge her reaction to my thinly veiled attempt to ask her on another date.

She shrugs, a smile on her face when she gently pushes me back with the hand on my chest. "Fine." She ducks into her car while I process the fact that she just accepted another date with me. I can't help the grin that breaks over my face as I round the car and hop into the passenger seat. She tosses her bag on my lap as I buckle my seatbelt. I let out an *oof* when it punches me in the stomach on the way down.

"Jesus, Summer. What the hell are you carrying in this thing?" I heft the offending bag. It must weigh at least ten pounds.

"My very necessary things!" she retorts, pulling out of her garage.

"Oh my God. There's a book in here isn't there?"

"Maybe," she replies evasively.

"Who are you, Rory Gilmore?" I ask, setting the bag between my feet.

"What?" She looks at me, confused.

"Rory? You know, from *Gilmore Girls*? She's always carrying a book around."

"I know who she is. It's my favorite show of all time. How do *you* know who she is?" She gasps theatrically and says, "You *are* stalking me aren't you?"

"My mom and sister love the show. I was subjected to it every fall," I say defensively, "They had the DVDs before Netflix was a thing and would binge it on the weekends every year starting in September." I shrug.

"Dean, Jess, or Logan?" she demands.

I sense this is an important question, so I think for a bit before

I reply, "It depends on where she is in her life. Jess was good for young Rory but Logan fits her more as an adult. Dean is trash."

She hums her agreement, then says, "You passed."

I try not to preen while watching the sky paint itself pink and purple through the windshield, rubbing my thumb across my lips to hide my smile.

* * *

We get seated at a table in the back of the small restaurant. I pull out her chair before rounding to my side and getting seated. To the left of us is a giant mural of the Italian countryside painted along the whole wall. Servers in white polo shirts bustle around carrying steaming plates and giant menus. It's a busy night, so the air hums with multiple conversations and the clatter of silverware.

"So," she says, sipping her wine after we've ordered, "If I remember correctly, you wanted more details from *Ghosted.*" She levels me with a playful smile as she whips the book out of her bag. I can see there are a few tabbed pages.

"You're going to give me those details here?" I ask incredulously, looking around. There's a cute old couple at the next table holding hands and chatting over their shared plate of mozzarella sticks.

She moves to the chair next to me and leans in closer, "Don't be a prude, Ryan. No one will even hear us. It's so loud in here." I think she's going to hand me the book, but to my horror and amusement, she opens it herself and begins to read, her voice taking on an over-exaggerated sultry quality, "'*Rae felt Dean before she saw him. He appeared in front of her, completely naked. Her pupils dilated as she took in his bare chest, mouthwateringly peppered with tattoos,*'"

I interrupt her, "Wait. Do you think ghosts can get dressed and undressed? Where do their clothes go?"

"Shh," she scolds, "We're not going for realism here. Now

listen, '*Dean reached out and touched her cheek. Even though she couldn't feel it fully, she could sense his hand there. 'Clothes off,' he demanded and stepped back to watch her strip for him...'*" Summer proceeds to read me a very detailed scene that will make me side eye anyone reading a book with a cutesy cover from now on. My jeans suddenly feel a little too tight. Hearing Summer read such erotic words in her raspy voice is almost too much to take.

Just as Summer is winding down the passage, our server swings by and sets our food on the table. While I'm cursing the interruption, it's probably for the best. My blood needs to be redirected back to my vital organs. "Thank you," Summer says demurely to the server as if she wasn't just reading erotica aloud in this crowded restaurant.

I stare blankly at the meal in front of me, blinking a few times to come back down to Earth. "Jeez, Summer. Warn a guy next time you plan to do that. Now I'm all hot and bothered and I haven't even taken a bite of my arrabbiata yet." She laughs evilly and stows the book away in her bag. Maybe I *should* start reading.

We dig in and I have to admit that it *is* pretty good and that my *nonna* probably won't be rolling over in her grave anytime soon. When I'm halfway through my arrabbiata, Summer surprises me by placing a hand over mine. I set my fork down and look at her, noting the nervous lines of her face. "Ryan, I want to talk to you about something," she says, meeting my eye, cheeks burning.

"Sure. What's up?" I ask, feeling her nerves invade me.

She takes a quick breath in before saying, "I know I've been sending you mixed signals and I'm sorry about that. Everything is still so fresh, and I wasn't expecting to find you —" Her cheeks recolor and she says, "Anyway. I know we're just getting to know each other, but I wanted to let you know that I'm open to seeing where things go if you are." She drops her gaze and fiddles with the napkin on her lap.

"So, you feel this intense pull, too?" I ask, feeling equal parts relieved and elated.

Her shoulders relax and she smiles shyly at me, "I do. I thought I was going crazy. I thought I was reading into things too much."

"Not at all. I've wanted you since the first time I caught you staring at me." I can't help the chuckle when her cheeks heat again. "When you asked to be friends, I respected it, but you have no idea how happy I am right now hearing you want to see where it goes. Does this mean I get to touch you?" I ask. I've been keeping a respectable distance ever since she asked to be friends. I didn't want to push a line she'd drawn. My heart races with the new possibilities.

"Please," she replies quickly. *Fuck.* Summer begging nearly brings me to my knees.

"You mean, if I kissed you right now, you'd be okay with that?" I ask, leaning in slightly.

"Yes," she practically whispers, wetting her lower lip in anticipation.

"Good to know," I say, reclining again and grabbing my fork. She mirrors me and crosses her arms, pushing her breasts up distractingly. She clears her throat, and I raise my eyes to meet hers, noting her raised eyebrow. "Make no mistake. I will kiss you, Summer. Just not here. I don't need eyes on us the first time I taste that sweet mouth of yours."

She nods dazedly, and I work to keep the cocky smirk off my face. Getting Summer to look at me like that after getting a taste of what she reads makes me proud. If I can bring lust to the forefront of her mind with just my words, I can't wait to see what'll happen when I use my mouth for other things.

CHAPTER 19

Summer

Ryan insisted on driving us home because I had two glasses of wine at the restaurant. I put up a fight, but it was half-hearted. It's nice to feel taken care of.

We pull into my garage and a mix of anxiety and anticipation flood my system. Even though I'm comfortable with Ryan, the feeling of being an actor on stage without her lines returns. I don't know how to do the adult dating thing. When Jared and I got together, we were still in high school and the rules and expectations feel very different when you're eighteen versus twenty-five. Is he expecting us to have sex right away? We haven't even kissed yet. Is he my *boyfriend*? Am I supposed to assume that he is or does he ask first? Is that juvenile thinking?

His voice breaks through the cacophony in my brain, "Hey, Summer?"

"Yeah?"

"Get out of your head. Let's go play some Scrabble." He gets out of the car, coming around to my side to open the door before I can even take off the seat belt. I sigh out a relieved breath and dig my teeth into a smile while I follow him inside. Even if he doesn't know what I'm thinking exactly, he still manages to center me.

We head inside and I turn on a couple of lamps in the living room. They both give off a soft glow and make the environment feel more intimate than it did earlier with painting supplies strewn about and bright daylight pouring in. "Do you want something to drink?" I ask, heading to the kitchen to grab a glass of water.

"I'll have whatever you're drinking," he says, setting up the game.

We both sit down on the couch with our Scrabble letter holders facing away from one another. For the next hour, we play Scrabble and joke around. It's nice to be so at ease with another person who isn't my child or long-time best friend. I beat him all three times, for the record. "Okay. That was *not* fair. What does 'quixotry' even mean? That is not a real word. No way!" He sits back and crosses his arms with a mega-pout taking over his handsome face.

"I'll take my winning twenty-seven points now, *thankyouverymuch*. I didn't peg you for a sore loser," I taunt.

"I am not a sore loser!" he says indignantly, eyes roving the board for a way he can scrape together a win.

"Are too," I sing-song childishly. Before I can blink, he's kneeling over me, pinning my hands down with his strong thighs over mine and tickling the life out of me. "Ryan! Ryan, stop!" I manage to get out between laugh-wheezes. Tears are streaking down my face as he takes his hands away but keeps me pinned. I blow out a breath and say, "See, you really *are* a sore loser." I can't help the smile that takes over my face when I see the forlorn look on his.

He gently swipes my tears that leaked out with his thumbs and laughs at himself. "Okay, I guess you're right. I'm a *little* competitive."

At the same moment, we both seem to realize that he still has me pinned and the air suddenly feels thick with static again. I could easily move my hands, but I don't. The room shrinks to just the two of us and all I can hear is our breaths and my pulse pounding like a war drum. In a blink, he's off of me and tugging me by the hips to straddle his lap. He must read the panic in my face as I wonder if I'm too heavy, because he says, "You're beautiful, Summer." He moves his hands up my sides, sweeping my rib cage, and grazing the sides of my breasts before his hands meet at the nape of my neck. He starts pulling me towards him and I lean in, closing the distance.

Our lips meet and my belly erupts in flames. The kiss starts out sweet while we learn each other. His hands in my hair gently tug, slanting my mouth over his, and suddenly the kiss isn't sweet anymore. It's ravenous. A month of careful restraint set free. All the doubts in my brain burn in the flames of this kiss, teeth tugging, tongues twisting, and breaths gasping.

Eventually, Ryan pulls back resting his forehead against mine. His breathing is heavy and his velvet timbre is an octave deeper when he says, "Summer, we need to stop if you don't want this going any further. You're in the lead on this, but I only have so much restraint."

I shift my hips, suddenly feeling the restraint that he does *not* have against me. We both groan. "Sorry," I pant, not sorry at all. I take a few deep breaths, hoping that some oxygen will clear my head, but it's infused with his warm scent and the mingling of our breaths. "I just—" I stutter, leaning back a little to get some breathing room, but not getting out of his lap, "I'm obviously not a virgin."

"Well, me either." His green eyes shine with mirth.

"But," I continue, not meeting his eye, "I've only had one other partner."

"I didn't know for sure, but I figured as much," he says, playing with the ends of my hair, sending tingles along my spine.

I sigh, "I'm not a virgin, but in many ways I feel like one. I'm guessing you've been with more than one person." I hold up a hand to stop what he's about to say. "I'm not judging at all. I honestly don't care if that number is two or twenty-two, but I feel really inexperienced in comparison and sex is kind of a big deal to me. It's not something I can be casual about."

Lifting my chin to meet my eyes, he says, "Yes, I've had more than one partner. But you and I are new to each other, so we both have learning to do. Our first time together, whether that's tonight or months from now, will be *our* first time. I'm happy to be a beginner with you." I grab his hand still under my chin to kiss his knuckles.

"You'd wait months for me to be ready?" I ask.

"Years. As long as I got to be by your side, I'd wait years, Summer. Though I might have to take a few cold showers a day. Especially if you keep wearing these jeans." His hands glide down to grab my ass while I laugh.

"You won't have to wait years. *I* don't have the self-restraint to wait years. Just, not tonight, not yet. I need a second to wrap my brain around this." I touch my face where his beard has rasped against my skin, leaving it feeling overly warm.

I expect him to be disappointed, maybe even upset despite his reassurances. Instead, he simply says, "Okay." He pulls me in for a much less intense kiss, our lips brushing together. Then, he lightly kisses the tender skin around my mouth in an unspoken apology.

We cuddle and chat until I almost fall asleep in his lap. He gently sets me aside and stands, intending to head home. "Stay a little longer?" I'm not ready for him to leave yet and the thought of going to my empty bed alone is unappealing at best.

He smiles at me, kisses me on the nose, and says, "I would love to."

CHAPTER 20

Summer

The next morning, I wake a little confused when I notice Ryan's solid arm thrown over my middle and a leg wedged possessively between my own. Then I remember after a movie marathon in bed last night, I vowed to close my eyes for just a little bit. I guess we both fell asleep instead.

I lay there for a minute, just enjoying the feeling of sharing a bed with someone who wants to be next to me. Last night, after deciding to move our watch party to the bedroom, we both wanted to change out of our jeans. He had stripped down to his briefs and undershirt. I averted my gaze because I felt I had to show some restraint for us both after my whole 'not tonight' speech. I threw on my own pajamas, a sexy but practical shorts and camisole set I had bought myself when Jared moved out, and it was his turn to look away, Adam's apple bobbing.

"Morning. Sorry, I didn't mean to fall asleep here." Ryan's gruff, barely awake voice greets me as he squeezes me impossibly closer.

I shrug a little in his arms, "It's okay. I fell asleep too."

I feel the press of his hardness against me and despite my best intentions, I wiggle against it. He groans, squeezing me harder. "Summer." There's a warning in his voice.

"What? It's not tonight anymore," I say. A girl only has so much restraint after all. I hear his quick intake of breath as he gently squeezes my breast, calloused thumb brushing over me through the silky pajama top. My own breath hitches and I press back against him. His leg wedged between mine presses up, exerting the sweetest pressure where I need it most. It's not enough.

"Fuck, Summer," he growls, before flipping me on my back and raising himself over me. My legs instantly fall open and he slots his hips into the welcome inlet of my thighs. He crashes his lips onto mine, the kiss rivaling our first last night. I grab his full bottom lip between my teeth and tug until he hisses in a breath.

He leans to the left, his other hand roaming under my shirt, lifting as he goes. I claw at his back, bunching his shirt in my hand, trying to pull it off him. He laughs against my skin, lifting onto his knees so he can yank it off himself. He tosses it off the bed and wow, does he look edible. His stomach has the causal definition of a man who does manual labor most days but also enjoys his food. I can't help but bite my lip as I stare up at him.

"Top. Off," he demands from between my legs, still on his knees. I pull it overhead, too turned on to be self-conscious about my soft belly and faded stretch marks bared to him for the first time. He exhales a strangled breath and presses a hand over my wildly thumping heart. "You are the most beautiful woman I have ever seen," he says so reverently I believe him.

"Come here," I say, pulling him down to me again, kissing him softly, sensually. Our tongues glide and teeth graze familiarly. He settles himself between my thighs again, the only thing separating us a few thin layers of fabric.

"You make me feel like a teenager. I don't think I've enjoyed just kissing this much since." He presses against me firmly, driving home his point. I'm too lost in the sensation of our bare skin sliding together for words, so I let out a sound of agreement as I wrap my legs around his hips to bring him tighter against me.

He starts a slow, reverent descent down my body, kissing and licking as he goes. He looks up from under his dark lashes before he starts tugging at my shorts. I allow him to pull them down and kick them off to the side. Just when I think he's going to rejoin me, his face returns to the line of my panties. "Okay?" he asks.

I nod, unabashedly wanting him to continue, insecurities be damned. As his mouth dips lower, I say, "Um. No one's ever... So, I don't know what I like." I feel a blush color me from the chest up.

He grins devilishly and says, "Let's find out together." Then, the man licks. His. Lips. I think I might faint from being so turned on. Before I can second guess myself, he tugs my underwear aside, lowers his head and presses his tongue to me, wide and flat so I feel him everywhere. He is both patient and ravenous. Responsive to my every sound and movement. Within minutes I'm trembling under him, an exquisite pressure building inside me.

Heat floods my core and my lower abdomen tightens, pleasure sparking along my spine. "Come for me, Summer," he demands against my skin. I climb a little higher, and then with one final well placed press of his tongue do as he says, breaking into a million glittering pieces. He gently kisses my inner thighs, replaces my underwear, and then climbs up the bed, laying his head next to mine. Smug male pride is written all over his face.

I go to my side and reach for him. Just as I pinch his waistband between my thumb and forefinger intent on revealing more of him to me, he places a large hand over mine, stalling it. "Today was for you. I have a feeling you haven't had many days like that," he says quietly. Because I can't resist, I reach my hand lower and squeeze a little before letting go, enjoying the groan that leaves his parted lips.

"I haven't," I say, curling into his side. "I feel guilty leaving you hanging, though." I trace a finger through the soft smattering of dark hair on his chest.

"Don't. Just because today was for you doesn't mean I didn't enjoy myself." He kisses the top of my head.

After attempting to convince him to get in the shower with me, I begrudgingly shower alone. I emerge from the bathroom feeling more blissed out than I have in a long time.

I pad into the kitchen in a pair of lounge pants and a bralette. Ryan is the picture of domesticity, puttering around my kitchen making us breakfast and coffee. He gestures for me to sit at the table where sunshine is limning everything in gold, feeding my many plants.

He comes over to me, plates and mugs in hand and I realize he gave me my favorite mug with the little suns. I have to wonder if it was just random chance or if he's really paid that much attention. He sets mine down, kissing me on the temple before sitting across from me. The sun gilds the outline of his frame and he looks so dreamy I almost pinch myself. I look down and see he's made us breakfast sandwiches with bagels, eggs, and some bacon I had in the fridge.

"Thank you," I say shyly, taking a sip of the coffee that he's somehow made perfectly without direction. "I'm not used to being taken care of." I take a large bite before I can say more, or more embarrassingly, cry since the lump in my throat is rising. It means more than I can express that he's just taking care of me without prompting or nagging. He's just doing it because he cares and he can.

He nudges my foot under the table and says, "You're welcome. I don't mind at all. I actually like cooking, and breakfast is my favorite meal. It's the only one you can have both savory and sweet as the main course and no one bats an eye."

"My kind of guy," I say, smiling at him. It still doesn't feel real that this man wants me.

We just finish breakfast when I see a truck pull up outside. To my horror, it's Jared's truck. "Oh, shit!" I exclaim, "Shit. You have to go." I stand so quickly, that I knock my hip hard into the edge of the table, making me wince.

"What? Are you okay?" Ryan asks, standing too and rubbing my throbbing hip.

"No! I'm sorry. That's Jared's car and he's bringing Emma," I pause to check the time on the microwave, "Two hours early." I start dragging him to the bedroom, halfheartedly thinking I can hide him and sneak him out once Jared leaves. *His truck, dammit.* I remember Ryan's truck is in my driveway.

"You're an adult, Summer. You don't need to hide the guy you're dating." Ryan rolls his eyes but comes along so he can throw his jeans on. I try not to get too distracted by the little flutter in my belly at the word 'dating.' I'm still adjusting to it and it makes me want to do a little happy dance.

"Look, I haven't told Jared anything about you beyond implying that we're friends."

"You don't need his permission," Ryan says, getting all gruff and protective.

"No, I don't. But, we did have an agreement that anyone we were serious about and wanting to introduce Emma to would need to be vetted by the other first. I need to do this right. I was planning on telling him today, but ideally without you almost naked in my house!"

He buttons and zips his jeans. "Okay, I understand. I don't want to mess anything up for you or Emma. I'll just say I'm here for the leak." He gives me a quick kiss and heads for the bedroom door just as the doorbell rings.

After throwing on a clean shirt, I rush to the door as Ryan carries the ladder we used yesterday to paint the ceiling into the hall under the attic access. I open the door and Emma bursts in saying, "Ew! It smells in here," on her way to her room, sparkly bag in tow.

"You painted," Jared says, stepping into the entryway. He

cranes his neck up at the newly white ceiling and whistles. "Man, you've been busy. Whose truck is that?"

"Mine," Ryan says, carrying his ladder into the room. An awkward beat passes while they size each other up like apes in the wild.

I'm about to whip out a ruler when Jared says, "Oh. Cool. You here for the leak?" When Ryan nods, a quick dip of the chin, Jared continues, "Yeah, I was going to fix that a while ago but just never got to it." He turns to me, dismissing Ryan with his back to him. Ryan's eyes go glacial and they narrow on Jared's head.

"Anyway, Summer. I brought you these." Jared thrusts out a bouquet of red roses, the petals browning around the edges. He says sheepishly, "I know they aren't the best quality, but it was all the store had this morning."

I look back and forth between Ryan and Jared, not sure if I should take them or not. I finally grab them and say, "Thanks." I set them on the coffee table and head to Ryan. "Let me walk you out."

He nods again, glaring over at Jared who has sprawled himself comfortably on the couch. I follow Ryan outside and shut the door behind us. "I am so sorry. I'm going to talk to him right now, I swear," I say, wringing my hands. I hope I haven't already messed this up. I know Ryan's past, and the last thing I want to do is poke at that insecurity.

"It's okay. It isn't your fault. I'm just trying to keep the caveman screaming 'mine' in my head at bay. I trust you, Summer. I do. Call me after, okay?" He kisses me softly before heading to his truck, ladder in tow. I know how much that trust means to him. He doesn't give it away easily after Lydia.

I take a breath before going back inside. From the direction of my kitchen, Jared says, "What the fuck, Summer?" I cringe when I realize he's seen the other bouquet that Ryan brought me yesterday, thriving and placed proudly in the middle of the table. He knows I never buy myself flowers, so he correctly guessed who they came from.

"Yeah. I was going to talk to you about that," I say, waving a hand at the flowers.

Jared petulantly throws his bouquet on the floor, petals scattering the wood planks in a mockery of romance. "Well. I was going to put these in water to be nice when I saw those. So, just fixing your leak, huh?" He crosses his arms, his brows drawn down over his dark eyes in anger.

"No, but I'm not going to talk to you about it if you're going to act like a child," I say, trying to rein in my annoyance.

"I'll act however I want when my woman is spreading her legs for another man!" he shouts. To my horror, his voice echoes through the house.

I whisper between gritted teeth, "Shut up, Jared. Emma's just down the hall and she doesn't need to hear you spewing your bullshit. Outside. Now." I head back for the front door, not waiting for him to follow. "I'm walking your dad out real quick, Em. Be right back!" I call, as cheerily as I can manage through the rage.

I hear her 'kay' just as Jared slams the door behind us. He opens his mouth and I jump right in, "No. you don't get to speak yet. It's my turn. First of all, don't you *dare* speak to me like that in front of our daughter. I don't care what you call me when she's not around, but if she's here, you keep it civil. We agreed on that. Second, I am not 'your woman,' and I can be with whoever I want."

He sighs, guilt flashing in his eyes, "I'm sorry. You're right about Emma. I lost my temper." His jaw ticks and his eyes harden again, "But you are mine, Summer. We just talked about this on Wednesday. I won't share you." He steps closer to me, getting in my personal space.

I am so stunned by the audacity that it takes me a second to react. I laugh humorlessly and say, "If only you cared this much when we were actually together." I scrub a hand down my face in annoyance. "We never agreed on anything. You made your feelings clear on Wednesday, but like usual, neglected mine. I don't want to be with you. Period." I'm trying not to be nasty, but I want to make myself clear.

"Oh, but you want to be with *Ryan?*" He spits his name like a curse.

"I do, actually. I was going to talk to you about it today. We're seeing where things go, and I want him to meet Emma eventually." I hug my elbows and watch a kaleidoscope of emotions play over his face.

"You don't even know this man. It's been what, a month since I moved out? Were you cheating on me?" He steps even closer, his breath mingling with mine and making me look up at him.

I take a step back, holding out my palm so he doesn't follow me. "No! I would never do that. You know me better than that despite whatever your anger is telling you. I'm sorry if it hurts your feelings that I've moved on, but I can't change how I feel."

He barks out a cruel laugh and I just know he's about to go for the jugular. "Damn, Summer. You're pathetic. You lay on your back for the first man to show you any attention after me. You think he's going to want to stay with *you?* I don't need to vet him. He's going to be gone soon now that you've already given him what he wanted. I won't take you back. I don't want sloppy–" he looks me up and down and sneers, "And I mean *sloppy* seconds." With that, he turns away. I don't even realize I'm crying until a tear drips off my chin. I take a few minutes to collect myself before I head back inside, his words weaving black threads through the bright tapestry of the last two days.

CHAPTER 21

Ryan

It's been nearly a week since that morning I spent with Summer in her bed. If it weren't for Jared, I'd be floating on cloud nine. Summer hasn't told me the specifics of what was said between them on Sunday, but I can just tell whatever happened wasn't good. She hasn't sounded like her usual self. Just when she seemed to be getting better, she saw him again on Wednesday, and her mood darkened again. She's going to tell me, but it isn't a conversation to have over the phone.

She's still trying to honor her agreement with Jared and not have me meet Emma until he approves, so when she has her I don't come around. I respect the rule, but man does it suck for me. This is the first time I've ever been with a woman who has a child and it's a whole different ball game.

I set out to clean my house since it's been a bit neglected the last few weeks. I throw in a load of laundry, blast my music, and go about scrubbing down my bathrooms and kitchen. I'm singing, *"'Strangers waitin' up and down the boulevard, their shadows searchin' in the night,'"* loudly into my broomstick when my phone rings, blaring through my Bluetooth speaker. It startles me so much I yelp and drop my broom stick/microphone.

"Hello?" I say after my soul returns to my body.

"Hey, man. Want to get some drinks and watch Victor and Chris annihilate each other at pool?" Luke asks.

I look around and shrug. My plans weren't great for this Saturday night, anyway. Being with friends will probably offer me a good distraction. "Sure. Let me hop in the shower and I'll meet you guys there. Taproom?"

"Yep. See you there." We hang up and I go get myself showered and dressed. I shoot Summer a quick text letting her know I'll be out tonight. She tells me to have fun and I grab my keys.

I pull into the Taproom and have a hard time finding parking. It becomes abundantly clear why there's so many people when I hear *Like a Virgin* by Madonna being sung off-key in a falsetto male voice.

According to the chalkboard sign above the bar, Karaoke Night is a monthly thing. A small stage has been erected in the back of the bar that typically has booths and tables. On stage is an older guy, probably in his mid to late fifties belting out the song. I quickly avert my gaze when he starts gyrating a little too enthusiastically and look for my friends.

I push through the crowd to get to the pool tables. I break through the thickest band of patrons and I see Luke laughing, a hand splayed across his chest as Victor fumes from the side of the pool table. Chris is wearing a smug look that tells me that he probably just won the game. "Hey, guys," I say, clapping Victor and Luke on the shoulders. "Guessing Chris just won?"

"For the third time in a row!" Victor yells over the still gyrating Madonna fan.

"I'm on fire tonight," Chris says, coming around to greet me. "Beer?" I nod and Chris gestures to Victor. "Go on, beer boy. Fetch us another round since you're losing so hard tonight." Victor rolls his eyes and cuts through the crowd to get to the bar.

"He'll probably be a minute," Luke says, pulling up a chair from the wall to sit on.

"Want to play a round?" Chris asks me a bit too gleefully for my tastes.

"I think I learned my lesson last time," I say, holding my hands up to ward off the offer. Chris shrugs and begins to gather the balls, already arranging them for another game.

"I've got ten bucks to spare since I'll definitely be buying you another round. I'll play," Luke says, standing from his chair. I take his seat gladly. It's much more enjoyable to watch someone else lose to Chris than to lose yourself.

In no time at all, Chris is poised to win and preparing to take his last shot. Just as he's lining up, a slurred voice behind me says, "Fuckin' bitch is cheatin' on him. Told him since she baby trapped 'im she was a no good whore." My lip curls at the foul language. I hate when men call women whores. I feel something cold splash down the back of my neck, and I jump to my feet.

"Ah, shit! Sorry, man," the drunk asshole in question slurs my way, half-empty beer mug tilted towards the floor, a slow drip of beer pouring out. He's got the look of someone who drinks too much, too often. His eyes are bloodshot and puffy. His clothes are a little too snug, with unknown stains marring the fabric of his t-shirt. His beard is scraggly and his hair is thinning up top. The guy he was talking to uses the distraction to slink away into the crowd.

"Woah, dude. Maybe you should slow down," Luke says, coming to stand behind me. The cold beer sluices down my back and soaks the band of my jeans.

"Here, Ryan." Chris hands me a stack of napkins to mop up the majority of the beer. I start scrubbing at my neck, keeping my temper in check. I'm not a bar fight kind of guy, and the Taproom isn't exactly a place for them anyway.

"Shuthafuckup Luke," the drunk slurs, half shutting one eye to focus on him.

"Go home, Duncan. You're beyond drunk. If Jared isn't here with you, call him to take you home," Luke says earnestly, obviously taking no offense. *Ahh, so this is the infamous Duncan I've heard so much about.* I instantly feel less forgiving. Then it really hits me. Summer. He was talking about *Summer* before dumping his beer down my back.

Before I can stop myself, I say, "You really shouldn't be running your mouth about something you know nothing about."

Duncan's glazed blue eyes turn to me and he spits, "Who the fuck are you?"

"Ryan Garett."

Something like recognition lights his eyes. "Oh shit. You're the guy that bitch is sleepin' with!"

"If you're talking about Summer, I'd use her name if I were you," I say, my voice lowering an octave.

Duncan steps up to me, nearly toe to toe, and puffs up like an overblown rooster. He's a much shorter man, so he has to look up at me when he's this close. He seems to lose a little steam when he realizes how much bigger I am. "Listen, man, there's no reason to throw a fit over *her.* I dunno what she told you, but she's still with Jared. How *she* can have two guys after her I'll never know, but get out while you can. I never trusted that b-" he looks at me and despite his drunkenness, wisely adjusts his words, "Woman."

I sigh heavily and say, "She's not with Jared anymore. I don't know what *he's* told you, but that's the truth. Summer wouldn't do that." I take a step back, not wanting to cause a scene.

He laughs, an ugly braying sound reminiscent of a donkey. "Damn. You poor sucker." He tips back his mug to swallow the last dregs of his beer. "She's got you wrapped around her finger too, huh? What is it with that chick?" He leans haphazardly against the wall, belching in a way that tells me his dinner isn't far behind.

"What do you have against her? You act like she broke up with *you,* not your friend." I cross my arms.

He flings himself off the wall in my direction, poking a finger into my chest, "Now you just shut the hell up!" Spittle flies in my face and I'm about two seconds from decking him. Luke must read my face because he gets between us and guides Duncan outside. Duncan sloppily pulls against him the whole way, but eventually follows him out the door.

I'm still fuming when Victor pops up, a pitcher of beer in hand. "What happened? Where's Luke going?" He sets the pitcher on the tabletop that lines the wall.

Chris says, "Duncan spilled beer all over Ryan and then insulted Summer. He said she was two-timing him and Jared."

Before I can say it, Victor says, "No way. There's no way she'd do that." I instantly like Victor even more than I did before.

"Exactly. She knows my relationship history. She wouldn't do that to me or anyone else," I say, pouring myself a beer. Despite my shirt sticking to my back, I won't let Duncan ruin the night for me.

"He was just piss drunk," Chris says, waving his hand, "He's never liked Summer either. No one gets why. I know our senior year of high school is when Jared and Summer started dating. Duncan didn't really pay her any attention until that. Jared started spending all his free time with Summer and I guess Duncan didn't like being on the back burner. Especially once they had their daughter, Ellie?"

"Emma," I correct.

"Emma, right. Anyway, once they had her, Jared obviously had even less time for his friend and since Summer didn't like Duncan either, they only ever got to hang when they played video games or on the occasional weekend." Victor and Chris start adding chalk to the ends of their pool cues.

"How do you know all this?" I ask, taking a sip of the cool beer and feeling my shoulders creep down from my ears.

Chris shrugs and says, "Most people in town know at least some of it. I work with Jared and have for the last few years, so I heard the rest from him. We aren't exactly friends but we talk at work sometimes."

"So, you don't care that I'm with Summer now?" I ask, now that it's revealed that he and Jared are acquaintances.

"Nah. As long as you guys are happy, who cares? Jared and Summer have been on a downward spiral for a long time. Maybe they'll both be happier apart," Chris says, shrugging and lining up his shot. I sit quietly for a while, watching their game unfold. The Taproom has gotten much quieter since it seems there's been a break on the karaoke stage. Music plays at a volume low enough to allow people to talk without shouting, alternating between pop hits and classic rock.

We're having a good time, but it's hard not to replay Summer telling me that he kissed her last week. I know she said that she feels done with him, but what if I really am just a rebound? Just a pit stop before getting back with him or finding someone better? Last I heard, Lydia and her British dude got married. Maybe that's all I'm good for: a last bit of fun before settling down. Even if Summer wouldn't do that on purpose, I can't deny that I worry about it.

Once their game is halfway over and my beer is nearly gone, Luke comes back shaking his head full of shaggy brown hair. "That guy is an idiot. Glad you didn't hit him," he says, pulling a chair up to sit next to me. I'm glad for the interruption because I was spiraling. Luke pours himself a beer and refills mine afterward. We clink our glasses in a silent toast that tonight hadn't ended in violence.

"Yeah me too," I sigh, "I wanted to though. Even if I wasn't dating Summer I'd want to punch him for talking about anyone like that." My anger stokes, remembering the words he said tonight as well as the things Summer has told me about.

"I get it. I really do. Honestly, I think Duncan had a thing for Summer before Jared got with her back in high school. I don't think he took too well to losing the girl he was interested in and his best buddy all at once," Luke shares, fiddling with his glass of beer.

I ask, "What makes you say that? Chris said he didn't pay her any attention until she started dating Jared."

"I was in the same class where they did that group project that brought Summer and Jared together. From an outsider's perspective, it was pretty clear that they both liked her, but I think she was just oblivious. I don't know if Jared and Duncan ever talked about it, but one day it just seemed like Jared and Summer were a thing, and Duncan all of a sudden hated Summer."

"If they were fighting over her, how did they stay friends?" I wonder.

"I honestly don't know. Like I said, I have no clue if they ever talked it out or if Jared just went for it. Duncan and Jared have been friends for so long that they probably were able to work it out." Luke shrugs.

"Doesn't explain why he hates her either. I mean, come on, a girl from high school rejects you and you hold a grudge for years after? Seems insanely petty," I scoff.

"Not to defend him, but Duncan didn't exactly have the best home life growing up. A drunk for a dad, and his mom never stood up for him when he got under his old man's foot. And I guess small towns make rejection a lot harder. Especially if that girl dates your best friend," Luke says. At my look of incredulity, he continues, "I'm not defending him. I think he's a total jackass. I honestly wouldn't have blamed you for decking him tonight if it came to that. I'm just thinking out loud."

"What'd you do with him anyway?" Chris asks.

"I made sure he didn't come back inside and waited with him until Jared could come pick him up. He didn't seem pleased to hear who Duncan almost got in a fight with, by the way," Luke says, eyeing me to gauge my reaction.

I shrug and say, "He can be mad, then. Summer and I aren't a secret, and I'm not going to let some drunken idiot talk badly about her." I clench my jaw and glare into my beer.

I see Luke's wide smile out of the corner of my eye. "So. You and Summer are a thing then, huh? I guess you caught her eye," he says, punching me playfully on the shoulder.

I can't help the dopey grin that spreads across my own face. "Yeah. Guess so."

CHAPTER 22

Summer

"Bye, Mommy!" Emma gives me a hug around the middle and then sprints towards Jared's truck.

"Bye, Em!" I call as she throws her bag into the backseat.

I awkwardly turn toward Jared. Things haven't been great the last week. He's still angry at me and I don't know what to do about it. He's been civil in front of Emma, but otherwise abrasive at best and downright mean at worst. He still hasn't apologized for what he said last Sunday, and the words still sting like a papercut doused in lemon juice. I decide to rip the bandaid off and ask, "So, are we ever going to talk about this?"

He huffs out a breath and chews his lip. "I don't know what to say, Summer." He looks away from me and watches the bees flit busily from flower to flower in my window boxes.

"You can start with an apology for what you said on Sunday," I say, crossing my arms.

"I'm not apologizing for being angry at finding out you're with another man." A muscle in his jaw ticks.

"You're allowed to be angry, but you aren't allowed to talk to me like that. We're going to be in each other's lives forever. We have a child together. That means we have to have a baseline of respect and be able to tolerate being around each other. I am not going to force Emma to have separate birthdays and holidays just because you can't be civil."

He sighs, scrubbing a hand over his short hair. After a painful beat, he says, "You're right. I lost my temper. I'm sorry. I'm not okay with Ryan though. Did you know that he tried to start a fight with Duncan last night at the Taproom?"

My head shakes side to side. "What? Why would he do that? They don't even know each other," I say, confusion pushing my brows together.

"According to Duncan, he said that you were still with me and Ryan didn't like that very much. Tried to punch him right after." Jared raises his eyebrows at me.

"Okay, well, first of all, we aren't still together," I say. He blows an annoyed breath out. "Anyway," I continue, "That doesn't sound like Ryan. He's not the violent type at all."

Jared scoffs, "You hardly know him! This is why he can't be around Emma. I can't trust that he's not some violent asshole." His lips tighten into a grim line.

"I know him well enough to know he wouldn't try to punch someone just because they lied, Jared. I don't think we're getting the full story. You know how drunk Duncan gets when he goes out. You've had to go pick him up a thousand times! Ryan would *never* hurt Emma. I understand you want to wait a while to introduce them. I'll respect that. I think you need to meet him first anyway, and we can go from there."

"I still don't like it, but fine." He spins on his heel and stalks back to the car. All in all, that went better than I expected. At least he didn't call me "sloppy seconds" again.

. . .

A few hours later, I'm stepping out of the shower when I hear a text ding my phone. It's Ryan, letting me know he's heading over. I wiggle in excitement and bite my lip. We're planning on having a date night in tonight.

I slip on a matching lilac boy shorts and bralette set and throw some black lounge pants over top. The loose-fitting lounge pants hug me at the waist while the bralette goes down my rib cage. It leaves an inch of skin exposed at the waist and it feels scandalous even though I'm mostly covered up. My lips spread in a smile when I think about Ryan seeing me like this.

I use a towel to scrunch the extra water out of my hair and exit the bathroom. I head to the living room where I've stashed the necessities for our date night. I spread my comforter and pillows on the floor in front of the TV so we can watch a movie and cuddle. On the coffee table, I've placed an array of snacks from salty to sweet. Ryan is supposed to bring dinner and we're going to eat on the floor like kids at a sleepover.

Ryan knocks on the front door and pops his head in, stopping in his tracks when he sees me. I smile at him self-consciously, wishing I'd thrown a cardigan or something over my shoulders. He shakes himself and comes inside. He toes off his shoes, closes the door, and walks towards me with purpose.

He tosses the Chinese takeout on the coffee table and yanks me toward him so quickly I yelp in surprise. His hands trace up my arms before he slides his thumbs under the straps of the bralette, making my breath catch at the possessive touch and look in his eyes.

He cups my jaw with both hands and brings my lips to his in a crushing kiss. I'm suddenly very glad I didn't wear the cardigan. I slide my hands up his back under his navy colored t-shirt as the kiss deepens. He pulls away first, keeping us close with the press of his forehead to mine. "Hi," he says, a grin in his voice.

I laugh out a breathless, "Hi." I lick my kiss-swollen lower lip as I pull back from him.

He takes a breath and says, "So. We should eat first or that's going to get cold." He gestures to the bag full of takeout containers. "If we keep going I won't want to stop and I know you've been craving Chinese." He sits on the blanket and pats the spot next to him.

"Good idea. I'm starved." I grab the bag and spread the containers between us. I hand him his chopsticks and a cold beer that I had pulled out of the fridge before he got here.

"Yeah, I'm hungry too. While we eat, why don't you tell me what happened last Sunday?" Jared asks, digging into the pork fried rice.

"Only if you tell me what happened last night," I quip, raising my eyebrow.

He gives me a sheepish look and says, "I swear I was going to tell you about it today. It wasn't a big deal and I didn't want you worrying about it when you were with Emma."

I take a bite of orange chicken and gesture with my chopsticks for him to go on. I'm not concerned about him being an "aggressive asshole" and am more convinced that Duncan over-exaggerated than anything.

"So, I went out to the Taproom with Luke and the guys like I told you last night. I was watching Chris and Luke play pool, and Duncan accidentally spilled his beer all down my back. He just came out of nowhere. I don't know if he was with friends or alone, but he was sloshed," he says before taking a swig of his beer.

"He was probably alone. Jared is pretty much his only friend that I know of. I can't even count the number of times Jared had to grab him from the bar after he had too much to drive," I say, rolling my eyes at the memories of Jared having to haul himself out of bed and drive to whatever bar Duncan had chosen for the night.

"That makes sense. Luke ended up having to walk him out and wait for Jared with him. Before he spilled the beer on me, I heard him saying some vile stuff. I figured out later he was talking about you. He was calling you names and saying you were cheating." Ryan looks at me and I can see the anger darkening his eyes.

"Just so we're clear, I am absolutely not cheating. I would *never* do that." I reach out and take his hand.

He squeezes mine and says, "I know. It's just hard for me sometimes. I trust you though." After a beat, he continues, "Anyway, Duncan realized who I was when I told him to stop talking about you like that. After he said some more bullshit, Luke walked him out. That was it." He shrugs and takes a huge bite of chow mein.

"So you didn't almost punch him?" I ask, sort of wishing he *had* punched him.

He swallows and says, "I thought about it, but I wouldn't have unless he hit me first. I thought he was going to before Luke walked him out. He charged me when I asked why he was so twisted up over you when you were with Jared, not him."

I snort a laugh. "Why would he be angry about that? Of all the things to punch you over." I roll my eyes and toss some broccoli beef in my mouth.

"I dunno, Summer. Luke seems to think he had a thing for you back in high school before you started dating Jared." I choke on the piece of broccoli in my mouth, sputtering and coughing. Ryan pushes my glass of water towards me and I chug it.

In a croaky voice, I say, "Is Luke okay? That's insane. Duncan does not and has never had a thing for me. Do I have to remind you of the time I overheard him calling me a cow?"

Ryan's jaw ticks and he states, "No, you do not. I *really* should have punched him." He clenches his chopsticks so tight I'm worried he'll break them.

I pat his thick bicep and say, "Down boy." He loosens his grip on the chopsticks and sets them on top of a container of fried rice.

He grunts and continues, "He's obviously immature. A lot of immature guys turn rejection into hurting the person who rejected them. Was he only nasty to you after you started dating

Jared? What about before?" He wraps an arm around my waist and pulls me snugly into his side.

"He was always on the periphery, you know what I mean? I was aware of him through school, but I feel like we hardly knew each other until we did that group project. He was nice enough then. We had to spend, like, a whole month working on that stupid poster and presentation. I don't remember him ever being rude until afterward. He even drove me to and from Jared's house after school a few times..." I pause as a memory hits me, "Oh my *God* I'm an idiot," I gripe.

* * *

"Thanks for driving me, Duncan. I'm trying so hard to get my license but my mom never lets me drive," I say, tossing my backpack between my feet in his passenger side.

Duncan gives me a radiant, recently braces-free smile and says, "No trouble at all, Sum. I like driving you around. If you need to practice driving or whatever, we could always do that. Together, I mean." He scratches the back of his neck. We pull into the line of cars queuing up to exit the student lot.

"That would be awesome! I'm kind of terrified of freeways, so maybe we can start out in the grocery store parking lot?" I smile sheepishly.

"Yeah, I wouldn't want us dying in oncoming traffic. Grocery store parking lot it is. It's a date." Duncan shoots me a grin and I feel thankful to have finally made some friends outside of Steph. She's amazing, but she's always busy with leadership things or cheer these days.

"I'll bring the crappy driving skills," I say, throwing him a thumbs up and laughing.

"And I'll bring the crappy car." He laughs with me. It's only a few minutes of comfortable silence later that we pull up at Jared's

house. "Do you want to do something afterward?" His hand fidgets on the gear shift while he stares straight ahead.

I turn to him now that we're seated in the driveway. "Like what?" I ask.

"Maybe we could grab di-" he starts, but Jared interrupts him by throwing himself dramatically on the hood of the car. We both laugh at his antics. Duncan clears his throat.

Jared opens my door for me and slings my bag over his shoulder. "What were you saying?" I ask, realizing Duncan never got a chance to finish.

Duncan looks between Jared and me. "Never mind. Let's get this shit done." He unbuckles his seatbelt and gets out. I follow suit, Jared tossing an arm over my shoulder as we walk to the front door.

* * *

I finish retelling the memory and say, "Duncan was trying to ask me out." I run a stressed hand through my hair. "Oh my God, *ew.* I mean he was nice enough then, but knowing what I know now, yuck." I grimace.

"Did you ever go driving with him?" Ryan asks, cleaning up the food containers.

"No. We never made a concrete plan, and it wasn't long after that that Jared asked me out. It felt weird being alone with his friend after I started dating him, so I passed on his offer when he brought it up."

"I'm guessing that's when he started treating you like shit."

"Yup." I shake my head and laugh humorlessly. The fact that Duncan has treated me like garbage for the better part of seven years because of a non-rejection rejection is just so *Duncan.* Leave it to him to twist something innocent around. At least he's moved on from the crush, even if it doesn't leave much room for anything but nastiness. "I don't want to think about him anymore. It's giving me the heebie-jeebies. Let's watch this

Marvel movie before I change my mind." I pull Ryan with me, so we're lying down, slightly propped up on pillows.

"*Guardians of the Galaxy* is a classic. If you don't like it, I don't know where this whole thing between us will go," Ryan says, tugging on the ends of my hair teasingly. I roll my eyes and we settle in as the dramatic opening music booms from the stereo system.

CHAPTER 23

Ryan

After the movie ends, I take a minute to clean up our snacks before sitting next to her again. I run my hand up and down her back, my callouses catching at the lace of her shirt/bra thing. I want to talk to her about Jared before we do anything else because I know she'll try to distract me otherwise.

"So, as much as having you sprawled all over me without a real shirt makes me want to do dirty dirty things to you, I think we need to talk about what happened last Sunday," I hedge, pulling back slightly so I can look at her. Mistake. Her eyes are hooded and before I can stop her, she's straddling me.

She leans down and peppers my face with feather-light kisses, nipping at my lips until I give in. I open to her and my hands roam over her lush curves. I pull back while my head is still getting some blood flow. "Summer," I chastise.

She buries her head in the crook of my neck and mumbles, "I don't wanna talk about it." She pulls back, sits on my lap, and looks down at my chest. She toys with the pocket of my shirt and says, "What Jared said was... painful. And I'm having a good time tonight, and I don't want to ruin that by thinking about it." She meets my eyes then. Vulnerability melts her expression into something soft, and now I want to punch both Jared and Duncan.

"You can tell me. It's important for us to be able to talk about things like this." I cup her jaw and pull her in for a soft kiss. I need to know what was said because I want to be in Summer's life for the long haul. That means Emma too, and Jared is unfortunately a part of that. "I promise afterward we can do whatever you want."

"Whatever I want?" Her eyes take on a wicked gleam and I feel myself go hard again. *Six times eight is forty-eight. Six times nine is fifty-four.*

"Yes, but before you distract me again, let's do the less fun part first," I say, trailing my hands up and down her hips.

She sighs and says, "Okay, I'll tell you what he said, but I need you to promise not to freak out and go all caveman. I'm a big girl and I need to handle my family drama on my own, okay?" She continues to run the tip of her finger along the edge of the pocket on my shirt.

I nod my head and squeeze her hips reassuringly. "Okay. I promise. If all you need from me is support, I'll do that."

She takes her time smoothing her hands over my shoulders before she sits back on my lower thighs and hugs her elbows. A frown creases her brow and she says, "So, he saw the flowers you brought me and freaked out because he realized they were from you and that you had obviously moved beyond just being my contractor. He accused me of cheating on him, and I had to remind him *again* that we weren't together just because he said so." She huffs out a humorless laugh. "Anyway, after that, I told him that you and I were serious or at least moving that way." She looks at me and I can see the insecurity she feels in the way she won't quite meet my eye.

"We're definitely serious." I lift her chin with my hand so she meets my eyes. She gives me a crooked smile that makes my heart break a little for her. For the way she struggles to believe that I'm absolutely feral for her. For what she's gone through that makes her doubt what's right in front of her. "So, I'm guessing that's not the end of it."

"No," she sighs and anger flashes in her eyes. "He said that you would be gone soon because I quote 'gave you what you want,' and he doesn't want your 'sloppy seconds.'" She drops the hands she was using to make air quotes into her lap. Her hazel eyes are made brighter with unshed tears. "He basically called me a whore and said that you'd be done with me after you slept with me. He also refuses to give you the green light to meet Emma because he's so sure you'll leave."

Anger roars up my chest and my jaw clenches so hard I worry about losing a filling. I take a few deep breaths in the silence to get myself under control. "Okay. I'm trying really hard to just be here for you because that's what you need from me, but I have to tell you that that is a load of bullshit. First of all, I'm not going to be done with you any time soon, no matter if we sleep together or not. I like you for a lot more than what's between your legs. You are one of the most selfless, kind-hearted, sweet people I've ever known. You're beautiful, inside and out. I think your ex," I can't bring myself to say his name, "Is just realizing what he's losing. All the nastiness is a product of that, not you. I'm sorry he's making it difficult with Emma. Is there anything I can do to make that easier?"

"Not really. We talked more today when he came to pick her up. He did apologize for what he said, but it still hurts. Today it was a new excuse about you, though. He said you were potentially violent because of the whole thing with Duncan. I told him that Duncan was probably over-exaggerating or leaving things out, but of course, he didn't believe me. He did agree to meet you eventually. I'm guessing that's his way of giving it time to see if you'll leave." I can see her physically closing herself off, curling inward like a wilting flower.

"I'm not going anywhere. You're going to have to work a lot

harder than that to get rid of me. I'm glad there's some distance between now and then because even though I'm not a violent guy, I wouldn't mind punching him straight in the nose for calling you names and making you feel bad. I need a little time before I see him. I don't want to give him any reason to say no to me meeting Emma. Is any of this custody stuff court-mandated?"

She shakes her head and says, "No, we decided to handle it privately because I thought we could be mature adults about this and put Emma first. I'm not going to take it to court yet because I think that'll make this whole situation worse." She sighs again and rubs her temple. "Anyway. Can we make out now? I'd like to forget about my problems."

Rather than answer her, I bring her face closer to mine, more than happy to fulfill her request. I take my time making my way to her lips, kissing along her jaw and over her cheeks and nose. I want her to feel cherished, important, and safe. She needs to *feel* how much she means to me because I know pretty words aren't enough for her.

I kiss down her neck and across her collarbone before I nip at her ear, earning me a gasp that goes straight to my groin. It's only then that I take her lips. I keep the kiss slow and sweet, all lips brushing and tongues exploring gently. When she starts to slide against me, I have a much harder time taking it slow. "You're killing me, babe," I say, running my hands down to grip her ass.

She pants into my mouth, tasting like the cherry sucker she ate during the movie and her own brand of sweetness. "Good," she says, bearing down harder against me. We both groan at the contact. Unable to help myself, I pull that pretty purple bra down, enjoying the way it frames her perfect breasts.

"You are so beautiful," I say between kisses on her chest. I work her over until she's practically melting into me. Her head is thrown back and we haven't even gotten started yet. I shift her off my lap and help her stand in front of me so I can tug her pants down, leaving her in a matching purple number that has my mouth watering. "Summer. Look at you." I hear the reverence in my voice and can't bring myself to be self conscious. I'll gladly get on my knees for her.

I lean in and press a kiss to the soft round of her belly. When she tries to shy away, I grip her hips and pull her closer, kissing and nipping under her navel again. "Stop that. You're the sexiest thing I've ever seen. All of you." She smiles, her cheeks going a pretty pink which makes me laugh. "So words make you blush, but not all this?" I gesture to her unclothed body.

Her eyes flare with heat. She takes my hand and pulls me up to stand in front of her. "Enough about me. Your turn." I whip off my shirt so fast she laughs and then sucks in a breath, trailing her hands down my chest, following the line of hair down until she reaches my belt buckle. "God, I forgot how stunning you are," she says, and now it's my turn to blush. No woman has ever called me stunning, and I think I like it. Sure, I've been complimented, but something about 'stunning' just holds a certain reverence to it.

Her red-tipped fingers make quick work of my belt and zipper. I'm down to my briefs with my jeans pooled at my feet faster than I can blink. I kick them off and mold my hands to her jaw, tilting her face so I can kiss her deeply. She opens on a whimper. I pull back to stare at her kiss-swollen lips. "Fuck," I groan, taking her in.

With a wicked smile, she drops to her knees in front of me and quickly has my briefs joining my jeans at my ankles. She leans in and places a chaste kiss on me and I think that'll be it until she grabs me by the hips and pulls me into the wet heat of her mouth. I gather her damp hair in my hand so I can see her better. The sight of her before me, head bobbing and hair wrapped around my fist is nearly enough to undo me. "You're gonna have to stop if you want to do anything else tonight," I eventually manage to say despite being unable to form a coherent thought. She looks at me through her lashes and releases me.

"Just thought I'd return the favor," she says, coming to stand in front of me. Her tongue darts out to lick her bottom lip and I think I lose my mind a little. "Come here," I say, sitting on the couch and gesturing for her to straddle me. While she slides her underwear off, I pull the foil out of my discarded jeans.

"Here?" she asks uncertainly, and I nod. She straddles me then and we both work to get situated. As she sinks down on me for the first time, our eyes lock and I can see the same disbelief I'm feeling at how good this already is reflected there. Her eyes are hooded and cheeks rosy with pleasure. We both moan as we move together, finding our rhythm.

Her nails dig into my shoulders as she leans down and tugs on my ear lobe with her teeth. I bring one hand up to palm her breast, bringing her to my mouth. I nibble and suck in tandem with her rocking over me, and I feel her muscles clench around me. "Ryan!" she breathes, coming apart with a shudder around me.

I take her mouth with my own again. I grind her harder onto me until pleasure crawls up my spine and I erupt, moaning into her mouth.

"The couch was a *great* idea," she pants resting her head on my shoulder.

When she sits back and looks at me, a shy yet satisfied smile on her face, I know then that I'm falling hard and fast for her and there's no turning back. This beautiful, amazing woman who has trusted me with her body and her heart is quickly becoming my everything. I almost say it, but I don't want it to come off as a post-sex confession that she might second guess.

I kiss her mouth softly and then press gentle kisses to her chin and cheeks where beard rash has made her red and tender. She slowly slides off of me and collapses on the couch, legs thrown over my lap.

I look down and say, "Let me just take care of this real quick."

I stand up and head to the bathroom. Just as I'm washing my hands, Summer comes in to clean up as well.

"Want to watch the next *Guardians of the Galaxy*?" I ask while she's washing her own hands.

She perks up. "There's more of them?"

I laugh and kiss her temple. "Ha! I knew you'd like them. Nerd."

"You can't call me a nerd for liking the movie you suggested," she says, smacking my butt before she leads me back out to the living room. A naked Summer walking around is a site I could definitely get used to.

CHAPTER 24

Summer

Ryan spends a few nights this week in my bed. While we agreed to take things slow, it's easy to have him spend the night when Emma isn't with me. I'm choosing not to evaluate it too closely because this is the first time in a while that I've done something just for me and I don't want to ruin it by overthinking.

On Friday morning after being woken up by Ryan's roaming hands and hot mouth, we both get ready for work. He's started leaving a few things here so he doesn't have to run home early in the morning. I insert my earrings while Ryan trims his beard next to me and am shocked by how natural it feels.

I could get used to this, I think. The thought scares me. I got so comfortable with Jared that I allowed myself to be treated terribly for years. I fell into what was comfortable and didn't have the foresight to know I deserved better. Jared wasn't always an asshole. What if Ryan turns on me too? I study him in the mirror and try to tell myself that even if things don't work out between us in the long run, Ryan isn't that kind of guy.

"What are you looking at?" he asks, leaning over the sink so it catches all the stray beard hairs.

"You," I say simply. It's true. This week he's caught me looking at him many times. I've also found him staring at me like he thinks I'll disappear if he blinks too hard.

"I know I'm pretty to look at, but you have a *look*. One of those doubting yourself looks," he says jokingly. When I don't respond, he tugs me into him, my hands landing on his deliciously bare chest. "Summer, what's up?"

I take a second to search his open, sleepy-eyed face and say, "Sometimes you just feel too good to be true. I worry that it'll all fall apart."

"I worry too. I think if you have a good thing going, it's natural to be a little afraid of losing it. The key is to push past the fear and enjoy what we have. After losing people or being hurt, it's easy to put your guard up and not let anyone in. It's a lot harder to be open again, so I think we're being brave." He brushes his hands down my arms and pulls me in for a hug. I smile and inhale his scent which is starting to smell like home.

"You're right. I'm sorry. I know my constant doubt is probably annoying."

"Not at all. I get it. You've been through it and it's hard to believe that things will be okay when your past proves the opposite. I'm going to work every day to show you that this is right and good. You're worth putting in the work, Summer." He tilts my head up with a hand under my chin and presses a sweet kiss to my lips.

We finish getting ready and head out the door. The summer heat is already creeping into May and the garage warms as soon as I open the garage door. I throw my bag on the passenger seat and try to start my car. It makes a huff of defiance, so I try again, turning the key to no avail. I groan in annoyance and jump out of the car to stop Ryan. "Hey!" I yell, waving my arms and walking down the driveway to catch his attention before he drives off.

He rolls his window down and says, "What's going on?"

"My car won't start," I say with a pout. The damned thing

gives me issues about once every few months. It's always something new.

"Shit. I don't have my jumper cables. They're at home. Do you want me to go get them, or do you just want a ride?"

"I'll just have a ride if you don't mind. I need to get in on time today. We have a staff meeting and I'll never hear the end of it if I'm late." I hold up a finger and jog to my car to grab my bag. My manager, Rachel, will be pissed if I'm late again. I try my best to be on time, but when you have a kid, it's not always easy.

"After work, we'll try to jump your car. If it doesn't start, we'll have the mechanic take a look. Have you had trouble with your battery before?" Ryan asks, pointing the truck in the direction of the bank.

"The battery, the brake lines, the air conditioning, and the carburetor," I reply sheepishly. Ryan laughs and interlaces our hands over the center console.

"Maybe it's time to get you a new car, or at least a new*er* car." He glances at me for a second before putting his eyes back on the road.

"Yeah, yeah, yeah. The old girl has been with me since I graduated high school. I have a hard time parting with her," I say affectionately, thinking about my little beater car.

It was my mom's before she gave it to me for my eighteenth birthday. Sometimes in the heat of a summer day after my car has been sitting in the sun, I swear I can still smell her perfume if I close my eyes and concentrate hard enough. Jasmine with a hint of musk. The glovebox still holds a tube of her emergency lipstick, melted beyond repair because I just can't get myself to throw it out. Every time I flip down the visor, I get a flash of her swiping on that coral shade and using the tip of her pinkie nail to clean up the edges of her lips.

When we get to the bank, I give Ryan a quick kiss goodbye and speed walk inside. "Good to see you on time, Summer." Rachel looks at me over her glasses, a silvery eyebrow raised.

Rachel likes to pretend to be a hardass, but she's really just a big softie. She took on a maternal role for me after my mom died, and I think she struggles to be as hard on me as she is on everyone else as a result. I'll never forget the way she closed the whole bank down so she could drive me to the hospital where my mom was taken after she passed. She's about as affectionate as a feral cat, but even still, on that day, she held me to her and let me sob until the tears dried.

Then, she took me by the shoulders and made me look into her eyes when she said, "I know this pain is unbearable. Unimaginable. So, you cry when you need to. You rage at the world when you need to. And you hold onto that baby of yours extra tight, because above all, she needs you. You are so strong, Summer. This hurts, but it will not break you because you won't let it." She's quietly been there for me ever since.

My heart squeezes with affection for my crotchety boss as I scuttle to the breakroom. My phone buzzes with a text message while I get seated with my coworkers at the large oval table. I subtly flip the screen over on my lap and see that it's from Jared.

JARED:

> Just letting you know I'm going to be out of cell range today. Going to check out a new site for work. Should be back in time to pick Emma up from school. If you don't hear from me by 2. Can you do pick up just in case?

> I think I can do that. Car is acting up again but I can get a ride from someone at work.

> Hopefully you won't need to. You need a new car. That thing is a piece of crap. Talk later.

I roll my eyes. *Men.* Always trying to tell me what to do. I shoot an apologetic look at Rachel who is going over new customer acquisition procedure changes. She gives me a pointed look but continues on. I sigh and lean back in my chair feeling like a sulky middle-schooler who just got caught texting in class. Today is *really* not going my way.

* * *

Just before lunchtime, I get a call from Lakeland Elementary. As soon as the school number pops up on my screen, my stomach bottoms out. The only other time I've had a call from them midday is when Emma had a high fever and strep throat at the beginning of the year. "Hello, this is Summer Evans," I say into the phone while walking towards the break room for some privacy.

"Ms. Evans, hello. My name is Janet. I'm the Lakeland Elementary school nurse. I have little Miss Emma here and she really doesn't seem to be feeling well. Her temperature is climbing and her stomach seems to be really bothering her. She complained of some pain when she was first sent to my office. I've been watching her for the last hour and it doesn't appear to be getting better. I'd suggest coming down here and taking her home."

I blow out a breath and sink into a chair in the break room, anxiety making the overstuffed bulletin board in front of me hazy. "Okay, I'll be there as quickly as possible. I probably need about a half hour or so to get there." She tells me she understands and will keep watch over Emma before we hang up.

Even though I know Jared said he would be out of range, I try his cell phone a few times just to make sure he didn't miraculously get back into town early, but it goes straight to voicemail. I leave him a brief message, "Hey Jared, it's me. Emma isn't feeling great, so I'm going to get a ride to pick her up. I know you don't want her meeting Ryan yet, but he's the only person I can ask right now to take me. None of my coworkers will want to catch whatever bug she has. I promise he'll just drive us and drop us off. I'll just take her home with me until you get back into town. Call me when you get this."

I call Ryan next and explain the situation. Even though he'll need to give me a ride hours before he expected to, he doesn't balk at all. He actually sounds just as worried about Emma as I feel. Luckily he's in the office today and can be here within a few minutes since it's close.

"Hey, Rachel?" I approach her desk as she types rapidly, not breaking eye contact with the screen.

"Yes?" she says, finally looking up from her computer. She takes in the worried look on my face, and asks, "What's wrong? Is everything okay?" She sits back from her desk, her posture ramrod straight.

"I'm sure everything is going to be fine, but I just got a call from Emma's school nurse. Sounds like she has the stomach flu or something and I have to go get her."

"Is there anyone who can watch her for you?"

"Well, Jared is out of cell range right now until at least two for work and his mom is at work also. I'm not sure who else I could ask."

She heaves a gusty sigh. "Alright, just make sure to use sick time so you get paid."

Now it's my turn to sigh. "Okay. Thank you." They say bad things come in threes, so let's hope my having to use some of my meager sick time is the last bad thing today.

"Oh, and Summer, keep me updated, will you?" she asks worriedly. I nod and close out my station.

CHAPTER 25

Summer

Ryan and I get to the school in record time despite stopping by my house to grab Emma's booster from my car first. I leave him in the truck and hustle to the front office. After dealing with the paperwork to sign Emma out for the day, the receptionist leads me down a short hallway and stops before a door with a homemade "Nurse's Office" sign dangling from a hook next to it. She knocks briskly on the door and leaves me to it.

I cautiously enter the dimly lit room after hearing a muffled "come in." The nurse has turned off the overhead lights but left on a dim desk lamp. The light of her computer gives her wrinkled face an eerie blue glow. She's seated behind a small desk in the corner of the room while Emma is laid out on a well-loved tan couch against the opposite wall.

Emma's eyes are closed, but her eyebrows are drawn together. Her little body looks so tense and I can tell even from across the room that she's feverish.

I go to her immediately. "Hi, precious girl. The school called and told me you weren't feeling well." I smooth her sweat-dampened hair away from her brow. She cracks her eyes open and looks at me. She gives me a little shake of her head and then closes her eyes tight again.

The nurse approaches us, rubbing hand sanitizer into her hands. "Ms. Evans. I'm Janet. I'm the one who called you earlier. Thank you for getting here so quickly." She gestures for me to follow her back toward her desk. "Sorry, I just don't want to scare her," she says in a whisper.

"What's going on?" I ask, my heart racing.

"Well, I'm a little concerned. After I got off the phone with you, Emma vomited twice in the time it took you to get here. Ordinarily, I would just write it off as a stomach bug, but what has me worried is that she keeps putting a hand over her abdomen on the right side. Has Emma ever had any issues with her appendix?" Her low, kind voice does little to calm me despite her efforts.

"No," I reply, trying to keep my voice as low as hers so Emma doesn't overhear.

"It could just be a pulled muscle from vomiting, but with all the symptoms she's having, I would advise you to take her to the emergency room. It's better to be safe than sorry."

My stomach drops to my toes. "Okay, thank you for calling me."

"Of course. I printed my notes for you already." She hands me a typed paper detailing Emma's symptoms and then says, "I'm also going to give you a few emesis bags for the road. The nearest ER is in Springview, and a thirty-minute car ride is likely to make her nausea worse." She hands me a few elongated blue bags with a ring at the top. She squeezes my shoulder and turns a worried eye on Emma.

"Thank you so much," I say, tucking the bags and paperwork into my purse.

I walk back towards Emma and squat down beside her. "Hey, baby girl. We're going to take a ride in my friend's truck to see some doctors at the hospital, okay? They want to check on you and make sure you're alright." She nods once. "Okay, sweetheart. I'm going to pick you up now."

I throw the paperwork and emesis bags in my purse and scoop her up in my arms as gently as I can. She lets out a low moan of pain and my breathing constricts. "I'm sorry. We'll get you to the doctor as quick as we can so they can fix you up." I nod my thanks to the nurse and then we head through the main office and out into the bright daylight.

* * *

Soon enough, we're walking through the large glass doors of the ER, Emma in my arms and Ryan trailing behind. Emma is so out of it, she barely paid Ryan any attention on the way here. He chucks the used emesis bag in the trashcan before hustling to keep up with us. I approach the desk, clutching Emma tightly, so I don't jostle her too much.

"Hi, can I help you?" The receptionist eyes Emma before turning her bespectacled eyes on me. I take a second to get her checked in with Ryan acting as an additional pair of hands to get the insurance card out of my bag.

I sit down with Emma in a nearby chair while she's still cradled in my arms. Luckily on this random Friday afternoon, there's only a few people sitting at opposite ends of the waiting room. One older Black man has an arm cradled against his chest, pain tightening his face. A young couple is sitting together across the room from us, her head resting against his shoulder.

Ryan comes and sits next to us after getting the paperwork for me. "Do you want to just tell me what to write and I can fill it out for you?" He clicks the pen when I nod and begins filling out the form while I quietly dictate Emma's information.

He takes the paperwork up to the desk and collects my license and insurance card. I run a hand through my hair and meet the older man's eye. He gives me a sympathetic look and returns his gaze to the flatscreen mounted to the wall.

"The receptionist said it wouldn't be long until they call us back," Ryan says as he sits next to me once again. He puts my things back in my bag and wraps a reassuring arm around my shoulders for a quick squeeze.

I nod and press my shoulder into him for a brief second of reassuring contact, hoping they'll call us back as soon as the receptionist thinks. I shift my arms a little, feeling them tremble with the effort of holding her for so long. I'm struck by just how big she's gotten. I used to hold her on my hip for an hour with no problem. Now, her long legs dangle over my arm and her sweaty head rests just under my chin. It's been a long time since I've held her like this. Time is a thief.

"Emma Forrester?" A nurse in colorful scrubs holding an industrial-looking tablet calls into the waiting room.

"That's us." I stand with Emma.

Ryan asks, "Do you want me to go with you or do you want me to wait here?"

"I think you should probably wait here. I'll shoot you a text when I know more. Thank you so much for doing this," I say as he hands me my bag.

"Don't worry about it. I'll be right here if you need anything." He settles back in his chair and pulls up a sudoku app on his phone.

Despite the circumstances, I can't help but tease, "Old man." The corner of his mouth ticks up and he gives me a gentle push towards the waiting nurse. I hoist Emma higher on my chest and walk towards the nurse.

"You're her mom?" she asks. When I nod to confirm, she leads me down a brightly lit, sterile hallway. The walls are painted a seafoam green and our shoes squeak on the gleaming, white tile. Her brisk pace has me scrambling to keep up, especially with Emma acting as a dead weight.

I follow her into a room labeled "triage." She directs me to lay Emma down on the bed and efficiently takes her vitals, all the while asking me questions about her symptoms.

When she pushes down on Emma's right side, Emma bucks and lets out a loud yelp of pain. She starts crying and reaches out for me, eyes wide.

"I'm so sorry sweetie. I had to do that as part of our tests to see what's going on." The nurse looks at me, her mouth pressed into a worried line. "We're going to get her admitted. I'll be back shortly with a gown and the doctor should be in after to talk to you." At my nod, she exits the room through an interior door that leads to what looks like a nurse's station. When she gets back, the nurse and I work together to get Emma changed into the light blue hospital gown and under the starched covers.

I know Emma isn't doing well when she hardly flinches as the nurse gets an IV going after we've been moved to a room for admitted patients. She normally throws a huge fit if she has to get poked. She just turns her head away while the nurse gets a few vials of blood and clutches my arm with her free hand.

The next little bit passes in a blur and suddenly they're wheeling Emma away for a CT scan and I'm left alone in the small, beige room. I tap my foot anxiously and repeatedly lock and unlock my phone, watching the minutes tick by at a snail's pace. When Emma was here, it was easy to be distracted from my own anxious thoughts because I was so focused on making sure she was okay. I might drive myself insane. After checking that Jared hasn't called for the umpteenth time, I leave him another message letting him know Emma is getting some tests done. Even though he probably won't get the messages until later, I want to keep him up to date.

They wheel her back into the room and let me know the doctor should be in shortly to discuss the test results. Once we're alone again I ask, "How are you doing, sweet girl?" I brush her hair back from her sweaty face. Luckily they gave her something for the vomiting so she hasn't been sick since before they took her back for the CT scan.

"It still really hurts," she whispers.

"I'm sorry, baby. Hopefully, they'll be able to help with the pain soon." I squeeze her hand and start humming the lullaby I used to sing her as a baby. It always calms her, even still.

"I'm scared, Mama," she whispers. My heart nearly shatters and I hold her hand tighter.

I say, "I know, Em. Going to the hospital can be scary. Just know that they'll take good care of you. You'll feel better soon." She nods and goes back to closing her eyes.

A young doctor enters the room after a quick knock on the door. "Hi, Emma and Mom. I hear you aren't feeling so great today. I'm Dr. Miller." She briskly washes her hands before pulling up the rolling chair next to the hospital bed. Emma shakes her head minutely. "I'm sorry to hear that. The good news is that we should be able to get you fixed up today and you'll be on your way to feeling better soon. How does that sound?" She leans toward Emma and gives her arm a small squeeze.

"Good," Emma states in a small voice, doing her best to muster up a smile.

The doctor grins brilliantly in response. "Great! Okay, Mom let me go over these results with you and our plan of action." She wheels towards the large computer monitor, enters her credentials, and pulls up a scan. She points to a blob amongst the other grayish blobs and says, "This is Emma's appendix. It's pretty inflamed and is the source of the pain. Considering her fever and the level of inflammation, I'm recommending we remove it today, as soon as our general surgeon, Dr. Watkins, is available."

My heart sinks. I knew it was a possibility, but it's awful to have it confirmed. "Okay. If you think that's the best course of action. I just want my daughter to get better."

"I understand completely. Dr. Watkins should be ready to take her back within the hour. I'll have my nurse bring you the relevant paperwork to sign in the meantime. I'll also order some pain medicine to make Emma more comfortable until they can take her back."

Dr. Miller stands to wash her hands again before giving me a reassuring smile. She says, "Don't worry, this is a very routine surgery and once she wakes up, she'll be a little sore, but feeling better than she is right now. She'll be back to herself in no time." I say my thanks and then go back to humming Emma's lullaby and stroking her hair.

CHAPTER 26

Summer

Ryan and I sit in the surgery center waiting room. They just took Emma back and said it wouldn't be long before she was out of surgery. The clock above the entrance to the recovery room says it's just after two in the afternoon. I can't stop the anxious bounce of my knee, or the way I keep glancing towards the double doors where the nurse will come out to update us.

"She's going to be just fine. I know it has to be scary, but at least they're confident they caught the appendicitis before it got more serious. My little cousin had the same surgery years ago. She was up and running around pretty quickly. Emma will be back to normal before you know it," Ryan says, rubbing his hand up and down my arm in slow, soothing motions.

"I know she's going to be okay. It just sucks that she has to go through this and that there's nothing I can do for her to make it better," I say, tears making my voice low and strained. Being a mother means having your literal heart walking around outside your chest. Knowing there is nothing I can do to take this away for her is the closest thing to torture I've ever endured.

"You already did everything you could by rushing to bring her here. Now you just have to get together some of her favorite things so she has something to do while she's recovering. Put your mind to that," he suggests. I nod, sniffling. I decide to take his suggestion to heart and create a list on my phone of some things she enjoys that she can do lying down. I order a few new toys and books from Amazon and take the time to update Rachel on Emma. I feel mildly better after being productive in the only way I can be right now.

A nurse wearing dark blue scrubs comes into the room and approaches us. She pulls her mask down with a smile and says, "Hi, are you the parents of Emma Forrester?"

"Yes, what's going on?" I say, not bothering to correct her assumption that Ryan is Emma's dad. There are more important things happening.

"Don't worry, the surgery is going smoothly. Dr. Watkins is almost done removing her appendix now. He just wanted me to come out and give you an update. He said that it's a good thing you brought her in when you did because it looked even more inflamed than the scans showed, and it had a good chance of bursting. That causes much more serious complications. Like I said, you guys did the right thing bringing her in. He'll be done with the surgery soon. I'll come out to update you again when she's headed into recovery. You should be able to see her shortly after that."

I rush out a breath and say, "Thank you."

"Of course! I know this is Emma's first surgery, and that's always nerve-wracking for the parents. Honestly, it's harder on you guys than her. She's taking a nice little nap while mom and dad are out here worrying." She gives me a reassuring smile. "Any questions you want me to pass along, Mom? Dad?"

Just as Ryan is opening his mouth to, I'm sure, clarify the mixup, I hear Jared's angry voice before I see him. "Dad? Who the fuck do you think you are?" Wild-eyed and face quickly morphing from fear to fury, he levels Ryan with a hard stare.

The nurse looks between the three of us and says, "I'll be back shortly. Please remember this is a hospital, not a dive bar. We expect everyone to act accordingly." She says this last bit to Jared whose jaw ticks in annoyance before he sits in the chair on my other side, nodding curtly in understanding.

"Thank you again for the update. Don't worry, we won't cause a scene," I say placatingly, shooting daggers at Jared.

The nurse heads back through the door she came from. I'm thankful we're alone in the waiting room because Jared immediately turns towards me and spits, "What the hell is he still doing here?" He flings a hand toward Ryan in annoyance. "You said in your message that he was driving you, but there's no reason for him to still be here playing dad with my kid!"

"Lower your voice." I stare at him until his arms cross and he leans away from me. "No one is 'playing Dad.' He's here for me while we wait. He's not here for Emma. He hasn't even said a word to her. It's not a big deal and definitely not the biggest problem we have today. Don't you think?" I gesture to the room around us.

He visibly deflates and says, "How is she? I know you texted me when they took her back for surgery, but did the nurse give any updates?"

"She just said that the doctor is close to finishing the surgery and that it was a good thing we brought her in. Her appendix looked close to bursting, I guess." I say with a shiver. I hate thinking of what could have happened if we hadn't rushed her here.

"But she's going to be okay?" He searches my face anxiously.

I soften a bit when I see the fear written plainly on his face. "Yes, she'll be fine. They want to keep her overnight for observation, but she should be good to go home tomorrow," I reply.

"Good. That's good." He rubs his hands down his thighs and looks at me out of the corner of his eye before he says, "I'm sorry I didn't get here sooner. I just got within range of cell service like twenty minutes ago. I hauled ass to get here as soon as I heard your messages." That's the only problem with living at the base of the Sierra Nevada mountains: the cell service is spotty at best.

"It's not your fault. There's no way you could have predicted this was going to happen."

He looks at me guiltily. "She did say her stomach hurt this morning before school." When I give him an incredulous look he rushes out, "But I swear she didn't have a temperature. I just thought she wanted to stay home because they did some sort of test for first-grade readiness today. I promise if I thought it was anything serious, I would have kept her home." I nod, because no one could have predicted the way this hellish day has turned out.

He leans around me and fixes Ryan with a stare. His voice is a near growl when he says, "You can go now."

Ryan ignores Jared and turns his attention to me, saying in a low voice, "Hey, I'm going to grab a cup of coffee. Do you want to come with me, Summer?" He places his warm hand on my shoulder.

"Sure." I stand quickly and turn to Jared, "I'll be five minutes. Will you call if the nurse comes back?" He nods sulkily then pulls out his phone.

* * *

RYAN

I lead Summer out into the hall and we walk a ways before I say, "Do you really want a cup of coffee? When my sister had her son and I came to visit, I remember it tasting like battery acid, but I'll still get you a cup if you want it." I interlace our hands and tug her to a stop.

She leads me to the side so we're out of the way of anyone who needs to get by. "I'm good. I just figured you wanted to talk. What's up?"

"Yeah, I guess I wasn't that subtle." I laugh and scrub the back of my head with my free hand. "I just wanted to make sure you're okay. Jared always seems to bring some major drama and you've already had a rough day."

"I'm as okay as I can be. Do I wish he didn't act like a child all the time lately? Yes. But it is what it is right now." She shrugs tiredly.

I squeeze her hand still tangled in my own, "Do you want me to head out? I know I'm not supposed to have much contact with Emma, but this seems like special circumstances. I want to be here for you if you need me."

She leans forward and gives me a long, lingering kiss that just borders on inappropriate for a hospital, and I don't mind one bit. She pulls back and rests her forehead on mine. "You have no idea how nice it is to feel taken care of." She leans back and looks me in the eye, a soft smile tugging the corners of her mouth up.

She says, "As much as I want you here for me, I have to think about Emma. Even if you didn't go see her in recovery, just waiting here is going to put Jared on edge. I don't want Emma to have anything else to stress about today."

"Okay, I can understand that. Are you sure you're going to be okay with him?" I loosen my grip on her hand so I can use both thumbs to sweep away the dark smudges her makeup left under her eyes from crying.

"I'll be fine. I've been dealing with Jared for a long time. He's more childish than usual these days, but I'm hoping if you head home, he'll dial that back. As annoying as he's been, he always puts Emma first." She leans into my touch for a second longer and then backs away, letting my hands drop from her face.

"Okay. How about I deal with your car? I'll go home and get my jumper cables and try to start it. If that doesn't work, I'll get it to the mechanics for you. I'm assuming Jared can give you a ride?" I feel better now that I have a purpose again.

"That would be amazing. I honestly kind of forgot about my

stupid car." She runs her fingers through her long hair, fluffing it back over her shoulders.

"I'll put the booster in your backseat again too. Will you please send me a text when she's out of surgery? I want to know that she's okay," I say earnestly.

Without warning, she tugs me in for another kiss that has me reeling. With a hand splayed over her lower back, I press her flush against me and relish in the feel of her soft body in my hands. I break the kiss before my lower half gets any ideas. "What was that for?" I ask, a little dazed.

"Sometimes I just think that you're too good to be true, you know that?"

"The feeling is mutual," I say, tucking a stray hair behind her ear and kissing her forehead. I allow myself a moment to inhale the scent of her shampoo - something floral with a minty kick before I pull back. "Text me, okay? I'll let you know about the car." She hands me her set of keys and nods.

"Thanks for everything today. It means a lot that when I needed you, you were here, no questions."

"Anytime, day or night." I brush my hand down her smooth arm before taking her hand in mine for a second, squeezing it in goodbye. She squeezes back before turning towards the surgery center. I watch her walk away, lush hips swaying, hair brushing the curve of her waist, and can't help the feeling of dread that hollows out my stomach.

CHAPTER 27

Summer

Emma is sleeping in yet another hospital bed in a private recovery room while Jared and I look on from uncomfortable plastic chairs. Emma's surgery went well, and her doctor told us to let her rest as much as possible for the next few days.

While we stand sentry over our girl, a nurse bustles into the room. She has brightly colored, floral patterned scrubs that contrast with her sienna skin. She sees that the lights are low and quiets her steps. "If you two want to run down and grab a bite for dinner, you should do that. I doubt Emma will even truly wake up for the next few hours. If she does, I can tell her you two will be right back. I'm happy to hang out for a half hour or so before I head out. My shift is over soon anyway," she whispers. She takes Emma's vitals without disturbing her – a trick that only a pediatric nurse could pull off.

"Are you sure?" Jared asks quietly.

"Of course. I don't mind at all. I can catch up on some charting while I'm in here and I'll just give one of you a call if she wakes up." The nurse heads toward the computer at the front of the room.

Jared's stomach grumbles loudly in the near-silent room. "Come on, we'll grab something from that cafe across the road. We'll eat and be back before she knows it," I say. I stand and let out a quiet groan as my muscles that have been hunched in uncomfortable hospital seating all day stretch out.

"You two go on, I got her," the nurse says, waking up the computer with a jiggle of the mouse.

* * *

Jared and I sit across from each other in a little cafe called The Drip. Apparently, it was opened by former doctors turned business owners who wanted to capitalize on the nearby hospital. The logo adorning every cup of coffee is an IV bag with the name of the place made out to look like a medication tag.

I have a side salad and turkey club in front of me while Jared is wolfing down a huge pastrami on rye. I don't know how he can even eat right now. Maybe because he wasn't the one having to catch vomit all day and see our daughter like that. The way she was curled in on herself in pain is an image that will haunt me for the rest of my life. I stir my iced chai with the straw before taking a small sip. It's delicious but I'm barely registering it. The adrenaline from the day is finally wearing off and it has left me feeling completely drained.

"Are you going to eat or what? We don't have a ton of time and anyway, you're not usually one to turn away from a meal," he seems to catch himself with his sandwich halfway to his mouth. He points at me with it, "That's not what I meant, and you know it. I just mean you never used to skip meals." At my eye roll, he continues, "Not that you should! It's just not like you."

I decide to put him out of his misery because watching him flounder is only fun for so long, "It's fine. I'm going to eat. I just still feel a little sick to my stomach. Rough day. Worse for Emma obviously, but it was really hard to see her like that and to know there was nothing I could do." I stab my fork into a plump cherry tomato before popping it in my mouth.

"I can't imagine. I'm sorry you had to do it alone," he says sympathetically.

"Luckily I wasn't completely alone, but yeah it was hard." I think of how terrible it would have been if Ryan hadn't been there to distract me when they took her back for surgery and to keep me calm when we were on the way to the hospital.

Jared wipes his mouth with his napkin and sits back, focusing his dark eyes on me. "Yeah, about that. I don't like that you went behind my back and had him meet Emma."

"Are you kidding me right now? Of all the shit to happen today, your takeaway is that I shouldn't have asked my boyfriend to drive our sick daughter to the hospital when I was out of other options?"

"So now he's your boyfriend?" He scoffs before sucking down his cold brew like it personally offended his mother. "Doesn't matter I guess. I told you I wasn't comfortable with him meeting Emma. This feels like a convenient way for you to get around that."

"You really think I was plotting against your wishes while Emma was doubled over puking in the nurse's office?" I take a bite of my sandwich for something to do and to give myself a second to calm down so I don't start yelling in this very cute coffee shop. "I told you my car wouldn't start this morning, so when the school called and told me Emma wasn't feeling well, I didn't want to risk getting any of my coworkers sick. At the time, I thought Emma just had a stomach bug. Ryan doesn't have kids and he didn't mind taking the risk, so yeah, I asked him to drive us. And you know what? He did it no questions asked. You heard what the doctor said - her appendix was close to bursting. Who knows what a difference even thirty minutes could have made?"

"Oh, Ryan, my hero," he sneers in a high falsetto, clasping his hands over his chest like a swooning damsel.

"Yeah. He really is."

"It isn't my fault that I wasn't here!" he exclaims.

"I never said it was. But do you see how we both did the best we could with the circumstances that were in our control? All that matters is that Emma got to the hospital in time and now she's safe and recovering. This is a petty-ass fight and you know it. Grow up. I'm over it." I push my chair back and stand. I can't eat any more anyway. I leave the half-eaten sandwich and barely touched salad and grab the chai, marching out of the cafe into the waning daylight.

I'm walking back towards the hospital entrance when Jared roughly grabs my shoulder from behind. He spins me around and says, "Hold on! We weren't done talking." His brow is creased in anger and his hand is digging into my shoulder in a way I really don't like.

"Get your hands off of me," I say quietly, trying to leash my anger. I don't want to make a scene when I've already had a rough day and I don't feel like having to Lady Macbeth my hands in the bathroom later— '*Out, out damned spot.*'

"No. You're going to listen to me." He keeps his hand clamped on my shoulder despite my nails digging in trying to pry it off. "I don't give a shit that on the weeks you're not with Emma, you're out spreading your legs for the first man who gave you attention." I try even harder to pull away. He continues, "But you know what? I'm sick of your demands and the way you make me feel like nothing I ever do is good enough. No man is going to do what you want. If he's doing it now, it won't be long before he realizes you aren't worth the effort." He releases me so quickly that I stumble back.

Before I can fall on my ass, a strong arm bands around my middle. When I look up at who caught me, Ryan is wearing an expression of wrath I've never seen on him before. He hands me the overnight bag I asked him to bring me via text a couple of hours ago and gently pushes me behind him. "You better watch how you speak to Summer. She's the mother of your child. Show some goddamn respect." His voice sounds low and dangerous, rumbling deep in his chest.

"Come on, man. Admit it. She was easy and she's a good lay, I'll give her that, but you don't want to actually jump when she says how high, do you?" Jared spreads his arms and laughs like this is all just a joke to him. I'm shocked and disgusted that he could say those things about me, *to* me.

"I would jump through any hoop she threw my way if it made her happy. Why don't you just admit that you realized you lost out and now you're pitching a fit because you can't have her back. You just aren't man enough to own up to your shit, so you have to take it out on her. I'm done letting you use her as your emotional punching bag. I'll say it again: Have some damn respect for the mother of your child."

"I'll show you respect," Jared snarls. Before I can even fully process what's happening, Jared is flying towards Ryan, fist slinging at his face wildly. Ryan bats it away before it makes contact. In a blur of motion, his fist connects with Jared's nose. Jared's head snaps back with a crunch that could only mean something is broken.

I grab Ryan's shoulders, not wanting it to go any further, but he's not moving towards Jared. He's just standing there looking at Jared who has backed up and is holding his nose, blood seeping through his fingers. Ryan shakes his hand out once before pumping it in a fist a few times.

"Fuck! You broke my nose you asshole," Jared screams in a nasally voice.

"Yes. I did," Ryan says calmly. He turns to me, "Summer, are you alright?"

"Me? I'm fantastic," I step around him and say to Jared, "It didn't have to go this way. We were doing so good until you couldn't stand that I moved on. I can't keep going like this Jared. It's escalated too far. I can't have you flying off the handle just because your pride is wounded. You were so worried about him being violent," I toss my thumb behind me towards Ryan, "But take a look at yourself. You're the one who keeps saying nasty things. You're the one that threw the first punch. You're the one who keeps a drunk around. I'm done. Done."

He looks at me, under eyes already turning a dusky blue, and says, "Say what you want, but he does not go near my daughter."

"I don't think you're in a place to make those decisions. I think we call this a wash and try to move on. I was respecting your wishes as a courtesy because you're her dad. But you haven't shown me any kind of courtesy in years. Go get your nose looked at and then go home. I'll start my week with Emma early. We'll talk next steps tomorrow when you can hopefully be more civil."

I leave Jared there, dripping blood on the concrete walkway. Only when I turn, Ryan in tow, do I notice we have quite the audience. I also feel my hands shaking and somehow in the past few minutes I lost my chai. Ryan nods toward a burly hospital security guard who is watching us from the entrance. As we pass him, the guard says, "Nice punch. Sounds like he deserved it." He winks at me and then goes back to looking serious and intimidating.

We make it almost to Emma's room in silence when I tug on Ryan's arm. He stops in front of me. "Are you okay?" he asks, looking me over as if my emotional injury can be seen on the outside.

I can't help the watery smile that takes over my face. "You keep asking me that."

"Well today has been one for the books, so I feel the need to keep checking." He brushes the tear from my lashes before it even has a chance to fall.

"I don't know what I am. Not okay, that's for sure. I need a second to process this day. It feels like it's been a year since we woke up in bed this morning." I rub my temples where my head has begun to ache. "How's your hand, by the way?" I grab his right hand and inspect the slightly swollen knuckles.

"I'm fine. Nothing a little ibuprofen and ice can't fix." He looks down at his knuckles and shakes his head as if he can't believe he actually punched Jared. He looks up at me and asks, "Do you want me to go in there with you?" He points to Emma's door.

"Nah. I know I talked a big talk with Jared, but I don't think the first formal introduction should be with her laid out in a hospital bed. I got this. It's what moms do. We rally when it feels like we have nothing left to give and then we give some more." I check my phone and inhale a sharp breath, "Shoot. It's been way over a half hour since we left Emma. Her nurse was only supposed to watch her for thirty. Okay. I have to go in there. Thank you. Again." I give him a quick hug that he turns into a sweet kiss.

When we pull away he says, "Okay. This is always at your pace. You're the one who has to think for two people, and I've just got me. I'm ready when you are. I hope she wakes up feeling a little better. I'm sorry the day ended the way it did."

"I'm not. If you hadn't punched him, I probably would have. I'll call you tomorrow when we get home." He nods and presses a quick kiss to my forehead before pushing the door open for me.

"Oh, by the way, I got your car to the mechanic and they're going to take a look when they get the time. I gave them your number to call when they figure out what's up," Ryan whispers before I can get inside.

I mouth, "Thank you," and squeeze his arm in goodbye.

I enter the room, overnight bag in tow, seeing that Emma is still asleep, and the nurse has a book in her lap. "Thank you so much for watching her. I'm so sorry it took longer than you gave us."

She waves my concern away, "I was just getting to the good part." She wiggles the book in front of me.

"Ah. *The Disastrous Duke*. Loved that one. Charles is hot."

She laughs quietly and her eyes scan over my face. "She didn't even stir. The poor thing might just sleep through to the morning. That's alright because her body needs the rest. You doing okay, sweetheart?"

"Everyone keeps asking me that." I sink tiredly into the hard plastic chair next to the bed.

"Well, you just have that look. I know today was hard. It's never easy to see your baby get hurt. When my son broke his wrist playing football, I damn near went ballistic on the poor kid who landed on it wrong."

I huff out a humorless laugh and say, "Yeah it's been a tough day. Between this and all the other drama, I just want to sleep for a good week."

"That man of yours cause issues?" At my look of confusion, she clarifies, "The blonde one. What was his name, Jacob?"

"Jared. How did you know?"

"Nurses talk," she says with a wink.

"Yeah, well, he's something else. He chose today of all days to be an even bigger ass than usual."

"When men are made to feel small they tend to lash out. Just like a damn dog." She huffs and stands, giving me a reassuring pat on the back. "It will all work out. It always does. It just may not look how you predicted it would in the end. That doesn't mean you're going down the wrong path." She spends a moment looking down at the still sleeping Emma, her face softening, "Get as much rest as you can on that crappy bed tonight, mama. Let the night nurse take care of your girl. You'll be on full nurse and mom duty tomorrow."

"Thank you for your kindness," I say, patting her hand.

"Of course. We mothers have to stick together." She exits the room as quietly as she entered.

CHAPTER 28

Summer

I press play on her favorite movie and sit back next to Emma on the couch. We've been home for the last couple hours and she's so much more relaxed here. She was not a fan of all the fuss at the hospital. Can't say I blame her, poor girl.

She's taken more catnaps today than she has since she was a newborn. Jared's mom drove us home from the hospital this morning (which was as awkward as you'd imagine), and even that short drive has her exhausted.

She snuggles into my side carefully, being mindful of the small surgical sites on her belly. She keeps her eyes on the screen when she asks, "Mommy? Why wasn't Daddy at the hospital when I woke up this morning?" She hadn't gotten to the question in the hospital because we were constantly bombarded with nurses and discharge paperwork. Small mercies.

"I'm sorry sweetie. He's okay, but he couldn't get to the hospital this morning. I think he'll be by to see you soon. Probably today," I reply, feeling like I'm walking over a field of landmines. How do you explain to your six-year-old that her dad is a jerk who got a long-deserved punch in the face without causing any trauma? You don't. *Sigh.*

"Whenever you say 'soon' it means it's not gonna happen," Emma says, finally breaking eye contact with the island princess to look up at me wearily.

I huff out a laugh and say, "Well, 'soon' this time just means I don't have an answer yet, but I'm sure you'll see your dad either today or tomorrow. I know he wants to see you too." I gently squeeze her to my side and kiss the top of her head.

She sighs out, "Okay." And just like that, her attention is back on the screen as the princess sails across the ocean.

I stand and go through the aging sliding door that leads to the small backyard and pull out my phone. Nerves ball my stomach into a knot I can't untangle no matter how many deep breaths I take. I don't want to make this call, but I have to.

"Hello?" The voice on the other end of the line is a little nasally and a lot annoyed.

"Jared, hey. How's your nose?" I'd rather just address the elephant on the line straight away.

"Bad. That asshole broke it," he says gruffly. I make a noncommittal noise that could hopefully be taken as sympathetic. "What do you want?" he asks.

I count to ten in my head before I answer, not wanting to start yelling again, "Well, Emma is asking about you and I don't know what to tell her. I figured we should probably come up with a plan."

"Yeah. Sure. I'll have my lawyer contact your lawyer and we'll go from there."

I was hoping to be the one to contact a lawyer first. I work hard to control the panic in my voice, and then say, "Lawyer? What are you talking about?"

"Yeah, a lawyer. We're going to figure out custody through a third party because I'm not going to stand by while he plays daddy to my little girl. Especially not after yesterday."

"You were the one that was going to punch him first! He

acted in self-defense you self-righteous piece of-" I cut myself off before I can stoop to his level.

"Doesn't matter. I'm the one with the broken nose and a filed police report. Good luck getting custody if you plan to keep him around."

I feel my heart pound out of my chest, and my ears ring with adrenaline. "You're going to leverage our daughter against me? That's how low you're willing to go?" I sit on the patio chair, pretzeling my legs on the seat. The warm May day had felt pleasant before, but now the heat was stifling.

"That's not what's happening, Summer. If you continue to have him around her, I have no other choice." His voice takes on a haughty quality.

"This is ridiculous and you know it. The only time he's been near her was when he was driving her to the emergency room!" I exclaim, raking my hand through my unkempt hair.

"Call it whatever you want. I'll be by around four to see Emma. Make sure that boyfriend of yours isn't around." Before I can respond, my phone beeps and the call has been disconnected. I pull it away from my ear and stare at the black screen blankly. *How much more can I take? How much more before I fall apart and can't find the pieces?*

I peek through the glass of the sliding door to see that Emma has fallen asleep on the couch. As I watch my innocent, hurting little girl rest, I feel my resolve come back. I refuse to go down without a fight. I sit back on my chair and start Googling lawyers around me. I recognize one of my frequent patrons at First Bank of Lakeland and give her a call.

Mrs. Lucas and I chat on the phone for a while before we decide to do a virtual meeting later this afternoon to discuss my needs in more detail. She sounded calm and reassuring over the phone, so I can only hope that our Zoom meeting will put me even more at ease.

I shake my head in disbelief that in such a short period, Jared and I have gone from co-parenting amicably, to whatever this is. It makes me wonder how much of his ambivalent pleasantness of the past few years would have disappeared if I had been the one to turn away first.

* * *

Despite his earlier nastiness, Jared is playing it remarkably cool while he's here visiting Emma. To be fair, I've made myself scarce and stuck to cleaning the bathrooms and kitchen, allowing them to have one-on-one time in the living room. He even got her to venture into the backyard and sit on the porch swing with him.

When she predictably asked what happened to his face, he said a tree from work got him in the nose. I did my absolute best to conceal my snort as a cough. Judging from his glare, I failed. Oh well.

I am elbows deep in the fridge, half empty condiments and produce everywhere as I scrub the glass shelves free of their crusted gunk. My house only gets this level of clean when I'm raging or anxious. That I'm both means I'm about to get on my knees and scrub the baseboards with a toothbrush when I'm done with the fridge.

I nearly jump out of my skin when Jared taps me on the shoulder. "Jeez! What?" I exclaim, turning quickly and wielding the filthy sponge.

Jared laughs, the quality having a nasal honk to it that makes me feel a little better about the fact that I almost peed myself. "I was just trying to tell you that I'm heading out. Emma is in her room resting. Since we already told her she is staying with you for the week, I'll just be back on Wednesday. I'll keep my calls at the same time too. But listen, I'm serious about this Ryan guy. I actually filed a police report and am going to pursue full custody if you have him around her."

I sigh long enough to prevent myself from going off like I

want to. "I think we both know what this is about, and it isn't about what happened to your face. Just because you want to punish me doesn't mean she deserves to get punished too. You know that seeing us equally is what's the absolute best for her. Don't give her unnecessary trauma just to be petty. She doesn't deserve that, and frankly neither do I."

I rinse my hands and the sponge in the sink to give myself a moment to think. If I can convince him not to go through a prolonged custody battle, I will. On the phone, Mrs. Lucas said that it's always better to handle custody out of court because it can be time-consuming and expensive otherwise.

He sighs and leans against the counter next to me. "You know I think you're a great mom. I just really think you're making a mistake with this Ryan guy. I mean, come on. What kind of guy swoops in knowing a woman just got out of a long relationship and has a kid? That's a lot of baggage to just accept. He clearly wants something from you."

I scoff, "Yeah, a good relationship with me. Hard to imagine, I know." I meet his dark eyes, "It's really, *really* sad to me that you couldn't see my worth until I was with someone else. I thought you loved me, but I think you just loved the idea of having someone who wanted you so bad that you could do no wrong. I'm not that girl anymore. I really, truly hope you find someone good for you because it clearly wasn't me." I dry my hands aggressively on the hand towel.

"I've always wanted you." He tries to place a hand on my shoulder but I shrug it off. With a sigh he continues, "You're right though. I didn't realize how good I had it. For that, I am truly sorry." I search his eyes, looking for the lie, but find only earnestness.

"Thank you. You've been so nasty to me lately..." Of their own accord, my eyes start to water. *Damnit.* I do not want this man to witness any more of my tears.

His face crumples too, and to my shock, I see tears well in his eyes mirroring my own. "Fuck, Summer. I'm so sorry. For every-thing I've said to you. You don't deserve it. I haven't been feeling myself since we split and I'm taking it out on you." I sniff back my tears and nod. He's been a completely different person since we broke up.

He holds out his arms tentatively, eyes shining. I step into them and allow him to hug me, chin resting on the top of my head. "I'm so sorry. You and Emma mean everything to me and I just can't deal with losing you."

I step back and he lets me go reluctantly. "I'm sorry too, Jared."

"For what?"

"Because you're hurting too. I'm sorry for that. I hope you find happiness. I think we can still work out a good thing for Emma if we get back to treating each other better." I pluck a tissue from the box on the counter and hand it to him.

He takes it, looking down. "You're still staying with him?"

"Yes. I think...I think I might be falling in love with him," I say, feeling a rush of exhilaration. The feeling has been taking root slowly in my heart, reaching curling tendrils out until the organ feels surrounded by him. Until now I hadn't named it. I feel like the only way for Jared to understand where I'm at is to be completely honest. I want him to realize that I'm not with Ryan out of spite or revenge, but because I genuinely think he might be my person.

Jared inhales sharply. He nods once before turning on his heel and leaving out the front door with a quiet *click*. I feel dread drop a leaden ball in my stomach. Jared always has to have the last word, and for him to say nothing terrifies me.

* * *

"Alright then, Summer, we'll be in touch soon. I'll probably give you a call to follow up with the details on Monday and I'll

180

shoot you an email with some documents I'll need your e-signature on. I'm positive we can get this settled in mediation rather than dragging it out in family court," Mrs. Lucas, my new lawyer, says to me with a reassuring smile through the screen. Behind her hang several certificates and plaques on a mint colored wall.

I nod, taking a deep breath. "Thank you, Mrs. Lucas."

"I told you, call me Nia," She chides gently, raising a dark brow.

"Nia, then. Thank you. You've made me feel a lot better. This is just such a one-eighty from how we started. No offense, but I never thought I would have to call you," I say sheepishly.

She tosses a handful of long braids over her shoulder and shrugs delicately, "Not many people assume that they'll need a family lawyer for much more than estate planning, but as you can attest, that's not always the way it works out."

She readjusts slightly in her office chair before leaning forward and says, "If I may, Summer, in my experience, people reveal who they truly are when going through a hard thing like separation and child custody. It makes you dig deep into who you are and what you value. There are people like you who genuinely try to do the best they can for their children and all parties involved, and then there are people like Jared. This darkness festers under the surface their whole lives until something brings the infection to the surface." She leans back again casually like she didn't just drop a hard truth on my lap.

I nod slowly and say, "It's just disappointing. I always thought that Jared, above all else, would put Emma first. It's a hard pill to swallow to learn that that isn't true. He might have been a bad partner, but he was always a good father."

"If men know how to do one thing, it's disappoint the important women in their life."

"That's the truth," I say with a humorless laugh.

She gives me a sympathetic smile and says, "I'll be in touch soon. Deep breaths, Summer. It's all going to work out. I'm fairly confident that things will go your way."

"Thank you. I'll get on that paperwork right away."

"Perfect. Talk soon." She waves an elegant hand, gold bangles tinkling merrily on her wrist before ending the call. I close my dinosaur of a laptop and sit back against the bay window, letting the heat of the late afternoon sun warm my back.

CHAPTER 29

Summer

My phone buzzes while I sit in the break room with my cold-cut sandwich and chips. I take a large bite and sigh through my nose. *I would kill for just one small moment of quiet.* My coworkers all decided to go out to lunch and I was not in the mood for socializing, so I told them I had some catching up to do. Really, I just wanted to enjoy the relative peace and quiet of the bank closed for lunch. I set down my sandwich after relishing in one more moment of silence and flip my phone over. I instantly brighten when I see the message is from Ryan.

RYAN:

Hey, are you free right now? I'm outside the bank in my truck. Wanna have lunch together?

Without a second thought, I jump up from my seat, gather my food, and weave my way outside. I see a huge grin spread across Ryan's face through the windshield of his truck and feel an answering smile appear on my own as I hurry to the passenger side.

He pushes the door open from the inside and grabs my water bottle from me so I have a handhold to haul myself into the truck. "Hello, gorgeous," he says while leaning toward me for a kiss. I let it linger longer than I normally would in a public space, his soft lips brushing mine in a caress. I just can't resist this man.

"Hi," I reply breathlessly when we pull away.

We talk about mundane things for a bit before I finally sigh and bring up what I've been too scared to. "So. A couple of things. I know you know that Jared threatened me with court and custody hearings, but it's really happening now. My lawyer is going to try to have us go through mediation first because that will be way less expensive. Second, there's the matter of the police report he filed against you." I wince at the last part, hating that he's included in my petty drama.

To my shock, he lets out a booming laugh that startles me "Yeah. I heard about that. Rina down at the station called this morning to give me a heads-up. I installed her new kitchen floor a few weeks ago."

"I thought they usually don't notify the person unless they need to do follow-up with them?" I ask while I open up my chip bag. I dig one out before tilting the bag towards him in offering, savoring the salty tang of my sea salt and vinegar chips.

He takes one and crunches down on it before replying, "They don't, but since Rina knows me personally, she gave me a heads up. Apparently, she's friends with the officer who was at the hospital and saw the whole thing. The guy who was standing at the entrance? They were buddies in the academy. He told her his play-by-play of what happened, so she called to let me know that it was a bogus report, but on file anyway. I wasn't even going to tell you since it won't amount to anything, but I guess Jared told you regardless." He scowls, his dark brows drawing down over his eyes.

"Why would you not want to tell me that?" I could feel my eyes bugging at the thought. I lightly smack his bicep in reprimand.

He sighs and laces our hands together over the console, "You've had more than enough stress to deal with over the last week alone. I didn't want to add to it. It really won't mean anything for me, so why bother?" He gives me a brief smile, stroking his thumb along the top of my hand.

His calm presence helps me relax, but I feel a stab of guilt all the same. I say, "You know, I am sorry that being with me has caused all this drama for you. I doubt you were expecting that when you came to fix my roof." I look down at our joined hands. Maybe I should have waited longer before dragging anyone into this mess.

"Hey." He lets go of my hand so he can tilt my chin up, forcing me to meet his eyes, "You are worth all the drama in the world. If this were one of your fantasy books, I'd say I would slay dragons for you, but since I'm just a lowly human, I'll say that I'll be by your side no matter what. I'm not going anywhere and there's nothing your ex can say or do that will scare me off." He smiles self-depricatingly at his own cheesiness and leans in kissing me once softly on the lips.

"Thank you. I feel like it's just been all about me and I haven't been able to be there for you."

"We take turns taking care of each other. That's what a relationship is. Sometimes you'll be holding me up, and sometimes I'll be holding you up. It just isn't my turn yet. Don't worry though, I have tons of abandonment issues that we've yet to deal with." He grins at me and squeezes my hand.

"Oh, twinsies! We haven't even *gotten* into those yet." We laugh and it feels nice to have some levity after the last few days.

"Eat your sandwich. I doubt you've been taking care of yourself much since everything happened with Emma. How's she doing by the way?" I relay how Emma's doing, making sure to detail how she thought she hallucinated a handsome stranger in the haze of her pain the day of her surgery.

He chuckles and says, "I'm just glad I could help. I'm assuming you didn't let her believe that she hallucinated me, so what did you tell her?"

I shrug and reply, "I just said that you were a friend of mine who was willing to help. I'm going to tell her soon, I promise. I just want to get through this mediation first."

He smiles a crooked grin that tugs at my heartstrings. "I understand. We're doing this at whatever pace you set, remember?" I reach up and caress his cheek, the softness of his beard tickling my hand. Just then a loud knock on the passenger side window startles the both of us. My hand flies to my chest as I whip around.

"Need to catch up on some things, huh?" Rachel's voice is muffled by the glass, but the raised eyebrow and disgruntled expression on her face is crystal clear. I wince sheepishly at being caught out and give a small wave through the window. Sherry is lurking behind my boss and is wearing a cat that got the canary grin.

"Hey, Rach," I say after rolling the window down, "How was lunch?"

"Good, but it would have been better if we had had the whole team there," she says slowly, eyeing Ryan over my shoulder.

I feel him lean closer on my side so he can see her better, "Hi, I'm Ryan, Summer's boyfriend. Sorry, I'm the one who convinced her to have lunch with me. She was very busy when I first got here." He places a hand on my shoulder and squeezes reassuringly.

When she gets a good look at him, her eyes widen a fraction and she clears her throat. "No problem at all. What Summer does on her break is her business of course. I just would have preferred if she chose to spend it with us. I can see why that maybe wouldn't be her first choice though." She raises both eyebrows at me in a *Damn, girl* gesture.

Sherry offers a two-thumbs-up and a wolf whistle when she catches sight of Ryan. If I could magically disappear right now, that'd be cool. I feel my cheeks flame and press my fingers to them hoping to dull the heat.

"Well, as cozy as this is, I should probably get back to work now. Thanks for keeping me company, Ryan." I give him a quick kiss on the cheek, gather my lunch, and hop out of the truck.

Before I can shut the door, Ryan says, "Hey, before you go, have you heard anything about your car?"

"It's supposed to be ready after work today. Emma's grandma is going to drive me to the shop when I'm done here," I reply.

"Oh good. We should definitely put car shopping on the agenda." He gives me a look that brokers no argument. I roll my eyes and wave, following my coworkers back inside, fully intending to do nothing about my geriatric car.

CHAPTER 30

Summer

The mediation date approaches faster than I feel ready for. With Emma back in school, time has flown by with all of the end-of-school-year madness. She is just about finished with her last week of kindergarten and I'm not feeling ready to have a first grader.

Today is the eighth of June and her last day of school. We're trying to get this mediation meeting done before she's home for the summer. Jared and I have stuck to our original custody plan thus far, but every time I see him, he vacillates between open hostility and cold indifference.

I can't help but feel that I brought this all on myself. Maybe I should have just been happy with what I had. I'm so glad this change brought me Ryan, but I'm also terrified of losing my daughter. I'm not someone that wants a lot out of life. Mostly, I want my daughter to be happy and I want to be a positive example for her. I'm not one for lots of material things or grand ambitions. I want a happy, slow life where I can savor the time with those I love. It feels like Jared is trying to take that from me. As I sit in front of the mediator's office in my car, I stare up at the dull rectangular building with trepidation.

I hope Jared will be reasonable. I can't believe that after all we've been through he can't move past petty jealousy. I can't believe that he's willing to sacrifice Emma's happiness just for the sake of his pride. I feel on the verge of an anxiety attack, my heart beat pounding like a war drum in my chest and my body breaking into a cold sweat. I close my eyes and do some breathing exercises that I learned in therapy years ago. I got here fifteen minutes early for this very reason. I knew I would need some time to calm down.

A light tapping on my driver's side window startles me. My eyes fly open and I stare into the apologetic face of my lawyer, glittery acrylic nail poised above the window to tap again. "Sorry," she mouths before stepping back to let me out of the car. She adjusts the smart blue suit jacket she's wearing that contrasts nicely with her umber skin before offering me a smile.

When I'm free of the car and not in danger of a heart attack, she steps in to give me a quick hug. We've really gotten to know each other well over the last few weeks. We've had many meetings both in person and over Zoom trying to be as prepared for mediation as we can be. "How are you doing, Summer? You look great! Er, well despite the fact that it looked like you were sleeping?" Nia pulls back, eyebrows drawn in a confused line, and looks me over.

"No! I wasn't asleep. I was doing some breathing exercises to calm down. I was feeling really anxious," I say, a little embarrassed at being caught in the act.

"I understand completely. It's normal to feel anxious, but I'm confident this will go your way." She squeezes my shoulders before dropping her hands and leading me to the door. "Come on, let's get inside so we can get settled before the meeting begins."

We step inside an office that clearly had its heyday in the 90s. Gray industrial carpet softens our footsteps, and the white walls and honey-colored furniture are broken up with both fake plants that look as if they haven't been dusted in the last decade and a few very sad-looking succulents on the secretary's desk. "Hey, Amy," Nia greets the secretary behind the desk.

"Oh hey, Nia. Greg is just getting things set up, but you're welcome to go back to the main conference room to say hello," Amy, a middle-aged blond woman says. Her vibrant pink lipstick is the brightest thing in this room. She gives me a quick smile and wave before returning back to her computer.

Nia gestures for me to follow her through a doorway to the right of the front desk and we walk down a short hallway with a few doors lining either side before arriving at the end. She gives the closed door a few light raps with her knuckle and we're invited in by a muffled, "Come in!"

We enter the claustrophobic room and sit on the left hand side of the long table. The room is dwarfed by the giant conference table situated in the middle with chairs all around. There's only one thin, long window at the very top of the rear wall.

"Hello, Nia, Ms. Evans. Welcome! Ms. Evans, it's a pleasure to make your acquaintance. I'm Greg Harbor, your attorney and mediator extraordinaire." He sweeps his arms out in a grand gesture from his seat at the head of the table, and I can't help but feel myself relax a little in his presence. He's an older man with slightly balding, gray hair. His face is open and friendly, his wide eyes made wider behind thick, wireframe glasses.

I hold out my hand to shake and reply, "The pleasure is mine. Thank you for being willing to handle our case so quickly. I'd love to get this sorted as soon as possible so Emma can get situated in whatever routine she ends up with over the summer." He gives my hand a few firm pumps over the table.

"Of course. Her best interest is my top priority, rest assured Ms. Evans," he says warmly before excusing himself to get some paperwork situated. I take a moment to smooth my dark pencil skirt over my legs and cross them at the ankles under my chair.

Greg comes back leading Jared and his lawyer into the room. Jared is in a black suit I haven't seen him in since his grandfather's funeral a few years ago. His lawyer is a thirty-something man with a bad combover and an ill-fitting, gray suit.

"Ladies, Mr. Forrester and his lawyer, Mr. Patterson." Greg walks to the head of the table and all three men loudly take a seat, chairs scraping gratingly over the dingy carpet and paperwork being set down in a flurry.

Greg jovially smacks his palms together and says, "Alright everyone, since this is our first rodeo together, I'm going to briefly explain how the rest of the meeting will go. Sound good?" We all nod and he continues, "Perfect. So, Mr. Forrester, Ms. Evans, I will take one of you with your lawyer into a different room. I will hear both sides out, offer my best advice, and go to the other party with your prospective custody terms. We'll probably have to go back and forth a bit to get things fully settled, but the goal is to keep you out of the courts and reach an agreement you both can live with that's in the best interest of your child."

Greg takes a second to arrange a stack of papers in front of him before continuing, "I'm stating now that I am a neutral party. My only goal is to help the two of you reach an agreement. Understand?"

"Yes," I say with a nod when he turns his wide, cornflower-blue eyes on me. Jared nods as well when Greg looks his way.

Greg stands, gesturing to the door. "Alright. Who wants to stretch their legs with me on a long luxurious walk down the hall-way?" He smiles and nods to Nia who stands.

She collects her things and places a hand on my shoulder, indicating for me to follow as she moves towards the door, "Come on Summer, let's go check out the other room."

"Okay." I stand and give a tight-lipped smile to Jared and his lawyer. I keep pace with Nia and Greg back down the short, dark hallway and into a smaller room to the right. Greg stays by the open door and gestures for us to walk deeper into the room.

My eye is immediately drawn to the large, slightly tinted window that takes up nearly the entire back wall. Despite the room's smaller size, the window makes it feel much less claustrophobic than the conference room we were just in. A smaller table, clearly only meant to seat four or so people, is in the center of the room with a few plush but worn office chairs surrounding it. Nia leads me to the left side of the table and sets her briefcase and folders down.

Greg smiles at me, the corners of his eyes crinkling behind his glasses, "Alright ladies, I'll be back shortly. I can have Amy bring you some coffee? Water?"

"Water please," I say, suddenly feeling the dryness of my throat.

"Same for me. Thanks, Greg," Nia says as he leaves the room and shuts the door. We can hear his muffled voice as he speaks briefly with his secretary.

Nia and I pass the time sipping on the small bottled waters that Amy brings us and rechecking the custody documents Nia had drawn up over the last few weeks. Just as I'm elbows deep in legal jargon (way too many heretofores for my taste), Greg knocks on the doorframe before entering the room.

"So, let's hear out your custody terms," he says, crossing the room to sit in the chair opposite us. He pushes his glasses higher on his nose and looks down at the papers on the desk with a concentrated frown.

We proceed to describe the same custody agreement I have now, with a few more specifications for holidays and weekly visits. Nia and I had discussed asking for more custody as a preventative measure since Jared threatened me with demanding full custody, but ultimately decided on what I think will be best for Emma. Even though her dad is an asshole to me, I know he's a great dad for her, and she deserves to have two equally present parents.

"That's basically what we have going now and it seems to be working well for Emma. Ultimately, that's what I care about. I just want to do what's in her best interest," I finish before taking the last, now lukewarm, swig of my water.

We had gone over point by point the details of both of our proposals and found only a few discrepancies that I was happy to concede to prevent a fight over ultimately pointless issues. I'm shocked that Jared didn't demand full custody or some other ridiculous concession, but I can only assume his lawyer or Greg talked him down.

Greg, who had been taking diligent notes on a legal pad throughout our discussion, makes a few last-minute scribbles and says, "Well. It seems like you and Mr. Forrester are on the same page for the majority. Although– and I have his permission to bring this up– he does have concerns about a certain Mr. Ryan Garrett whom you are currently engaged in a romantic partnership with. Here's a copy of the police report he filed with the local PD he gave me. Now, when I went and looked up the police report, it seems as though the investigators found nothing to charge Mr. Garrett with as Mr. Forrester allegedly began the fight and Mr. Garrett acted out of self-defense."

I cross my arms and say, "That's exactly what happened. Jared was going to hit Ryan and Ryan hit him first so he would stop fighting. Is this police report anything that could hold up in court?" I gnaw on my lip worriedly.

"Likely not. You aren't married to Mr. Garrett, nor is he currently living on your property. Who you spend recreational time with isn't truly of his concern."

"What is his concern though? Can he object to Ryan spending time with her?" I ask.

He tilts his head back and forth before stating, "Yes and no. He could technically stipulate that Emma not meet Mr. Garrett until your relationship has progressed past a certain point. Usually, six months is the standard for such an agreement, providing that said romantic partner doesn't pose a risk to the child."

"He's trying to say that Ryan poses a risk though, isn't he?" I feel my temper rising with each word. He just can't let me be happy. He *has* to drag me down into his miserable bullshit.

Nia places a soothing hand on my arm, "He is, but as Greg said, the police report won't hold up in court and honestly could even backfire since he's the one who instigated the altercation. If that's all he has against Ryan, it's not much. No judge would agree that Jared has a say in your private life." I take a deep breath and nod, feeling slightly better.

"So, Mr. Forrester obviously has an issue with this new romantic relationship of yours. How do you feel about a six-month stipulation like I mentioned earlier? It would be a compromise, I understand, but it might be worth it to keep this from going before a judge. We can even ensure that the six-month rule would apply to him as well." Greg flicks through some forms when he finishes speaking and hands one to me.

As much as it sucks, it seems like the best alternative. "Okay, I can do that. If that will end this and keep it from getting worse, I'm fine with that. That's only another three-ish months anyway." I'm choosing to be petty and count from when I first met Ryan rather than when we started dating.

Greg nods and says, "Alright, just know that if you're found in violation, it could mean Jared has the right to take it to court and it could be used against you. Just have to let you know." I nod back and bend my head over the form, signing next to the highlighted areas. "Perfect! Back in a jiffy. I'm just going to make sure this works for Mr. Forrester, then after meeting with you all again, I'll draft a new custody agreement and have it to your lawyers over the weekend." He scrapes the paperwork together into a tidy pile and bustles out of the room.

* * *

As I drive home from the mediator's office, I let out a loosening breath, feeling each muscle unclench one by one. Jared had (grudgingly I'm sure) agreed to the custody agreement including the six-month wait on introducing new significant others. While Nia's legal fees took a chunk out of my savings, it was nothing compared to what it could have been if Jared had pursued litigation. I'm still pissed he brought that bogus police report to the meeting, but I'm trying to let it go. I need to be civil for Emma's sake. *For Emma* has been my constant mantra as of late.

I grab a celebratory overpriced coffee and pastry on my way home and decide that Emma and I will spend the rest of the afternoon doing "spa day." It's something we've done since she was two. We put on face masks, take a bubble bath, and when she holds still enough, paint her nails. I could use some relaxing girl time after all this. I pull into the driveway and sit back in the peace of my car, relishing the quiet before going inside.

The large oak tree out front is dappled with late afternoon sunlight and the grass has that lime green, nearly yellow tint that it gets in the summer. I watch as bees buzz lazily around the lavender in front of the porch, gilded by the golden light. It feels a little like magic. I can almost hear my mom saying, *It's going to be okay.* And this time, it really feels like it.

CHAPTER 31

Ryan

I slide a deep blue button-down short sleeve over my shoulders and make quick work of the buttons. I clasp my dark, slim profile watch onto my left wrist and take a cursory look in the mirror. I'm supposed to grab Summer for the Springview Fourth of July festival in less than ten minutes. We're meeting my sister and her family there. I'm running a little behind because my sweet, elderly next-door neighbor had some issues with her wiring again.

I smile to myself at the memory. I'm pretty sure nothing is wrong with her house's wiring. I suspect she's loosening her lightbulbs to give me a reason to come over. When I suggested that it appeared two of her lightbulbs just needed to be tightened (and how odd that it's a different set of lightbulbs than last week) she adopted a confused look, brows drawing together while she put on a show of leaning heavily on her cane.

I told her I'd be happy to spend some time with her whenever I was available, but she just said, "I'm not sure what you mean young man. Are you suggesting I did something untoward to get you over here? Alone?"

"Yes," I said, laughing. I told her again that I would stop by in a few days. I caught her sly smile before she covered it with a cough into her elbow.

"Well, I never. See you soon then," she harrumphed and ushered me out the door, demanding that I change my clothes before picking up my "lady friend." She reminds me so much of my *Nonna* that it hurts a little to interact with her.

I shake my head and chuckle while getting in my truck. In just the few months I've been here, I've felt so at ease. I had been so starved for an actual community these last few years. It feels so nice to have one again between Summer, my sister, old friends, and my nosy neighbor.

I feel a sense of purpose and belonging I haven't felt in a long time. I let Lydia cut my tethers and I'd been drifting ever since. I'm more than happy to tie myself to this place. To Summer.

When I pull up to Summer's house, she's sitting on her porch stoop, freckled legs outstretched and crossed at the ankles. She has her phone out and her eyes rapidly scan back and forth, devouring her ebook. She bites her lower lip (red of course because my girl loves a theme) and her eyebrows raise in a way I know means she just read something spicy.

I pop the truck's door open and hop out. She looks up at the noise and her cheeks color prettily, confirming she just got to the good part in her book and knows she's been caught. I raise my eyebrow playfully. "They finally did it?"

"God, yes. Finally! I'm, like, eighty percent of the way through the damn book. I like a slow burn, but this was downright glacial." She stows her phone in her small purse and stands. I get the full view of her now and it nearly knocks me on my ass. She's wearing jean shorts and a red sleeveless top studded with tiny metal stars. It's tight over her chest and flares out over her hips. The bare expanse of her legs is distracting and I'm about to suggest going back inside so I can peel those shorts off her.

"Ah-ah," she chides, seeing the look in my eye, "We are not

missing the festival and my chance to meet some of your family because you can't keep your hands to yourself."

"Who said anything about hands?" I smirk as she stumbles a little on her way to me.

Her lust blown eyes close and she shakes her head, poking me in the chest. "No. Nope. You're not going to use sexy words against me. You know they're my weakness."

I laugh and wrap my arms around her, inhaling the clean scent of her shampoo, and say, "Okay, fine. I was going to suggest a reenactment, but I see you're not interested." I lean down and capture her lips with a kiss and feel my pulse quicken. I wonder when or if it'll ever feel routine to kiss her. I hope it never does. I love that even after months with her, it still feels brand new.

She pulls back, "I have to actually *read it* first before it can be reenacted." She pouts, twisting her fingers through the hair at the base of my neck, giving me goosebumps.

"Do you want me to give you twenty minutes before we leave so you can finish reading?" I ask earnestly. "I do need to spray the weeds again." I look over the front lawn with a critical eye, seeing a few pesky but resilient weeds creeping in from the edges.

She beams up at me, "I love that you asked that and meant it, but no. If I pick up where I left off and you're here... Well, I don't think we'll be going anywhere." When she sees my pleased smile she says, "I want to go to the festival and meet Layla, Hudson, and Todd. If I stick around here, it's just going to make me sad that Emma isn't with me. This will be the first holiday of hers that I've missed. I need to do something different than the usual."

"Festival it is," I say before leaning down to press a kiss to her forehead. "Let's get going. I doubt parking is going to get any better." I tug her towards the truck and open the door for her.

Once we're both settled in I ask, "Do you know what Emma is doing with her dad today?"

"She's going with him to his parents' and I think they're going to barbecue and shoot off fireworks. She'll have a good time," she says with a tight smile. I know today is going to be hard for her, so I'm working overtime to make it special. I know nothing can replace spending time with her daughter, but I hope I can at least take her mind off it and make it fun.

"Sounds like she'll have a blast. Let's try to do the same, okay?" I reach over and squeeze her thigh, letting my hand rest on her warm skin. Her smile turns more genuine, and it gives me what I need to put the truck in reverse and head out.

When we get to the multi-block festival in downtown Springview, parking is just as I suspected. Terrible. We end up having to park several blocks away and walk hand-in-hand towards the booming music and red, white, and blue bedecked crowd. I have an old backpack slung over my shoulder with a few essentials.

We missed the start of the parade, but it looks like we'll catch it in the middle. Intricate floats featuring local clubs and interests roll by, interspersed with dance teams, fire trucks, cheerleaders, and the local middle and high school bands. Everything is classic Americana, down to the cherry red vintage Mustang acting as a float for the previous years' prom king and queen.

Once we reach the main road, I scan the crowd for my sister and find her with Hudson on her lap in a camping chair by the road. I tug Summer with me, glad that it seems that Layla and Todd saved us a small bit of real estate near them. The entire street is packed tight as sardines, most people sitting or standing shoulder to shoulder in the blistering heat. "Layla, this is my girl-friend, Summer," I say when we get close enough to be heard.

"I'd get up to hug you, but this barnacle is a little people shy and his favorite person had to run back to the car for more water. Nice to meet you, Summer. I've heard so much about you," Layla says warmly, tucking Hudson in closer when it seems he wants to be back inside her skin as a result of Summer smiling at him.

"No problem. It's great to meet you, too. Ryan has also told me a ton about you and this little cutie," Summer replies, waggling her fingers at Hudson who has peeked one eye out from the refuge of his mom's neck.

"Don't listen to anything he says unless it's glowingly positive," Layla jokes.

I roll my eyes and spread out a picnic blanket under one of the last shady trees available near my sister, glad at least that they seem to be hitting it off. Both women are amazing, so I wasn't really worried, but it's always a little scary introducing your girlfriend to family for the first time. I'd never tell Layla this, but her opinion matters more than anyone else's to me.

Summer and I take a second to arrange ourselves on the blanket before we down some ice-cold water bottles. After we cool down as much as possible, I pull Summer in front of me so she can lounge back on my chest. She comes willingly and instantly relaxes into me despite our sweat-dampened skin.

"Hey, Ryan," I hear Todd's deep voice say from behind me. Summer and I both turn our heads to see him heading for the open camping chair next to my sister. I say hello and make the introductions between him and Summer. I catch Summer giving Layla an approving nod and a thumbs up.

I try to hold in my snort of laughter and tickle Summer's side briefly. She grabs my hand and kisses the back of it before placing it back around her waist. Hudson careens from Layla's lap to Todd's and watches the parade in wide-eyed amazement.

Looking around at the festive chaos with Summer snuggled up to me and my family nearby, I feel a moment of pure peace. This is what I've been looking for. I didn't know it at the time, but she is the reason I came back to Lakeland.

I'm pulled out of the moment when one of the high school band members trips over her feet, tuba letting out a loud *squawk* as she rights herself. I'm impressed by the way she throws her shoulders back and keeps going. Her resilience reminds me of Summer. We watch the rest of the parade in comfortable silence. When the last float goes by, long silver streamers reflecting the setting sun, we get up to stretch and walk around.

Summer shakes out the picnic blanket and we work together to fold it quickly. "Want to go check out the booths?" I ask, looking across the street at the pop-up tents that seem to stretch as far as the eye can see.

Her face lights up when she says, "You mean you'll willingly walk around, mostly window shopping and potentially paying an exorbitant amount for something that you could find anywhere else for much less?"

"As long as I'm with you. You should know by now that I'll follow you anywhere," I say, lessening the sentimentality with an eye roll. She grins in response and grabs my hand.

"You guys want to come?" Summer asks as Todd and Layla work to get their chairs folded and put in the carrying bags.

"We have to get these back to the car, but how about we meet you guys for dinner? That way we don't slow you down," Todd suggests.

"Sounds good. I know there's supposed to be a big line of food trucks somewhere. Want to meet there in an hour or so?" I ask, slipping the straps of my backpack over my shoulders. Todd and Layla agree and then lead Hudson back towards the side street to find their car.

We spend a long time weaving through the labyrinth of booths. It feels part farmers market, part craft fair, part music festival. Summer pauses at most of them, running her navy-tipped fingers over shirts, crystals, jewelry, and all manner of handmade tchotchkes. She picks up a tiny bracelet dripping with a rainbow of rhinestones for Emma and definitely pays more than I thought possible for such a small thing.

I get swindled into purchasing a handmade beard oil when Summer says she likes the scent. The man behind the booth (sporting a fantastic beard himself) looks at me and winks saying, "Trust me, you'll be going to our site for more as soon as you run out. Women are addicted to the scent and the softness." He gives me a knowing look and slips his business card into my hand.

Summer assesses me and says, "Your beard *could* be softer." I sigh and fork over my credit card.

As we approach the exit of the vendors and move towards the scent of carne asada, funnel cake, and hotdogs, I realize she hasn't gotten anything for herself.

When I point out as much to her, she tries to wave me off, "It's no big deal. I'm trying to keep my excess spending to a minimum. I don't want to dip into my savings more than I've already had to. There will always be more time to buy little things I don't need."

"Wait, are you saying I *didn't* need the beard oil?" I dangle the brown gift bag accusingly in front of her face.

She laughs and pushes it away, "No, you definitely need it. Maybe I won't get so much beard rash once you start using it."

I scoff and tug her back to my front, rubbing said beard playfully along the side of her exposed neck. "See? Plenty soft," I whisper into her ear before pulling back to look at her. She looks up at me, eyes crinkling before schooling her expression and rolling them.

We break into a clearing lined with food trucks and I spot my sister and her family in line at a taco truck. We wave and then decide on corn dogs and beer to really go for the all-American experience. Unfortunately, it seems like lots of other people have the same idea, so the line feels a mile long. There are at least fifteen people in front of us and the line slows as a large family of eight approaches the window. The parents are trying to corral their children while also ordering food to feed their small army.

As we stand melting in the heat, I get an idea. "Hey, I'll be right back, okay? I just have to use the restroom. If I'm not back by the time you're close to the front, give me a call." She nods and smiles at me. I give her a quick peck on the lips before dashing back through the vendor booths.

I weave my way back to a stall we spent a long time looking over. Crystal bookmarks made of obsidian, agate, rose quartz, and ones I can't even name spread across a section of the table. They are thin enough to be placed in a book but delicate enough that they have a translucent quality to them. I select a rose quartz one that has a heart-shaped hole drilled through the top of it with a heavy tassel attached. I know Summer didn't get it because of the price. It wasn't outrageous, but enough to make her turn away after she spent a few minutes turning it around in the light and playing with the tassel.

"That's the one your girl was eyeing earlier," the woman running the booth says with a smile. She's petite, almost birdlike, with a large nest of curly dark hair piled atop her head.

"I know. I paid attention," I say, smiling at her in return.

"Good man. I'll even throw in a worry stone for free. She looked like she could use it. Clear quartz will help absorb negative energy."

"Maybe I'll strap a few dozen to her myself then," I say with a chuckle. She laughs with me as she carefully wraps the bookmark in tissue paper and places it into another brown gift bag. She picks up the worry stone, wraps that one up too, and sets it on top. "Thank you," I say, after signing my name on her card reader.

"No problem. Take care of that one. Lots of bad energy hanging around her, but I can tell she's usually full of sunshine. Stick close to her, I think she's going to need you." I smile and nod, a little spooked at the accurate reading. I'm not one to believe in much outside of what I can see with my own eyes, but that damn near sent a chill down my spine. I pause to shove the two bags in my backpack on top of the picnic blanket.

I head back through the booths and am back in the food truck alcove just as I feel my phone start to vibrate. I jog up to Summer and give her a loud, smacking kiss on the cheek. She laughs, ending the call. "You're just in time." She gestures to the food truck ahead just as the couple in front of us steps out of line to wait for their order. I grab her hand and entwine our fingers together while we come up to the window.

A young guy leans out with a harried smile and asks, "What can I get you, folks?" He has sweat beading his brow and I hope he's had at least a small break today. This heat is no joke.

Summer cranes her neck to meet his eyes and says, "I'll take a footlong with nacho cheese dip, please."

"Make that two," I say, digging my wallet out of the back pocket of my shorts. Layla, Todd, and Hudson join us as my card is returned to me. Layla and Todd are each holding a burrito that looks like it could feed three people a piece.

"Thanks for buying me dinner," Summer says as we all walk over to the pick-up window on the truck.

"Only the fanciest for my woman," I say with a cheeky smile. I catch Layla's eye as she mouths, '*I like her,*' behind Summer's back. I wink at her in acknowledgement and go back to looking at Summer. She laughs at my dumb joke, the setting sun catching the side of her face and making her glow.

I am absolutely fatal for this woman. We haven't said "I love you" yet, but I know we both feel it. We've been in such a whirl-wind since we got together that there just hasn't been a good moment. I know Summer would never ask for it, but I want to give her a book-worthy moment. She deserves to have a few fantasies played out in real life. That's what tonight's for.

CHAPTER 32

Summer

Hudson gets the last bite of my corndog, and I'm glad it was even bigger than I was expecting since he ended up eating nearly half of my meal. He had decided a carne asada burrito didn't live up to his culinary tastes. Layla and Todd asked me a million times if I was sure about sharing my food, but I don't mind one bit. I can never eat much in the heat and it's boiling hot today.

After we all demolish our meals and drain the last dregs of our drinks, we get in line to grab a special holiday beer from Reaper's Reserve, a local craft brewery. We've been seeing people with their holiday edition drinks, tiny American flags sticking out the top of the cups with the brewery's Grim Reaper logo emblazoned in red, white, and blue, and Layla seems really enthused about trying them.

"Two Raucous, Witty, and Brewed, please," Ryan says to the tattooed twenty-something woman taking orders in the sleek black and silver food truck. His cheeks color a little at having to order the ridiculous-sounding beer, and I feel love swell in my chest to near strangling proportions.

I haven't told him yet because I've been enjoying every second with him. I want to drag out all the good and make it last. With Jared, everything moved at lightning speed. Partially because we were in high school and relationships tend to run their course in dog years, and partially because we had a baby so young. I'm savoring this second chance.

"This beer better be worth it," he grouses as we rejoin Layla, Todd and Hudson, beers in hand.

I take a sip, ripe raspberry and yeast bursting on my tongue, and tip my head side to side. "I mean, it's pretty damn good. The name could be better, but at least the beer is good."

He takes his own sip and nods grudgingly, "Okay, that's delicious. I can forgive the name."

"I told you it would be good. Reaper's Reserve is known for their seasonal beers," Layla says, leading us through the crowd.

We meander toward a live cover band playing some classic rock. "What are we doing next?" I ask. We're two amongst a decent crowd with families spread out on picnic blankets or camping chairs surrounding us.

"Well, once we polish these off, I figured you and I can head out. I have something special to show you." My interest is piqued, but now's not really the time for conversation as Metallica's *Enter Sandman* blares through the speakers. The lead singer gets drowned out by the *bang* of the drums. Despite the sound not being attuned properly, the band is actually pretty great.

We stay through a few more songs where they play everything from Queen to Creed. I enjoy dancing with him as he holds me close by the waist, swaying in time with the music. Todd and Layla dance with Hudson between them, and he giggles every time they spin him in a circle.

He's warmed up to me a bit after I shared my food with him, but he's still a little weary. I admire the standoffishness towards strangers to be honest. Emma has always been way too friendly. The girl hardly has any stranger danger and it's always made me nervous. Hudson is much more discerning and I bet Layla rests a little easier as a result.

Eventually, we drain the last of our sweet beers and Ryan looks at me with a smile. He pushes some stray hairs behind my ear and says, "Ready for a quick little adventure?"

"I thought this was the adventure," I reply, gesturing to the still undulating crowd around us and his family.

"Part of it. We'll see you guys later," he says to his sister and her family.

"It was so nice to meet you all," I say, leaning in to give them both hugs and Hudson a fist bump.

"You too. Seriously, I'm so glad I finally got to meet you. Ryan never shuts up about you and I'm happy to see he isn't exaggerating. You're as sweet and beautiful as he says," Layla states, reaching out to squeeze my shoulder. I smile and thank her, flushing slightly with the blunt compliment. "I pestered him to give me your number, but he wouldn't budge. Maybe he will now that he can see we get along," she says.

"I think that's a great idea. I'd love to chat and hang out," I say earnestly. Layla is like the more intense, feminine version of Ryan, and I've had such a good time hanging out with her today. It was nice to meet someone who is so important to him.

Ryan facilitates another round of goodbyes and promises he'll give me his sister's number. He starts tugging my hand and leading me back through the crowds, clearly trying to make an escape. Once we're in the truck with the AC cranked up, he waits for a gap in the cars and backs out.

"My sister really does like you. She's not just blowing smoke up your ass. She doesn't do that, so if she says something, she means it," he says, eyeing me for a second before returning his attention to the road.

"I really like her too. And Todd and Hudson both seem really sweet."

"They are. I was so thankful when Lay found him, because he is truly one of the nicest guys I've ever met."

I nod in agreement and then get distracted by the road. I don't recognize where we're headed, because Lakeland is the other way. "Okay, I can't take it, where are we going?" I ask, lifting the heavy weight of my hair off my sweaty neck.

"You'll see. Can't you wait for a good surprise?" He takes his eyes off the road briefly to smile at me and puts his palm on my thigh.

"Fine," I acquiesce, drawing out the middle of the word like a sullen teen. He laughs and we fall into a comfortable silence, the radio playing softly in the background.

We weave up through some foothills until we pull off at a service road. I look over at him, eyebrow raised, as we bump over the unpaved road. "Is the surprise murder?" I ask jokingly.

He snorts, "*No.* I like you alive, thanks. It's just up ahead." He takes his hand off my thigh so he has better control over the uneven dirt road. We meander through a thicket of trees, the path barely visible, until suddenly we're in a clearing and I can see all of Springview laid out below us. The service path continues on to the right, but up ahead, there's a turnout that Ryan backs into.

"Wow," I can't help but say, "How did you find out about this place?" We hop out of the truck and Ryan instructs me to look at the view while he gets some things ready in the truck bed. I stare out at the town just lighting the streetlights below us in wonder. It looks like a little doll town with well-manicured buildings interspersed with large trees, patches of grass, and a blacktop grid. I can even make out the large park where the festival is.

I can hear him puttering around behind me when he says, "Well, one of my coworkers whose brother is a firefighter mentioned that this is a great lookout spot that very few people know about. Really only some of the local firemen know of it because they want to keep it hush-hush. They don't want a bunch of people up here causing issues since this is technically a service road. Anyway, he told me the view for tonight's fireworks would be fantastic." I nod in acknowledgment and he says, "Okay, you can look now."

I turn to see that he's lined the edge of the truck bed with fairy lights, and there are a few small solar-powered lanterns emitting a soft yellow glow poised on the edges of the open tailgate. In the truck bed, he's laid out the same picnic blanket we used at the festival along with an open sleeping bag for extra cushion from the hard surface. He's also thrown several pillows up by the cab of the truck. Sitting in the middle of it all is a tray with a small char-cuterie board for two with meats, cheeses, crackers, fruits, and chocolates. Next to the board is a small bottle of champagne and two plastic champagne flutes decorated with red, white, and blue fireworks.

When my eyes finally find their way back to his, I find that they're blurred with tears. "You did this for me?" I can't quite process it.

"Of course I did," he says, coming up to catch my tears on his thumbs. He leans in and kisses me softly. Just as the kiss is turning into something more, we jump at the *pop! Boom!* of a firework exploding behind me, over the town.

We break apart with a laugh and Ryan takes my hand. "Come on, let's go watch from the truck," he says.

As I get closer, I notice something shiny leaning up against the champagne bottle. "You went back and bought it," I state, a hitch in my voice. I take the beautiful bookmark in my hand and run my fingertips along the cool length of it reverently. The bookmark is made of rose quartz and has the prettiest, heaviest tassel I've ever held.

When I finally look up at him, I find him studying me just as adoringly as I was looking at the bookmark. "I did. You wanted it," he says simply. I hug him hard before tucking the bookmark safely in my bag in the truck.

He gives me an effortless boost into the truck bed and I crawl back towards the cab so that I can lean against the pillows. He follows close behind and drags the tray with our snacks and champagne closer. He makes quick work of the cork and pours us each a glass while the sky ahead of us lights up in technicolor. "What should we toast?" I ask, snuggling into his arm and looking up at him.

"To love and a future of endless, happy little moments just like this," he replies, his eyes softly tracing my face.

"Cheers to that," I say, clinking my glass to his before we both take a sip. Despite the fireworks exploding ahead of us, I can't take my eyes off of him. The way he's completely focused on me, the gentle upturn of his full lips, a swath of hair sticking out of his backwards ball cap and covering his forehead.

The air explodes with a continuous stream of *bangs! W*e turn to look at the fireworks again, the sky covered in glittering sprays of red, blue, gold, and white. We watch the finale in companionable silence, sipping on our champagne and picking over the charcuterie.

The sky lights up with one last display and just as quickly as it started, the sky goes dark and quiet. All that's left of the show is the slight smell of smoke and gunpowder on the breeze. The truck bed feels bright and cozy with the warm-toned fairy lights shining around us. Ryan pushes the tray with our now empty glasses and picked over charcuterie to the side.

He turns to me and cups my cheek, thumb tugging gently on my lower lip. "I love you, Summer. More than I ever thought possible. Today I kept thinking about how incredibly grateful I am to be with you. The last few years left me feeling so untethered. Like, no matter where I was or who I was with, it wouldn't matter if I faded away. Here, with you, makes me feel grounded. You give me a purpose I've been missing." His eyes, dancing with the twinkling lights around us, search mine.

I reach up and rest my hand on his wrist. "I love you too. So much. I can't tell you how lucky I feel to have found you. I honestly thought I would be alone because I was terrified I was too much. Too much to love. Too much work. Too much baggage. When you came into my life, it was like coming home. It's like my heart said 'Oh, there you are.'" I smile a little at him.

He takes hold of my wrist and places my hand over his heart. "It's yours. As long as you want it." I leave it there for a minute, the pounding beat matching my own. I slowly slide my hand up his warm, broad chest until I'm cupping the back of his head. I pull him in close and kiss each cheek, his nose, his closed eyelids, his forehead, before pressing my lips to his. I want him to feel as cherished as he always makes me feel.

He hooks a hand around my thigh and pulls until I'm straddling him. I abandon the kiss and he groans in protest which makes me smile wider. "Ryan Jacob Garrett, did you bring me out here so you could sweet talk your way into my pants?" I lean back and give my best scolding face.

His returning grin is somehow both proud and sheepish as he says, "Maybe?" At my raised eyebrow he continues, "Okay, yeah, getting in your pants was definitely on the hopeful agenda for tonight, but mostly I just wanted to give you an experience and tell you in the most romantic way I could that I love you."

I feel as though the champagne we drank has made its way into my chest, little fizzy bubbles popping joyfully at his words. "I love you too," I reply, smiling fully now.

"I know. Now kiss me," he demands, his voice taking on a gruff edge. He runs his hands up my bare arms and locks them together behind my neck, pulling me roughly to him for a kiss. When our lips meet, the fizz in my chest catches fire and I can't get enough of him. His hands are everywhere, his mouth on mine, on my neck, my jaw, nipping at my exposed collarbone.

He runs his hands under the hem of my shirt, breaking his searing kiss on my neck just long enough to whip my shirt over my head. He tosses it somewhere behind us and then his warm, wet mouth is on me again. He follows a path lower, making me gasp and writhe when he takes a rosy bud into his mouth.

I work to unbutton his shirt and push it down over his shoulders, baring him to me. He looks like a golden god in the light and I can't believe my luck. Sweet, kind, smart, and hot? I must have done some Gandhi-level good deeds in a past life to be here right now.

Soon, there's nothing between us, and the feel of his warm skin flush against mine is dizzying. His kisses are drugging in their slow, but insistent pace. When I finally sink down on him and we move together, I swear I've never felt anything better. He breaks the kiss and looks me in the eye. "You're fucking perfect, Summer. This. Everything. I want it forever." My eyes flutter at the mix of the feel of him between my legs and his heady words. He cups my face, making me look at him. "Say it. Forever." There's a vulnerability in his eyes that I've rarely seen.

"Forever," I say with a breathy sigh. He smiles and picks up our pace, hands on my hips guiding me through it. I lean forward, kissing and nipping at his neck, relishing the noises he makes in the back of his throat. We both climb and climb, until at last, we shatter one after the other.

Later, while he's holding me close and we're looking up at the stars, I feel a contentment settle deep in my bones. I've never felt so right about where I was going, but as I look up at him, his eyes still focused on the stars above, I know that my only way forward is with him. *Pop! Fizz* go the bubbles in my chest.

CHAPTER 33

Ryan

August is in full swing and with it, everyone's air conditioners are going out or needing repairs. The heat wave that hit us last week knocked out what feels like every single household. I took an HVAC course a few years back to expand my services, but I'm regretting that now that I'm staying in one place. Most of the local HVAC companies are booked out, so I've been doing what I can to patch up our client's ACs until they can get out to replace them or do more long-term repairs.

I mop my brow with the cooling towel slung around my neck and chug the last of my water. I was able to patch this apartment unit's AC, but it'll need a full replacement in the next few weeks or so. I stand from where I was kneeling by the hulking unit and gather my tools into my bag. I start in the direction of the apartment's management office to tell them as much and squint against the high noon sun.

As I cross the lawn towards the office, I hear, "Hey, asshole!" I keep walking, assuming they aren't talking to me and not wanting to get involved in some petty neighbor squabble. "Hey, you, Summer's new bitch!"

At that, I spin around and narrow my eyes. I see a drunk, stumbling Duncan who looks like he's off a fresh bender with his sweat-stained t-shirt and basketball shorts. His flip flops smack the back of his heels as he speeds towards me when he sees me notice him. I take a deep breath of the searing August air. *It's way too hot for this shit.* "Hey, Duncan. Why don't you go back home and sober up?" I hold my hand out so he stops an arm's length away.

"Fuck you, man," he slurs. My lips flatten into a line and I turn to keep walking. I just want to get this job over with so I can go home and take a cool shower. "Hey, I wasn't done talking," he says, grabbing my shoulder from behind and turning me halfway to him.

"Don't touch me," I bite out, swiping his clammy palm off my shoulder.

He raises his hands, apparently knowing enough in his drunken haze to see that he wouldn't win in a fight against me. "What're you doin' here?" he asks.

I hold up my toolbag and jiggle it, making the tools inside shift and clank. "I was finishing a job. I'm heading out," I say curtly.

"No, wait. Just listen to me. Now that I have you here without *her* nearby..." At that, I roll my eyes. It's about Summer, of course. *What is this guy's problem?* "You gotta get out while you can. She'll either baby-trap you or dump you when she gets bored."

"Why do you always act like an angry ex?" I ask, raising an eyebrow and inching away from him.

"Shuddup about things you know nothin' about," he warns, grubby finger pointed at me.

"Listen, I get it. She's an amazing woman and you're upset you lost your chance with her however many years ago, but you have to let that shit go. Sober up. Be happy. Life is too damn short to waste it being miserable," I say, clapping him a little harder than necessary on the shoulder.

His expression goes dark and ugly, lip pulling up in a sneer, "Yeah. Miserable. What do you know about that, pretty boy?" He spits at my feet and stumbles away, back to whichever drunken hole he escaped from. I watch him go and sigh. I honestly feel a little bad for him. I shake my head and make my way to the blissfully cool office.

* * *

Once I'm in my truck with the doors locked, I shoot off a text to Summer.

RYAN:

I just saw Duncan and it didn't go well.

OMG are you okay???

Yeah. I'm fine. He was just spouting off more bullshit and drunk off his ass.

If he wasn't such a dick, I'd be more worried about him. Seems like he's drunk more often than not these days. Every time someone mentions him, he's always wasted.

Yeah.

Ugh. I don't want to, but I'm going to reach out to Jared and see if he's aware of how bad it's gotten. Maybe he can get him to an AA meeting.

You're a good person.

Yeah, yeah. Just doing my civic duty and all that.

I toss my phone on my passenger side and head for home, more than a little excited at the prospect of a cool shower and an even colder glass of water. I don't usually work Saturdays anymore, but I feel bad letting people cook in this heat. The overtime pay is a nice perk.

My mood lightens at the thought of the FaceTime call we have planned for tonight when Emma is in bed. I feel my cheeks heat as our last late-night FaceTime replays in my mind and shake the thought off so I can focus on my drive.

CHAPTER 34

Summer

Oh, now you care about my friend? Why don't you and that little boyfriend of yours mind your own damn business? I scrub the coffee table harder, being mindful of the chip in the corner from where my mom did one of her numerous craft projects and got a little overzealous with the box cutter. I am determined to work out the anger I'm feeling in a productive way. Even when I'm trying to be kind to Jared, he has to be a dick. The last couple of months since our mediation appointment have been a constant flip between hot and cold. I never know which side I'm going to get from Jared when I see him. One minute, he's laughing with me and treating me like we're friends, and the next he's snapping at me. It's like he moves on and then remembers that he hates me.

I'm still trying to be as neutral as I can in the face of his anger because I know if I start down that path, it'll be hard to go back. I'm just thankful Emma is at her grandma's house so I can have an afternoon to rage and work it out of my system before she's back for dinner.

I'm trying to keep Emma's future in mind. I want to be able to attend birthday parties, graduations, holidays, and maybe even

217

her wedding one day without her worrying that I'll blow up on her dad.

After rage-cleaning, I decide to give Ryan a call to update him on how the talk with Jared went. I find his contact in my phone and press call. "Hello?"

"Hey, babe. Just wanted to let you know what Jared said. Are you busy?" I take a seat at the kitchen table and absently look over my plants, making a note to water the pothos later.

"For you? Never. So, it went super well, right?" Ryan asks sarcastically. It pulls me out of my angry stupor and I snort a laugh.

"Yeah, *so well*. He thanked me for my concern and reminded me what a fantastic mother I am. He's putting me up for a good citizen award."

"No way. You'll definitely win," he deadpans. Both of us laugh and I enjoy the break in tension, feeling my jaw unclench for the first time this afternoon. Once we sober he pushes, "No really. How did it go?"

I sigh and respond, "Not great. He accused you and me of meddling and told me to mind my own business. He, and I quote, 'can handle his friend without me and my little boyfriend.' Can you hear my eyes rolling? He's literally the most dramatic person ever. I swear, if you had met him a year ago, you would think he was level-headed and dependable, if not a little self-centered some-times. But that was overshadowed by the fact that he was such a good father."

"I know, sweetheart. I'm sorry that he isn't turning out to be the person you thought he was," Ryan says softly.

"It's just crazy how much a person can change when they don't get their way." I sigh, trailing my fingers along my string of pearls plant. "I cleared my conscience. I told him that I was worried and that he should see about getting Duncan some help. I can't do any more than that."

"Nope. You did what you could for a person who has been nothing but rude to you for almost a decade."

I nod even though he can't see and ask, "So what are you up to tonight?" I'm sick of talking about Jared.

"I'm going to go out with the guys. They said something about a new action movie. As long as it's indoors and has air conditioning, we could be watching paint dry for all I care."

"Yeah, you were in the heat again today, weren't you? I'm sorry," I say sympathetically, "I hate the idea of you working outside in the middle of the day when it's hotter than satan's left tit."

"Is his right tit known to be cooler?" he asks dubiously.

"Smart ass," I retort. We laugh again, and it feels good. When our laughter dies down, I say, "Okay, I'll let you go so you can get ready to watch people get blown up or whatever."

When he speaks, I can hear the smile in his voice, "Thanks, babe. I'll see you soon, okay? I miss you."

"I miss you too. Have fun tonight," I say.

"I will. Love you." No matter how often I hear it, I can't get past the swarm of butterflies that take flight in my abdomen when he tells me he loves me.

"I love you too. Bye." When we hang up, I feel so much more at ease. It's amazing how much just speaking to him grounds me. He always knows how to calm me down and make me feel better.

I breathe in through my nose and wrinkle it when I realize I smell like dust and dirty dishwater. I decide a bath is in order, even if it *is* hotter than satan's left tit out there. I head to my bedroom where I strip off my biker shorts and t-shirt and start the bath.

While it's filling up, I go back into the bedroom to grab my newest book, *Obsession*, off my bedside table. I could only get a chapter or so in last night before giving up and going to bed. The one thing that hasn't changed in the last six months is how exhausting motherhood is, especially solo parenting. It will never stop to amaze me just how much energy my daughter has and how much it feels like that energy gets funneled directly from my own reserves.

I step into the steaming bath and sink down into its warmth. After drying my fingers on my nearby towel, I open the book and gently set my rose quartz bookmark down on the side of the tub. I fully intend to read until my toes are pruny and the water is cold.

CHAPTER 35

Ryan

I'm putting the finishing touches on my time card for this week and the fluorescent office lighting is making my eyes ache. I hate the damn time card even though I understand its necessity. Billable hours and all that. Still, I wish there was some automated way to do it instead of having to go into explicit detail over every working hour, attaching each one to specific jobs. I always forget to do it until the last second and I spend the last couple hours of the pay period scrambling to get it together. I'm reading over it one more time, the ache in my eyes getting worse as I try to focus on the tiny typeset in each of the Excel spreadsheet cells when my phone starts buzzing across my desk.

I let out a sigh of relief, glad something is pulling me away, and answer, "Hello, this is Ryan."

A voice crackles down the line, sounding muffled and a little far away. "Ryan, hey man, this is Jared."

My head rears back in shock and I clarify, "Forrester?"

"Yeah."

"Uh. What can I do for you?" I'm trying to stay as polite as I can in my bewilderment. I don't want to give him any ammunition.

His voice breaks up again, and all I can make out is, "Can you...Emma?"

"Sorry man, you're breaking up pretty bad. What about Emma?"

"Sorry, heading out to a work emergency. Better?" His voice sounds a little clearer, but it's still tough to make out. It makes sense that the call quality is so bad if he's headed off to some lumber emergency. Summer usually has to rely on text messages when he's at work to communicate about Emma. When I confirm I can hear him better, he continues, "Can you pick up Emma from gymnastics in, like, twenty minutes? I can't be there and I already tried to call Summer. She didn't answer."

I'm stunned by the request seeing as he's had a long vendetta against this very thing: Me having casual contact with Emma. "Are you sure?" I ask slowly, wondering if this is a test.

Even through the poor reception, I can hear his annoyance, "Yes. Just take her to get ice cream or something and I'll pick her up after. There's a place just down the road. I shouldn't be long."

I think for a beat before saying, "Okay, I can do that." Maybe this is how I show Jared that I can be helpful and that Emma and I can get along okay. I have to think long-term about this. We hang up and I release a tight exhale. I'm nervous, but I can't pinpoint why. Maybe I just want Emma to like me. It feels sort of strange to be meeting her formally without Summer.

I try to give Summer a call even though Jared said he couldn't get ahold of her. Her phone goes straight to voicemail, and after the tone, I leave a brief message saying, "Hey, so I'm going to pick Emma up from gymnastics. I'll explain later. Love you."

After I hang up, I wonder if I should have mentioned Jared but decide against it. I don't want to bother her at work and I figure since Jared asked, she'd be okay with it. I'll just tell her when she calls me back. I don't want to leave Emma waiting for long, so I click save on my timesheet, power down my computer, and head out of the office, waving to our receptionist as I go.

When I pull in front of Oasis Gymnastics I turn off my audiobook (one of Summer's favorites) and shove my phone in my pocket. I quickly get out of my truck because I'd hate to be late *and* unexpected.

I open the glass door and am greeted by an icy blast of air conditioning, a front desk, and a waiting area full of parents either looking down at their phones or watching the kids through the large glass wall separating us from the rest of the gym. "Are you here to enroll a new student?" the teenage girl behind the desk asks me, boredom rolling off her in noxious waves. She has her hair pulled back in a thick blonde ponytail and her crossed arms have the toned definition of an athlete. She must be one of the older students here.

"No, I'm here to pick up Emma Forrester?" I realize I end the sentence with a question and mentally roll my eyes at myself. I need to get it together because right now I sound like a confused old man.

She narrows her dark brown eyes at me and pops her gum once before replying, "You're not her dad."

"No, I'm not. I'm a - um - friend of her mom's," I fumble. My god, who knew teenage girls could be so intimidating?

She sighs and holds out a hand, palm up, "Let me see some I.D. and make sure you're on the approved pick-up list." I take out my wallet and slip my I.D. out from its slot, slapping it into her open palm. She makes a show of squinting at the picture, then up at me, "You look old." I feel my ears turn hot and I grumble something about not taking a new picture for my license in a while. "I'll say," she responds while clicking around on her computer. "Okay. Looks like Ms. Evans put you on the approved list a few weeks back. Lucky you," she says the last part so dully, you'd think she was talking about her least favorite class in school.

I look over her shoulder to see that Emma is finishing up. I take my I.D. back and stand by the wall near the exit.

Emma follows a few other students through the glass door

and comes to a stop to scan the room. When her eyes land on me, I wave awkwardly (I swear I hear the girl behind the desk snort) and her brows draw together in confusion. She slowly approaches me and asks, "Do I know you?"

"Sorta. I'm Ryan, your mom's friend. You might not remember, but I drove you to the hospital the day your appendix got removed." I sit in the chair nearest me so I'm not towering over her.

She frowns again before her expression clears. "Oh yeah, I kinda remember you. What're you doing here?" She looks around, clearly searching for her mom or dad.

"Your dad called and asked me to pick you up. Said he was running a little late from a work thing. He thought we could go get some ice cream and then he'll get you from there soon."

She shrugs and says, "Okay," in the easy, accepting way that children often have. I've always admired how they can just roll with the punches. I lead her out towards my truck, and when she looks at the backseat she says, "Where's my booster seat?"

I mentally facepalm. I don't know how I forgot that little detail. "Well, I don't have one for you, but we can probably just walk to the ice cream place. Your dad said it was nearby?" Didn't think I'd be asking for directions from a six-year-old, but here we are.

"Oh! We're going to Swirl? Yes! Come on." She excitedly slams the door, takes hold of my hand with a surprisingly firm grip, and then tugs me back on the sidewalk. As she leads me (hopefully) in the right direction, she prattles on about all the different flavors she's tried and warns me away from a flavor called Curd Your Enthusiasm proclaiming it's, "yucky."

A few minutes later, we stop at a storefront with windows painted in bold swirling patterns of every color. I pull open the door and am immediately assaulted by sweet-smelling, cool air. "Come on, kiddo. Let's get you a scoop. Do you want it in a cup or a cone?"

She looks at me like I must be missing a few brain cells and says, "Cone," in a way that implies "idiot" was tacked on at the end in her head. She must be getting sass lessons from the front desk girl at her gym.

Despite the heat, there's no line, so we walk right up to the counter. I order her a watermelon lemonade flavored ice cream in a cake cone and get a scoop of strawberry cheesecake in a cup for myself. Once we have our ice creams in hand, I lead her to a spot where the seating is made up of two giant swings on either side of a picnic table hanging from the ceiling.

The decor looks like something they threw together in the hopes that it would photograph well on social media and attract more customers. They have a silk flower wall with an orange neon "Swirl" sign glowing in the middle. Inexplicably, there's also a stuffed animal section in the back corner with one massive teddy bear whose head nearly touches the ceiling surrounded by his much more appropriately sized minions. It looks vaguely like something I've had a nightmare about once or twice. I shiver and tell myself that it's just from the cold.

I pointedly angle my body away from Nightmare Corner and feel the bench swing sway under me. "So, how are you enjoying your summer?" I ask, hoping the neutral question will launch her on another tangent and I can avoid any awkward conversations.

She purses her ice cream covered lips and looks me over shrewdly, "Are you really my mom's friend?"

"What else would I be?" I ask back after swallowing an admittedly delicious bite of ice cream. I suppose I can ignore the horrifyingly large teddy bear for this. Maybe I'll bring Summer here one night on a date. I glance again at the gargantuan bear and I swear it moved positions since I last looked at it. Okay, maybe we can get our ice cream *to go*.

"Her boyfriend?" Her retort comes quickly and ends with a titter I was not expecting. Oh god. I do not want to lie to this kid the first time I'm officially meeting her. That sounds like a recipe for disaster.

I gracelessly switch topics, "So, what's your favorite part about gymnastics?" I breathe out a sigh of relief when she brightly discusses the balance beam, bar, and bouncy floors to practice tumbling. Her favorite skill is doing a cartwheel on the balance beam even though she was scared to try it at first. I'm about to ask a follow-up question about a bar maneuver she called a "backward hip circle" while scraping the edges of the cup to get one last bite of soupy deliciousness when the door bangs open. In storms an irate-looking Jared.

"What. Are. You. *Doingwithmydaughter*," he growls, approaching like a storm cloud. The last bit is said so quickly that the words bleed together, but I get the gist. He walks over to Emma's side of the table and wraps a protective arm around her.

I feel my eyes go wide as I look at him glowering over the table, "Um, what you told me to," I say like a question because I am genuinely confused right now.

His head rears back and a puzzled look draws his brows together. In his current state, it makes him look like a bull getting ready to charge. "What are you talking about?"

"You *just* called and asked me to pick her up less than an hour ago. You said something about a work emergency and not being able to get ahold of Summer," I say as calmly as I can.

"I never called you! I don't even have your number." Emma is watching the exchange, head bouncing back and forth like she's watching a tennis match.

"Well *someone* called me and said they were you and that you needed help."

Jared laughs, a sharp sound that seems like it hurts coming out, and says, "Even if I needed help, you are the absolute last person I would call."

"Well, if you didn't call me, then who did?" As he scoffs, I pull out my phone and check the call log. I turn my screen to him, pointing out his incoming call. "See? You called."

"That's not my number. It's not even the right area code," he says slowly. His brows draw together in confusion before he types something into his phone. After studying it for a bit he says, "This is one of those throw-away numbers that you can use as long as you have a wifi signal. How do I know you didn't call your phone from your computer just to make this all up?"

I shake my head, genuinely taken aback. "Because that's insane?" I stretch out the first word, not able to help myself. What the fuck is going on?

"Daddy, it's true. He said you told him to come pick me up," Emma says, eyeing her dad, tiny hand clutching at the arm banded around her shoulders.

"Shh baby, this is between the grownups, okay? Why don't you hang out with the teddy bears and I'll come get you in a second." He presses a kiss to her brow, helps her down, and gently pushes her in the right direction. Or the wrong direction if you ask me. I shiver at the thought of her sitting in that thing's lap.

Jared sits across from me and takes a deep breath. "Look, I don't know what's going on, but I do know that I didn't call you. I showed up a couple of minutes late to pick my daughter up from class because I *did* have something come up at work and couldn't find her. Then when I panicked and asked the girl at the front desk where Emma was, she said she left with some guy and they mentioned something about ice cream. When I exploded on her asking why the *hell* she let my six-year-old daughter leave with a man who wasn't me, she said you were on the approved list, and showed me your sign-out signature. If you weren't setting this whole thing up, why are you suddenly on the approved pick-up list when it hasn't changed since Emma started there two years ago?" His voice gets more and more heated, but I can tell he's trying to keep it down.

I spread my hands out in front of me and say, "I didn't even realize I was on the list, or that there even was a list. Summer must have added me at some point. Listen, I didn't introduce myself as Summer's boyfriend or anything, okay? I just told her that I was picking her up and her mom knew me. No harm, no foul." I am trying to be understanding because I can't imagine how terrified he was to get to Emma's class and find her missing. Still though, I wish he would calm down so we can get to the bottom of this.

I see his jaw clench once, twice before he says, "You know what I think? I think you orchestrated this whole thing so you could soften up my daughter. Make sure she likes you so she's on your side when the whole six-month clause is up. Which is, conveniently, in about a month. I think you just couldn't wait to come in and be Prince Charming or whatever. I think you want to push me out and make one happy little family." He sneers the last part. I blink, stunned. Does this man think that I'm some sort of Bond villain?

I shake my head vehemently. "I promise you, not at all. I truly want what's best for Emma. I think that means having you and Summer here for her. I'm sorry this was such a fucked up thing. I genuinely thought you called me and that I was helping. Can I have your actual number so nothing like this ever happens again?" I ask, trying to show I'm not the bad guy here. He grudgingly gives it to me and then stands to leave.

Just before he goes to Emma, he knocks once on the sticky table and says, "I still don't think I believe you. I'll be talking to Summer and my lawyer about this." A lead ball drops in my gut, but before I can say anything more, he's got Emma and is hustling her out the door. She gives me a meek wave and a small smile before following her dad out. *Well, shit.* I scrub my hand through my hair and hope I don't get charged with kidnapping or something equally as ridiculous. *This won't be good.*

CHAPTER 36

Summer

I grab my phone from the "phone jail" basket in the middle of the scuffed mahogany conference table and turn it back on as the rest of my coworkers file out in various stages of disgruntlement. We had some team building expert come in and she enthusiastically insisted that our phones should be off and inaccessible for the whole day because we needed to, "be fully unplugged so we could plug into each other." While it sounded vaguely sexual, nothing that interesting (or scarring) happened. It was mostly a lot of icebreakers that felt completely unnecessary since most of us have been working here for over five years. I *did* find out that Rachel's favorite animal is a guinea pig during one rousing round of two truths and a lie. Riveting stuff.

I sit back, eyes going wide as my phone buzzes with more notifications than I've ever gotten at one time. I'm scrolling through a CVS-receipt-long string of texts from Jared where I gather he got to Emma's gymnastics class to pick her up and found her not there, only to see that Ryan checked her out. My brow furrows in confusion. *Why would he do that?* Apparently, Jared found them in Emma's favorite ice cream store, Swirl, and took her home. Judging from the last string of angry texts, he thinks I have something to do with it.

Knowing that Emma is safe, I feel my heart rate start to slow, and I go to my missed calls and voicemails next. I see a missed call from a number I don't recognize, several from Jared, and two from Ryan. Both Jared and Ryan left me voicemails and I decide to rip the band-aid off and listen to Jared's first. I then listen to Ryan's two voicemails, the first saying he's picking up Emma and will explain later, and the next has him profusely apologizing and explaining there was some sort of weird mix-up. I shake my head in confusion and decide to call Ryan back first once I get outside.

The phone rings once before he picks up, and with just his "Hello," I can tell he's extremely anxious.

I start my car and lean back, letting the old girl warm up before I head home. "Hey. Wanna tell me what happened?" I ask gently. I know there's no way he would have just picked Emma up like that for no good reason.

He explains the weird phone call he got and that he didn't want to leave Emma alone for long, so after he couldn't get ahold of me, he just went for it. He figured since it was Jared calling him, there was no reason not to do it. His voice is tight with frustration at the end of his explanation, and I wish he was here so I could soothe him. I make the split-second decision to go see him at his place so I can do just that. After confirming with him that he's home, I hang up and make the quick drive there.

On the way through town, I call Jared and manage to have a restrained conversation where we agree to meet up tomorrow to figure out what happened. I hang up with him right as I pull into Ryan's driveway. He's already outside waiting for me, sitting on his front porch, his hands dangling between his spread thighs.

When he hears my car door shut, he looks up and smiles at me. He stands so he can give me a bear hug and I push up onto my tiptoes to kiss him. I get a little lost in the kiss and pout when he pulls away. He groans and I feel it zing through me. He gently presses me further away with a hand on my shoulder, "You shouldn't be kissing me like that. I'm trying to be repentant."

"What sins did you commit?" I ask playfully. It sounds like there was a weird mix up and some wires got crossed, but ultimately everyone is safe and okay. He's acting like he burned down the building.

"Too many to name, but most recently pissing off your child's father and maybe almost getting arrested for kidnapping," he says into his hands.

I snort a laugh and push his hair back from where it falls in his eyes. I lean in and whisper, "And would you like to make up for it on your knees?"

He tips his head back with his eyes closed, looking almost pained before he opens them and says, "Stop being sexy, I don't deserve it." His face crumples in a genuine pout and I drag him by the hand into his place. I kick off my work pumps by the door and hang my bag on the coat rack.

We sit on the black leather couch, my back to the armrest and legs draped over his lap. He draws little shapes on my exposed knees and down my shins with the tip of his calloused finger. We don't spend much time here, but his little house already feels like home to me because its an extension of him. The place is masculine with clean lines and an air of comfort with the pastoral pictures on the wall and multiple throw blankets draped over the couch.

We relax in silence for a while before something dawns on me and I ask, "So, what was the number that called you again?"

He shows me the number on his phone and I say, "You know what's weird? A random number called my phone just before you called me. They didn't leave a voicemail or text me. Let me see if it's the same one." We put our heads together over my phone as I pull up my call log. I sit back defeated when the numbers don't match.

Ryan fiddles with his phone before turning the screen to me

and saying, "This is another one of those random numbers you can use with a wifi signal. Remember how I told you Jared said the same about the one that called my phone? Your random caller called ten minutes before they called me. It was almost like they were seeing if you would answer your phone."

I get the chills because suddenly this doesn't feel like a weird misunderstanding anymore, this feels like a targeted attack. "Who would do that though? Why would they want you to pick up Emma?" My stomach trembles when the seed of anxiety plants firmly in my gut. *Is someone trying to hurt my daughter?*

Ryan shakes his head slowly side to side and squeezes my legs. "I don't know. I guess in the grand scheme of things it was pretty harmless because they called me and not some random person. I'm obviously not going to hurt Emma."

I've seen way too many true crime documentaries because my next question is, "But what if that was just the first step? What if they just wanted to see if they could pass as Jared so they could do something worse?"

Ryan notices my visible trembling and takes my hands in his, giving them a squeeze, "Hey. We don't know what their intentions are, but let's not jump to the worst conclusions. What else could it be?" I shake my head mutely. I don't know who would do this. If Jared did it so he could say I violated the clause in our custody agreement about romantic partners, I wouldn't be scared right now, I'd be furious. It makes the most sense, but from the way Jared sounded genuinely panicked in his voicemails and over the phone I don't think he was behind this. He's not that good of an actor.

I hardly slept last night. Between worrying over whether or not Jared would use this against me for custody, worrying about Emma's safety, and being alone in my house, I could not get settled. I stupidly insisted on sleeping in my own home because I knew Ryan had to be up early today to get to work on some roofing projects before it gets too hot. I regret my benevolence because I know I would have slept better if he had been next to me. I wouldn't have been so freaked out over every noise.

In my sleep deprived state, the work day passes in a blur. The door jingles while I'm zoning out over new client intake forms. I look up blearily and see Jared striding towards me with a giant to-go cup of iced coffee in one hand and a bag from the cafe down the street in the other.

"Hey," he greets, tentatively.

"Hi," I reply, eyeing the giant coffee that looks suspiciously like what I typically order.

"Do you want to come sit in my truck with me? I brought lunch and a coffee. Figured you'd be tired too. I hardly slept last night because I kept getting up to check on Emma. It felt like she was a newborn again when we'd get up randomly to make sure she was still breathing."

Even though he doesn't say it outright, I can sense an under-current of apology in his words. He hands me the coffee and I take a sip, *yep, definitely my order.* I nod and round the high-top desk. I wave to Sherry on the way out who is giving Jared the stink eye. She just narrows her eyes further and mimes slitting his throat with a thumb dragged across her own. I press my lips together to hide my smirk and turn to follow Jared.

Once we're settled in his truck, lunch sandwiches spread out around us I hedge, "So, yesterday was weird."

He snorts and sputters over a bite of sandwich. Once he has himself together he says, "Understatement of the fucking century."

I can't help the half smile that tugs at my lips. I miss being able to joke with him. This is what I hoped we would have after splitting up. "I know, but, like, how do you bring up what happened yesterday when it feels mostly harmless, but also kind of terrifying?" I take a sip of my coffee and look at him pointedly.

"True. But really, what the hell was that?"

"I have no clue. Ryan said it sounded like you on the phone, but the call quality was bad and he's not exactly super familiar with your voice," I take a bite of my sandwich and chew contemplatively before continuing, "So, does this mean you believe us? We didn't do this out of some weird desire to push you out," I reiterate for what feels like the hundredth time since yesterday.

He breathes out a heaving sigh and says, "Yeah. I believe you."

I mime checking his temperature and he playfully bats away my hand. "What changed your mind?" I ask, hoping I'm not looking the gift horse in the mouth on this one.

"Well, I started seeing someone." My eyes must bug out of my head because he says a little uncomfortably, "A therapist, not a woman. Well, she is a woman, but Ruth is about sixty years old and happily married. Anyway, I asked for an emergency appointment this morning because I was kind of spiraling, and she helped me think a little more clearly about the facts. I realize now that you wouldn't have benefitted at all if you and Ryan had done this on purpose, especially since we have it in our custody agreement."

I nod and say with as much genuine care as I can, "I'm really proud of you for getting help. What made you finally take the plunge?" I have been trying to convince him to see a therapist for years. After my mom passed, I spent a solid couple of years in weekly appointments, and I'm a firm believer that everyone needs it. We ended up working through not only my grief but a lot of my other issues as well.

"I made an appointment with her for the first time after our custody mediation. I was so angry because I felt like you were getting everything you wanted, and I was getting nothing." He gives me a look to silence the argument I'm sure he can see brewing in my expression. "I know. Logically, I know that isn't fair to you. It's just hard to remember that sometimes. Hence the 'frequent outbursts.'" He puts bunny ears around the words, and I can tell he's quoting his therapist. "Anyway, I was suddenly so angry that I was scaring myself. You know that I've never been an angry person. I didn't want to *be* that person anymore. I didn't want that for Emma either, so I finally bucked up and made an appointment. I've never been so afraid of a sixty-year-old woman in my life." He smiles at me tentatively and for the first time in months, I feel like we might be able to be around each other again.

"Well, I'm really glad she's helping you. And not just because it seems to benefit me," I offer. Even though I'm still upset at the way he's behaved since splitting up, I'm happy to see him working to better himself. Now all his hot and cold behavior over the last few months makes sense. He's been trying to work on it, but it's going to take time.

After a few minutes of surprisingly comfortable silence where we wolf down what's left of our food, Jared says, "So, about yesterday. If it wasn't you, and it wasn't me, who the hell was it? And why would they do it?"

The sandwich feels like it congeals in my stomach. Every time I think about it, it makes me nauseous. "I don't know. I mean, as far as Emma was concerned, it was mostly harmless. Despite what you may think of him, Ryan is a good guy and really just thought he needed to help."

"Yeah, yeah, right-hook Ryan and his fantastic adventures saving damsels or whatever—"

I can't help but snort at "right-hook Ryan."

Jared rolls his eyes at me and continues, "Anyway, just because I don't think he had kidnapping in mind yesterday doesn't mean I'm ready to be a big happy family. I need more time, okay?" He goes from sarcastic to vulnerable in a blink and I work to school my expression and give him a nod in affirmation. I want to keep this version of Jared around. It's better for all of us. Now that I know he's working on it, I'm going to do what I can to help.

"Okay, back to the topic at hand. If it wasn't a way to hurt Emma, then what could it be?" I muse.

"I mean, it freaked me the fuck out. Maybe it was a way to scare me?"

"But who would want to do that? It would have to be someone who has some knowledge about our schedules, where Emma does gymnastics, and that you would be late. Who's that mad at you? Or maybe it's me." I think for a second and then say, "Do you think it could be Duncan?"

His expression shutters and he says flatly, "No, I don't. He wouldn't do that to me."

I see that I'm on thin ice, so I change the subject. "Okay, if you're sure. Do you think it's someone at work?"

He scratches along his stubbly chin with the palm of his hand. "I mean, most of the guys I work with know at least that much, especially the guys who were on shift yesterday. They knew I was running behind because I talked about how I needed to hurry so I could go get her from her class."

"Well, does anyone there not like you?" I ask.

"Not that I know of. I've been working with most of them for at least a few years and have never had anything like that come up." His brow furrows and he stares out the windshield as if he'll find the answers painted on the hood of the car.

I check the time on my phone. "Shoot, I have to go, my lunch ended like, five minutes ago. Let's keep thinking about it and talk again later. Maybe ask around at work, see if there's something you don't know there."

He nods and seems lost in thought, "Okay. And you think, too. It could be someone with something against Ryan. I could have caused a way bigger scene and called the cops on him. He could have potentially gotten in a lot of trouble. Especially because he would have had no way to prove that his story was true." My stomach sinks at that, and I nod in return. I hadn't thought that it could be Ryan they were after. I get out, wave to Jared, and close his truck door.

CHAPTER 37

Summer

A week goes by fretfully but uneventfully. Jared can't find anyone at work with a big enough grudge to mess with his kid and risk losing their job. Ryan has been combing through six months' worth of clients and has found nothing of interest. It feels like whoever did this vanished in the wind.

The waiting is killing me. I'm on edge any time Emma is out of my sight or if I see someone unfamiliar around town or at work. So, basically, I'm on edge all the time.

Today is Sunday, and while I'm exhausted from the lack of sleep, I keep finding small tasks around the house to keep busy because if I stop and let myself think, I'll spiral. Emma is playing in the back yard and I keep staring out the window at her while I fold Mt. Laundry on the couch.

The sound of the doorbell makes me jump out of my skin. I toss the shorts I was folding on top of the pile and go to the door. I put my eye to the peephole and breathe a sigh of relief when I see Jared standing there, leaning against the pillar.

I unlock the door and pull it open for him. I got back into the habit of locking my door all the time after the weird phone calls.

"Hey," I say as I lead him into the living room, "I think Emma's bag is mostly packed, but let me just double-check real quick. She's in the backyard if you want to go say hi." I hear him slide the back door open and step out, calling a greeting to her as I round the corner into Emma's room.

I check through her bag making sure all of the essentials are there. We've done our best to make sure she has a base at both houses with all of her necessities, but she still likes to bring certain things back and forth like her stuffed unicorn that she's had since her first birthday, some favored clothes, and whatever toy she is currently obsessed with. I also make sure to tuck in a little note to her from me. Even though we talk every day she's not here, I like leaving her something to find when she misses me.

I zip up her bag and heft it over my shoulder, turning off the light on the way out of her room. Emma and Jared are standing in the kitchen chatting while I set her bag by the front door. She's chugging a glass of water and her cheeks are rosy from the August heat. "Hey, Em, why don't you go to the bathroom before we leave? We have to run a few errands before we get home," Jared says to her, plucking the glass out of her hand.

She shrugs and says, "Okay!" She skips out of the room and down the hall towards the bathroom.

The door clicks shut and Jared turns to me while I enter the kitchen. "What's up?" I ask, knowing this was just a tactic to get me alone for a second.

"I was thinking, what if you, me, and Ryan have dinner or something this week?" he asks in a rush. He's clearly nervous about this, but I admire the effort.

I narrow my eyes into slits, "Why would you want to do that?"

"Well, I'd say that at this point Ryan isn't going anywhere." He looks at me, "Right?"

"No, he's not. I'm pretty stuck on him."

He nods and says, "That's what I thought. Anyway, it's safe to say he and I got off on the wrong foot,"

"Or fist," I interrupt with a snort.

He levels me with a look and chooses to be the bigger person, "Right. Anyway, the six-month relationship stipulation will be up soon, and I'd like to actually have a conversation with him before he formally meets my daughter."

I can't help the way my head tips back in shock. Even though he's been better since our conversation a week ago, it's hard to reconcile this man with the one who was hurling insults my way only a month ago. The hot and cold attitude has dissipated a lot. It felt like once he shared his therapy appointments with me, he released a lot of the pressure off himself. Maybe *I* should be paying his therapist. "Okay," I say slowly, waiting for the catch.

He's right that the six-month stipulation is coming to an end soon, but I thought he'd drag it out until the last day. I clarify, "This isn't like a 'gotcha' thing is it?"

He laughs through his nose, "No. I promise. I know I've been acting out since we split up and I'm sorry about that. I think when I realized you were serious, it shocked me, and I didn't know how to handle it. I really want to try to be better for Emma. Since you're serious about this guy, I need to be cordial with him," He shifts on his feet and scratches the back of his neck, "And, I want to apologize for how I treated you. The things I've said to you. It's not okay. After Ryan decked me, I stewed on his words and he was right, which just made me more angry. I can't disrespect you like that. You don't deserve it, and none of the things I said about you were true. I'm just — I'm really sorry, okay?" He finally meets my eyes again, his sincerity softening them.

"Thank you for apologizing. If you keep showing an effort to be civil, we can definitely move forward. I'm not saying we all have to be best friends, but I'd like for us to be in the same room without hurling insults."

"Or fists?" A corner of his mouth kicks up in a rueful smile.

I laugh this time, "Yeah, or fists."

"I'm trying to get over us and move forward. I want to be happy too."

"I hope you find that, Jared. I really do." A beat passes and then I look at him with wide eyes and say, "Oh shit, Emma."

We both say, "Dammit," and rush towards the bathroom. She's been in there a suspiciously long time. Jared gets to the door first and yanks it open. We find Emma and her most favorite Barbie coated in hair gel and cosmetic glitter.

"I did a makeover," she exclaims happily while gobs of clear hair gel slowly slide down the sides of her head.

"Emma," Jared and I groan simultaneously. We have quickly learned that unsupervised bathroom time lasting longer than a few minutes is always cause for concern. One time, she was flushing Legos down the toilet. *That* was a fun call to the plumber. Another time she was writing on the mirror with a tinted chapstick and it took me several rounds of Windex and a whole roll of paper towels to clean it. This time, it's gobs of gel and glitter.

Jared sighs and says, "I'll start the shower and you grab her new clothes?" I nod and go to get her a change of clothes.

I grab Emma a sun dress and underwear and head back to the bathroom to see Jared hosing her down with the shower head in his hand. Glitter is now coating the front of his soaked shirt and coursing down Emma's body in sparkly rivulets. I laugh at the absurdity of it all and cover my smile with a hand when Jared turns a glare on me.

I am always the one to laugh when Emma does something wild. It's either laugh, cry, or scream, and laughing seemed like the most appealing option. I clap my other hand over my mouth and leave the room so Emma won't see me laughing and decide to do it again.

When I see Steph tonight, she is going to lose her mind when

I tell her what Jared just suggested. I am finally getting a chance to hang with her before the school year craziness starts. She's been doing prep work for the last couple weeks and hasn't been able to get away. We're hanging at her place this time since being alone at mine still gives me the heebie-jeebies. She might even call Jared herself to make sure he hasn't been replaced with a body snatcher.

CHAPTER 38

Ryan

When Summer first approached me about having dinner with Jared this week, I have to admit that my first reaction wasn't exactly kind. I know that she is quick to forgive, and I love that about her, but I tend to hold a grudge whether I like it or not.

One time in the eighth grade, while waiting in the lunch line, my friend came up to talk to me. I let him go in front of me and he got the last slice of pizza. Later on, I learned he did that on purpose to mess with me. I didn't speak to him for a week. Over cafeteria pizza. While I like to think I've grown since then, getting chummy with my girlfriend's ex who put her through hell might be pushing it too far.

Today is the day, and I'm feeling pretty apprehensive about the whole thing. Jared hasn't proven to be the most even-keeled, so I'm hoping tonight goes okay for Summer's sake. Emma is being watched by Jared's mom, so it will just be the adults.

I fill a glass of water from Summer's tap and drain the glass. I set it in the sink when Summer pads into the kitchen on bare feet. She's wearing a brightly patterned sundress that falls just below her knees with the hair around her face pulled back. Stunning as per usual.

She presses up on her toes to peck me on the cheek before going behind me and wrapping her arms around my middle in a hug that allows me to keep doing what I'm doing. "Hey," she says, pressing her cheek between my shoulder blades. Even though I'm nervous about tonight, having her near gives me a sense of instant calm.

"Hey, yourself. Are you ready for tonight?" I ask as I turn to face her in the circle of her arms.

"As ready as I can be, I guess. Go get changed so we can leave." She releases me and steps up to the counter, gently pushing me aside.

"You got it," I say, leaning in and stealing a lingering kiss on her lips.

I throw on a casual t-shirt and shorts, reapply some deodorant, splash my face with water, and then assess myself in the mirror, hoping my apprehension isn't as clear on my face as it feels. To my horror, it is. I work to school my expression into one that says, *I know I punched you in the face a few months ago, and I know you're kind of an asshole, but we can get along, right?* I grunt at my reflection when my expression doesn't do what I want and turn from the mirror.

* * *

We pull up outside a local diner called Pete's Place. I take a deep breath and will myself to relax my shoulders which have crept up to my ears. Summer gives me a small smile and pops open her door. I follow her into the mostly empty restaurant. Other than a few people sitting at the counter, the rest of the homey diner is deserted.

The walls are dark and wood-paneled, making it feel more like a cabin than a diner. Lots of fishing bits decorate the walls, old-fashioned fishing baskets hang next to quaint artwork of the local fishing hole. Each of the pendant lights above the booths have fishing lures dangling from them, creating a rustic chandelier.

"Hey, man," Jared says when we approach, standing from the booth in the far corner and sticking his hand out. I give it a firm, but not aggressive shake and let go. "Hey, Summer," he says, giving her a small smile.

We exchange greetings and then sit for a while in a silence that feels like an itchy tag on your shirt. We make small talk about the menu and then dwell in the palpable collective relief when our waitress comes by. After we place our orders, Jared says, "So, um before we get talking about anything else, Ryan, I just want to apologize for being so rude to you. My therapist has helped me see that you did nothing wrong and I was just taking my anger out on you."

"And Summer," I can't help but add. If he was just pissed at me, I could have taken it no problem, but he's been downright foul to her.

His eyes narrow, brows drawing down before he takes a breath and his expression clears. He says, "And Summer. You're right. I've already apologized to her and will continue to. If you had met me a year ago, you would know that this isn't who I usually am. It's not an excuse, but it's been a hard adjustment. Anyway, I'm sorry for how I acted and the things I said."

I hold out my hand and say, "I forgive you, man. It's been a hard run for all of you. Clean slate?" He shakes my hand and smiles tightly. The tension surrounding our table releases slowly and we're able to make pleasant small talk. Forgiving him is easy if it means it will make things better for Summer and Emma.

We all dig into our meals and chat, feeling out this new dynamic with tentative hands. Honestly, when Jared's not being a dick, I can see why people seem to like the guy. He mostly talks about his daughter (with a glowing reverence reserved only for goddesses and Emma apparently) and briefly mentions football with an eye to Summer who checks out the moment team affiliations are compared.

We're all leaning back, pleasantly stuffed with greasy diner food and sipping on our sodas when Jared's phone rings. He pulls it out, scowls at the screen, silences it, and places it face-down on the table. A few seconds later, it kicks up again. He releases a long-suffering sigh and answers it. "What's up, Duncan?" I catch Summer glaring down at the condensation ring her Coke leaves on the table and lean into her a bit so she knows I'm here with her. She nudges me back in acknowledgement.

"What? I can't hear you, dude." He looks around the diner, clearly not wanting to disturb anyone. Jared's frustration is written in the angry slash between his brows as he stabs at a button on his phone.

Suddenly, Duncan's voice is loud and clear when he says, "Bro. I got so shitfaced—" and with that, Jared slides out of the booth and strides across the diner towards the exit. Summer looks even more pissed, but I'm absolutely frozen.

She nudges my foot. "Ryan? You okay?"

I turn my widened eyes from the table to her, and her eyes widen in response. "That's the voice," I all but whisper.

"Huh?"

"The one who told me to pick up Emma," I say quietly. Her face pales and her eyes get impossibly wider.

She hisses, "Are you sure? That's the voice?"

"Almost positive. It was a little hard to make out like I said, but it sounded the same."

Summer stands, breaks into a light jog across the restaurant, and yanks a bewildered-looking Jared back towards our booth. He plops down in his seat across from me and shoots her an incredulous look when she wrestles the phone from him. All the while, Duncan is bragging about grabbing some poor serving girl's ass and describing said ass in excruciating detail.

"This jackass is the voice you heard?" Summer quietly clarifies one last time.

I wrinkle my nose in disgust as he starts describing how he plans to get her number before leaving and nod. Jared looks between the two of us, and says, "Sounds good, Dunc. I'll call you back," before ending the phone call.

"What did you say?" he asks me, brows drawn into a confused pucker.

"I said, that's the voice I heard last week telling me to go pick up Emma," I say, looking him in the eye.

His whole body recoils and he says, "No. There's no way in hell that Duncan would do something like that. I know he's had some issues lately—" Summer's scoff cuts him off, but he continues, "You have to have gotten it wrong."

"I told you it was him. I had a bad feeling," Summer says, looking at Jared accusingly.

I shake my head adamantly. I would know that voice anywhere because I've replayed it in my mind a thousand times since then. "No, I don't think I'm wrong. I swear, other than some of the stuff I've heard about him and Summer, I don't have any bad blood with him. He was annoying at the bar, but it's not like it went anywhere. I have no reason to lie to you."

"Didn't you say the call sounded like whoever made it had bad service? You probably just didn't hear it clearly enough," he reasons, leaning back in his chair with his arms crossed.

Summer throws her hands up and hisses, "Why are you always so prepared to defend that asshole?" I wince as two of the older men sitting at the bar turn their heads to look at us.

Jared fixes her with a hard stare. "Because he's like a brother to me. You know that! We've been friends since preschool. Like I said, I know he's been struggling with getting his drinking under control, but he would never do anything that would jeopardize Emma."

"But this didn't jeopardize Emma. As much as you didn't like me, you knew that I would never harm your child. I'm sure if you and Duncan are as close as you say you are, he knows that too," I reply.

Suddenly, Summer sits straight up. She covers her mouth with her hand and says, "Jared. Oh my God. Don't you remember back in high school, when we first started dating, Duncan and some of your other friends prank-called me? Duncan pretended to be you on the phone. I can't even remember what he said, but I know it was something dumb and I was sure it was you. You spent the next few days convincing me it wasn't. Remember? You even had him call me on the phone while you were next to me. That's the only reason I believed you."

I watch as the color slowly drains out of Jared's face and then returns, turning it nearly purple. "That motherfucker," he growls. He narrows his eyes at me, "He did this because of your run-in at his apartment. He called me afterward all up in arms because he said you were being a dick."

"I wasn't! I just told him that maybe he should lay off the drinking because he was stumbling around drunk in the middle of the day. How does that man even work a job? It seems like he's always drunk," I say, shaking my head in exasperation.

"He works with me," Jared says uncomfortably. "I let him sleep it off in my office if he seems too out of it."

"That is so beyond dangerous. For both of you!" Summer explodes.

"I know! Okay? Save the lecture. Can we get back to the more important thing?" Jared shoots a furtive glance at the old men who are now conspicuously turned with an ear towards us.

"What, that he tried to get me arrested for kidnapping?" I scoff.

"I wouldn't say that. I bet he was just trying to make you break the custody agreement. He probably just wanted you two to have to jump through more hoops for me. His twisted way of helping me get some revenge," Jared says.

"I don't think it was that innocent," Summer retorts leaning forward, "He didn't know the sign-out procedure for Emma's gymnastics, and even if he did, he couldn't have known that Ryan was on the approved list because not even you knew. I only put him on there because I wanted to make sure Emma would always have someone who was able to pick her up. My car has been acting up so much and you've been out of range pretty often with the new job site, so I wanted to make sure she had someone with a reliable car on there. I wasn't going to actually ask him ot pick her up unless it was an emergency."

Jared's mouth pinches and he visibly deflates. "I really don't think he meant to hurt Emma," he reiterates weakly, scrubbing his hands over his hair.

"No, I don't think he did. As screwed up as he is, I don't think he would ever try to hurt her. But, I could see him trying to hurt Ryan if he thought it would help you, and if he felt that Ryan belittled him," Summer says gently. "I know you care about him, but this is more than a step too far. I'm not going to tell you what to do about your friendship with him, but you also have to think about the fact that he impersonated you, called me to see if I would answer, and then messed with our kid. That's not right, and it shows a level of premeditation that tells me this wasn't random. I really think you need to confront him and see if you can get him to get some help. There's something seriously wrong with him, and I don't want him anywhere near Emma."

"Okay, that's fair. Let me talk to him, please," Jared says, looking hollowed out.

Summer nods, then tilts her head to the side in consideration. "Maybe we both should since it's about Emma and my boyfriend," she says. He nods his agreement and sighs, looking like he just aged a few years.

After a beat of silence, I ask "What I'm not getting is how did he know you were going to be late to pick up Emma?"

"I was with him before then. I spent some time watching

Emma, but since the class was a couple of hours long, I went to see him and check in on him a bit. I've been worried lately and I hoped that if he had someone popping in on him, he would shape up. He's not close with any of his family, so I'm kind of all he's got," Jared closes his eyes briefly and then continues, "I was with him when they called me into work. I told him about it because he saw me take the call. He even asked if I thought I would be back in time to get Emma. I thought he was just being a concerned friend." He huffs an unamused laugh. I incline my head in acknowledgment because I don't know what to say. How do you respond to that kind of betrayal?

"I'm really sorry, Jared," Summer mumbles.

"Yeah," he replies, "Me too. I had no idea he would ever do something like this." He rubs a hand over his mouth. "Okay, well I should probably get Emma from my parents so I can get her in bed. I'll give you a call tomorrow Summer, okay? We'll get with Duncan soon. Whenever my parents are good to watch her again, I guess." With that, he stands from the table and slouches toward the door. I've never seen a man look so much like a kicked dog before in my life.

CHAPTER 39

Summer

Ryan spends the night with me and I finally have a solid eight hours of uninterrupted sleep. While I'm so beyond angry at Duncan, I also feel a huge sense of relief that it's not some unknown psychopath plotting Emma's kidnapping. When I wake to a slow Saturday morning, I feel peaceful for the first time in weeks. I leave a still-sleeping Ryan in bed and pull on a thin, waffle-knit robe.

I start my ancient coffee maker and sit in the breakfast nook bathing in the warm, buttery sunlight that pours through the window. My various plants stretch towards the sun in supplication, and I close my eyes soaking in the peace. After a few moments, the coffee maker dings, letting me know it's time to pour a cup. I open my eyes and go about fixing my coffee the way I like it. I decide to make some pancakes for the two of us even though Emma isn't here. Saturday pancakes are a tradition I carried over from my mom and began when Emma was just a toddler. Even when she's not here, I find myself reaching for the ingredients.

After I flip the first couple of pancakes, Ryan walks into the kitchen shirtless and mouthwatering. Of their own accord, my eyes trace down the lines of his chest and stomach, then back up to his smirking, cocky mouth. "Hungry?" he asks, voice raspy with sleep.

"Starved," I reply, swatting his pec with my spatula. "I made coffee," I say, gesturing to the half-full pot. This moment brings me back to the first time I had him in my kitchen. *'Thirsty?'* he had asked. I had been too shy to tell him then that I was the Sahara, and he was the rush of clouds promising rain.

"I know, the smell woke me up. Thank you for making breakfast." He grabs a mug dotted with Christmas trees and candy canes from the cabinet above the coffee maker and fills his cup. It's his favorite one. I finish the pancakes and we sit down at the table to have breakfast together.

After we spend most of our meal chatting, Ryan nudges me with his elbow and asks, "When do you think you and Jared will talk to him?"

"Maybe today? Jared's mom is always happy for a chance to watch Emma since she's the only grandbaby, so I'm sure she wouldn't mind another few hours of babysitting duty."

He cups the back of my neck and gently pulls me in, teasing featherlight kisses over my whole face before pressing his lips to mine. "Mm better make good use of the last of our alone time this weekend then," he says in a low rumble. He slides his lips along mine before angling me so our mouths can slant together. He kisses me deeply before pulling away with a chuckle when I whimper in protest. "What do you say?"

He kissed me into confusion, so I blurt out, "please?" assuming he wants me to be polite about asking for more. He groans and pulls me to stand.

He leans in close, breath tickling my neck and sending goosebumps down my arms, "I meant, devious woman, does spending some time with me inside you sound good?" He pulls me close, hand on the small of my back so we're pressed fully against each other.

I feel my face split into a teasing smile because I know how much of a hold my next words have over him, "Yes, please."

* * *

A few hours later, Jared and I are sitting in his truck in front of Duncan's apartment. Luckily, Jared's mom was more than happy to take Emma for the afternoon.

"So, what's our plan of attack?" I ask when I can't take the silence anymore. I rub the worry stone that Ryan got me in rhythmic circles with my thumb. The smooth texture is soothing. It's something I've been relying on to help ground me the last few weeks.

He scrubs a hand over his hair, making it stick up. "I don't know. I guess we'll go in together. Just let me do the talking, okay? I think he'll listen better if it's coming from me."

"Does he even know I'm going with you?"

"No, I figured he wouldn't agree if I told him," Jared replies sheepishly.

"Well, this is going to go well," I say sarcastically.

"Let's just get this over with," he states, pushing his door open. I sigh and get out as well. We walk across the grass toward Duncan's apartment and Jared knocks on the door in a five-knock pattern they've used since they were kids. The door opens and the smile that stretches Duncan's swollen face drops the second he notices me.

"Oh God, you're back together again aren't you," he says with a sigh. He steps aside and gestures for us to follow him into the cluttered space. "I *thought* we were just having a boys day," he says, casting a bloodshot glare in Jared's direction. He hikes up his black basketball shorts and tugs down his t-shirt.

Jared shuts the door behind us and says, "Sorry, man. We have something to talk to you about, and no, it's not that we're together again. We're not, and that's probably not happening."

"Definitely not," I say. To which, both men glare at me. "Sorry, just wanted to clarify."

"Anyway," Jared says smoothly, leading me over to the stained couch on the back wall of the living area, "Like I said, we need to talk to you." I choose to perch on the arm of the couch rather than sit on the cushions that would probably scream in horror if they suddenly gained sentience and a voice.

Duncan sinks down into a low-lying gaming chair that he's had since he was a teen. The black leather is so worn out that you can see the metal framing in some spots. "Okay," he says, the end of the word tilting up in question.

"We know you've been going through a hard time lately, and it seems like you're drunk more often than not. I'm afraid it's affecting your ability to think clearly and I'm worried about your health," Jared says, leaning forward, hands clasped between his knees. Jared has always gotten straight to the point, and it seems he's not going to treat this any differently. I shift uncomfortably on my perch and grip the worry stone harder.

Duncan rocks back in his chair like he's been physically struck "I'm fine. I can stop whenever I want. I haven't even had a drink today," he says eventually. He eyes me, clearly wondering what I'm doing here for this talk.

"It's only one o'clock," I point out helpfully. He scowls at me. Jared gives me a look as well and I raise my hands in defeat, my left one still curled around the stone.

"Even still. You know I've been having to cover your ass at work just about every week. And think about how many times I've had to pick you up from the bar in the last month alone. What do you do when I'm not able to get you because I have Emma?" Duncan casts his eyes down and shifts uncomfortably in his seat. "Please don't tell me you're driving yourself," Jared says in a stern voice I've only ever heard him use with Emma when she's doing something dangerous.

"Sometimes. But I swear, my driving isn't affected. It's only a few miles away anyway," Duncan says flippantly, sitting up straighter.

Jared drops his head into a hand and rubs at his temples with his thumb and forefinger. "Oh, Dunc. Can't you see how bad it's getting?" He looks at his oldest friend with the saddest eyes I've ever seen. I, for one, am beyond furious that he's putting other people at risk because he can't control himself or be bothered to call an Uber. I'm trying to stay true to my word, though, and keep my mouth shut.

"I'm fine," Duncan responds with a hard edge, and a challenge in his voice.

Jared pleads, "I don't think you are. I know you like to party, but it's concerning me that it seems like you're always getting drunk by yourself and making decisions I know you wouldn't normally make." I have to physically bite my lip to stop myself from talking.

Duncan heaves himself up to standing, a vein popping out in his forehead. "Listen, I don't get in your business, Jared. Stay out of mine." He points a finger in Jared's direction, and I find that I've had enough of being silent.

"Really? You stay out of his— *our* business Duncan? Is that what we're going with?" I ask, crossing my arms.

His eyes slide to mine and for a second there is so much hate in them, I'm actually a little afraid. "Yes. It is," he replies through clenched teeth. "I don't think I was talking to you anyway. And you know what? Now that you aren't together anymore, I can say what I've wanted to say for a long time. Out of respect for him," he throws a hand in Jared's direction, "I kept my mouth shut."

I scoff at that, remembering all the times he made subtle and not-so-subtle digs about me. He spits, "You think you can judge me? Meanwhile, you're over here reading porn and leaving a good man because he doesn't follow you around like a whipped puppy. You don't want a real man, you want a pet that'll bend to your every whim. That new idiot you have on a leash will learn eventually." He stands there, chest heaving as though he's just exited the pulpit.

I react as calmly as I'm capable of. In a level voice, I ask, "If you mind your business so much, why are you talking about me with anyone who will listen? Why are you even speaking to Ryan? Why are you impersonating Jared and trying to get Ryan in trouble?" At the last question, his face fades from a deep red to a sickly pale.

His eyes dart to Jared and he licks his lips. "I don't know what you're talking about," he says quickly.

In the tone of a disappointed father, Jared says, "We know it was you, dude."

Seeming to shrivel in on himself, Duncan sinks back down in his chair and runs a hand through his stringy hair. He finally looks at Jared and says, "Okay, so I might have played a prank on him. I was drunk and I thought it would be funny." He winces when he owns up to being drunk.

"How did you get drunk in the twenty minutes after I left here?" Jared asks incredulously.

He admits abashedly, "I was already halfway there when you got here. I just asked to watch TV so I could hide it."

"Hold on. Let's get back to the 'prank' thing," I say, making air quotes. "How in the hell is having our daughter taken without our permission a prank? Do you think it's funny that Jared was out of his mind with worry when he realized Emma wasn't where he left her?"

"I didn't really think about that. Like I said, I was drunk," he says flippantly. Jared shifts on the couch and I can tell from the set of his jaw that he's getting angry.

"It wasn't funny. I thought for sure something had happened to her. When I realized who she was with it just pissed me off. You know that I want Emma to have the best life possible. If I had let my anger make my decisions, Emma wouldn't be very happy right now," Jared bites out.

I lean back, my shoulders against the wall, "Can we just be honest here, Duncan? You didn't think it was funny or a prank. You were deliberately trying to get Ryan in trouble and trying to make sure Jared had a case against us." I am suddenly so beyond exhausted with this overgrown toddler and his games.

"You don't deserve to be happy!" he explodes, standing in a rage. He paces back and forth, "All you do is take, and take, and take, Summer. With no care for the people around you!"

I rear back so far that my head bumps the wall with a dull thud, "What are you talking about?"

"First you take my friend, then you baby trap him. Then, when you're sick of that little life, you drop him on his ass and move on to a new guy you can use."

I stand and take a step forward. Jared grabs my wrist and tugs so I can't go any further. "I didn't take your friend! Last time I checked, you and Jared are *still* close which is why I'm sitting here in this apartment that stinks like beer and piss to make sure you get nowhere near my kid! You're fucking deranged to be acting like this over something that happened almost ten years ago now." I pull my wrist out of Jared's grip and cross my arms.

Duncan shouts, "I was in love with you!" And then it's so quiet, I can hear his upstairs neighbor's TV running through a local commercial. My arms drop to my sides and I freeze.

"What?" Jared asks dumbly. I drop onto the couch beside him, disgusting cushions forgotten.

"I was in love with Summer," he says more quietly, looking down.

"When?" Jared and I ask at the same time, twin expressions of shock on our faces.

Duncan stalks to the small kitchen to the right of us and opens the fridge. He pops open a can of beer, chugging half of it down in one glug that would have been impressive if we were twenty-one in a frat house. He belches and turns the stink eye on us, "Don't judge okay, I need some liquid courage."

He leans against the counter that divides the room from the kitchen and stares at us. His eyes meet mine briefly, and for a second I can see the pain behind the dislike that he's worn like armor. "Do you remember when we first met?" he asks me quietly.

I think back through the years and try to pinpoint it. In a small town like Lakeland, it feels like you know everyone forever. "I don't know, maybe fifth grade?"

"Second. I sat next to you in Mr. Juarez's class. On the first day of class, my notebook got ruined because my water bottle lid wasn't screwed on right, and it spilled inside my backpack. It soaked through all the pages and the paper couldn't be used because it got so warped. When Mr. Juarez asked us to take out a piece of paper for writing practice, I started to cry because I didn't have one that wasn't ruined. I took out my messed up notebook, ready to use what I could save. I knew my parents wouldn't buy me another one because they would want to teach me a lesson, and I thought Mr. Juarez would get mad at me.

You saw me crying and gave me a piece of your own paper. The next day, you set a brand new notebook on my desk without saying a word. It had some weird rainbow animals on it, but I didn't even care because it meant that I wouldn't get in trouble with my parents for ruining my own. I kept that stupid notebook until you got pregnant."

"Are you saying you've been in love with Summer since the second grade?" Jared asks quietly. Duncan looks down at his feet, not saying anything.

To be honest, I don't remember the interaction at all. We must not have talked after that until later. I *did* have a Lisa Frank obsession all through grade school though.

Finally, he looks up at me and says, "Yes." I am so completely floored that I feel like I'm watching this play out from above.

He seems to be waiting for some sort of reaction and I finally mutter, "I don't know what to say. So when you said that I just take and take and that I would break Ryan's heart, you were thinking about yourself?" He nods once, jaw ticking under the day and a half's growth of stubble. I am completely flabbergasted.

Jared, who has morphed from shock to rage, says, "So all the time you spent trying to convince me to leave her was really because *you* wanted her?" Duncan says nothing, just takes another large gulp of beer. "You know that if you had mentioned it at *any point* leading up to us dating, I would have backed off, right? Why would you not have said anything?"

"I could see the way she looked at you! She had spent the last ten years at the time hardly looking at me, but when you start showing interest, she goes all gaga. She would just throw me little crumbs of kindness every once in a while to string me along. What would have been the point?" he finishes dully. I stiffen at the implication that my being *kind* to him was me stringing him along. *Fucking men.*

I blow an unamused laugh through my nose, "I don't know, it may have saved us all from this gigantic mess." I don't think there was ever a possibility that I wouldn't have dated Jared, no matter what he says to Duncan. We were crazy for each other at the time in a way that only hormonal teenagers can be. I just wonder if Duncan had ever told me and I was able to let him down gently if he could have moved on healthily instead of letting his pining turn into a sickness that rotted something fundamental inside him.

"Well, I didn't. So, here we are," he says glibly, crushing the now empty can of beer and setting it beside others on the scuffed counter.

"Here we are," Jared echoes with a faraway look in his eyes. Finally, he turns to me, "Summer, can I talk to Duncan alone? Here are my keys. I'll only be a minute." He drops his truck keys into my hand and I stand.

I look at Duncan and nod, I have nothing left to say to him. Nothing excuses his behavior, and honestly, it almost makes it worse that he thought he was in love with me. Maybe he was once, but it twisted into something sinister. He started to view me as an object. If he couldn't have me, no one could. And if I didn't want him, then he wanted me to suffer.

Before I walk out the door, I pause, finding I do have one last thing to say to him, "Whatever your relationship is with Jared after this is none of my business, but I want you nowhere near my daughter. I am sorry you were hurting, *and* it's no excuse for the constant bullying you subjected me to over the years and the way you've tried to interfere with my happiness over and over again. I really hope you get help, Duncan, but please, stay away from me and my daughter."

With that, I leave the small, dingy apartment and walk dazedly to the truck. I feel emotionally spent as I turn it on and get the air conditioning going. The sun is high in the sky, and I feel it baking through the windows of the truck.

Would Jared and I have had a better relationship if we hadn't had someone constantly poisoning the well? His actions are his own, but no one is free from the influence of their closest friends. He always thought that Duncan had his best interest in mind. I feel sorry for him that he's learning that that hasn't been true for a long time.

Within a few minutes, Jared leaves the apartment, shutting the door gently behind him. He walks toward the truck and hops in the driver's side. Without a word, he starts reversing out of the parking spot and driving me home. We say nothing the whole way, both processing what just happened. When he parks in front of my house, neither of us moves.

Finally, he says, "I told him I couldn't be close with him anymore. Not until he got help anyway. I feel like shit saying that when he obviously needs someone, but I just can't do it anymore. Not after–" He breaks off, inhaling sharply.

"Summer," he says brokenly, "I'm so sorry. I listened to him for years telling me over and over that you were bad for me and that you baby-trapped me. I think part of me started to believe it, even though I knew it wasn't true. It's no excuse, I know, but maybe things wouldn't have gotten so bad if I hadn't had him in my ear." He swipes at his eye with a fist.

I reach over and squeeze his shoulder, "Maybe. But, Jared, we both weren't making the other person happy. Can you honestly say that even without Duncan interfering, you actually enjoyed being with me by the end? Were you even excited to spend time with me after the first couple of years? I know it felt familiar, and in a way, that was comforting, but we both deserve more than that. We both deserve to find people we're crazy for and who feel the same about us. I'll always love you. You're the father of my child, and without you, Emma wouldn't exist," I find myself getting choked up too. I swallow through it and continue, "I wish it had worked out between us. I really do. But all we can do now is move on and be the most kickass co-parents around."

He chuckles wetly at that, clears his throat, and says, "I'll always love you, too. I'm sorry I didn't see what a good thing I had until you were gone. And I'm sorry I kept someone around who said such bad things about you."

"I forgive you. Now let's move through this and try to be happy. Life is so fucking short and it's not worth wasting time being this miserable," I say and mean it this time. I wrap my arm around his shoulders and tug him in for a brief side hug. He squeezes my waist and lets go.

"Okay. I promise to be better about Ryan. I want to get to know him, too. And listen, you can have him meet Emma whenever you want. I know the six-month thing is still a few weeks away, but I trust your judgment. I always have. I just forgot there for a little bit." I feel the hard walls he forged around my heart start to crumble. We have a long way to go, but this is a start.

"Thank you," I say earnestly.

He smiles at me, "Be happy, Summer."

CHAPTER 40

Ryan

I'm still reeling from what Summer told me yesterday when she rehashed everything with Duncan, but I'm trying to put on a happy face with her so she can relax. She seems totally emotionally spent today. I made her breakfast and we ate together in bed, enjoying a slow start to the morning. We watched some dumb comedy that pulled a few halfhearted laughs out of her.

While the credits are rolling, I finally ask her, "Do you want to talk about it?"

She sighs and snuggles deeper into my chest, "I'm okay. Things are going to be so much better from here on out. I think Jared finally realized what a colossal ass he's been and I know deep down he doesn't want to be that guy. I'm just kind of sad for Duncan, you know?"

I pull back so I can look down at her upturned face. "Duncan?" I ask incredulously.

"Listen, I know he's done some truly terrible things and I don't want him in our lives, but I can't help but feel for him. Jared never told me everything, but I know Duncan's home life was pretty awful growing up. I just wish we could have been friends instead of him twisting every kind thing I did into some sort of signal."

I squeeze her shoulder, "You know that isn't on you though, right? It was not up to you to change how he behaved."

"I know that. I just can't help but feel bad that I was the source of his pain for so many years, whether I meant to be or not," she says, eyes downcast.

"I get it. You hate to see anyone hurt. Remember that one time you accidentally closed the car window on my hand when we were going to dinner? You cried so much, I was mad at my hand for bruising." She laughs and nods. "He's an adult though, babe. It sucks that he had a bad childhood, but at some point, you have to start taking responsibility for your own actions. I love how much you care for others, but let's let this one go, okay? Please don't hold onto guilt over someone who doesn't deserve it." I kiss the top of her head.

After a beat, she says, "You know what would be a fun way to move on from this nightmare?" I roll on top of her in answer, pressing kisses over her cheeks and settling into the cradle of her lush thighs. She cackles and pushes my face playfully away from hers, "Yes obviously that, but I was thinking about a family dinner where I introduce you to Emma as my boyfriend." She shyly lowers her eyes and bites her lip to contain a nervous smile.

I feel a giant grin come on, splitting my face in half. "Seriously?" I ask. She nods and I give her a smacking kiss on the lips before rolling off of her and sitting up. I don't think the *most* clearly with her under me.

I'm so excited to meet Emma and move into this new phase of my relationship with Summer. I love being a part of her life, but I know I've missed out on a huge chunk of it since I haven't been able to be around her daughter. From everything Summer has told me about her, she's a little firecracker.

"When?" I ask. A huge smile stretches her lips and makes her eyes crinkle, and I realize once again that I am so completely, irrevocably in love with this woman.

"How about this week?" she asks. I can't help myself; I launch back on top of her and roll so she's straddling me. She squeals and laughs out, "What are you doing?"

"I'm just so excited to meet her under normal circumstances. I love her already and I haven't even had more than one conversation with her."

"How can you possibly know that?"

"Because she's half you. And I love you so much it actually physically pains me sometimes. I just know she's going to be amazing," I say truthfully.

Her eyes soften and she reaches down to stroke my cheek above my beard, "She really is. It means a lot that you're this excited."

"Of course I am. She's the most important person in your life," I say, holding her hand to my cheek. I pull it back and kiss her fingertips.

"I love you," she says, leaning down to kiss me deeply. I murmur it back against her lips and then the world shrinks down to just her and I and all the points of contact between us. She shivers and I pull the blanket over us. We fall into each other.

CHAPTER 41

Summer

Emma's shriek is piercing but joyful as she leaps over the sprinkler toy, getting splashed with cold water from the hose. She'll start first grade tomorrow, and for a second I allow myself to mourn the passing of time and that she'll never be as tiny as she is today. After that second, I shake it off. I want to be excited about all of her milestones, not dreading them. My mom only got to live so many of mine, and I just want to appreciate the ones I get with Emma.

The sliding door opens behind me making me gasp and jump. A warm arm bands around my waist, and a beard catches in my hair when the man behind it presses a kiss to the crown of my head. "Back to not locking doors, I see. It's out of spite isn't it?" Ryan asks teasingly in my ear. I laugh, give his arm a squeeze, and then gently peel it off. We decided to avoid PDA in front of her at first. I don't know how jarring it will be for her otherwise.

"Hey, Emma," I call, "There's someone here I want you to meet." I gesture to Ryan, who is now a respectable distance away, and she stops frolicking in the water to tilt her head at him.

"That guy?" When I nod, she shrugs her tanned shoulders and says, "I already know him. He got me ice cream, remember?"

I shift a bit on my feet and am suddenly uncomfortable. Why does it feel like I'm about to tell my parents about a new boyfriend? "Can you just come here please?" I plead, holding out a wide seahorse-print beach towel. Her sigh is audible over the din of the neighborhood winding down for dinners and bedtimes. Children's screaming laughs, thumping feet, and parents calling out to their kids to come eat permeate the balmy, late summer air.

She covers herself in the beach towel and plops in the nearest chair. She pushes her wet hair back and looks at Ryan, "I *did* forget your name, sorry," she says sheepishly.

He smiles and sits down in the chair opposite her. "I'm Ryan."

"That's it! I knew it started with an R, I just didn't know if it was Riley, or Robert, or something. I had a boy in my class last year named Roscoe. I told him it sounded like a dog's name and he got pretty mad at me. I thought I was being nice. I love dogs!" She says this last part to me meaningfully, and I close my eyes briefly to avoid rolling them. She's been begging for a dog forever and I haven't felt ready for it with all the changes we've had. Coconut comes to mind though, and I feel myself thaw a little at the idea.

"Dogs are pretty cool," Ryan says sagely. Emma grins at him so wide, you can see her missing lower tooth. I release a long-suffering sigh and sit in the free chair between them.

A scheming glint enters her eye and I work to get us back on topic. "Dogs are wonderful pets that are a *lot* of work. Anyway, Emma, Ryan and I have something to tell you."

She sits up straighter, the towel falling from her shoulders, "Are you gonna have a baby?"

"What?" Ryan and I both gasp in unison. I collect myself and say, "No, sweetie, not at all." She visibly deflates. "Did— did you want me to be pregnant?"

She nods, bottom lip pouting out, "Vivian from my gymnastics class is having twin baby sisters. Twins!" I heave a sigh of relief as understanding hits me. She is obsessed with babies and used to frequently badger Jared and me to have more. It never felt like the right time. But now... I look over at Ryan and pictures of a little mini him flash through my head. I smile a little, *maybe one day.*

"Ah, I see. Well, I'm sure once Vivian's mom says it's okay, you can go over to play with her and meet her sisters," I say. Emma nods and adjusts her posture again, sadness forgotten. "Back to the point. Emma, Ryan and I are dating and have been for almost six months now," I end in a rush.

"Oh. Okay," she says with a shrug. Then she turns narrowed eyes on Ryan, "Hey, you told me you were just friends at Swirl!"

Ryan raises his hands defensively, "It wasn't up to me to tell you. That was between your mom and dad." I subtly kick his shin under the table for throwing me under the bus.

I give Ryan a look and turn my eyes back to Emma, "We wanted to make sure things were serious before we told you, hon. You've already gone through a lot of change."

Emma rolls her eyes in a way that sends a shiver down my spine because she looks *exactly* like me when she does it. "I'm not a baby anymore, Mama. Besides, it's pretty cool to have two bedrooms. Other than missing you or Daddy, it's been kind of fun."

"Well, I'm glad," I say, and it's true. I am so happy that despite everything I've gone through, the only thing she's gotten out of it is that it's fun to have two rooms. I'm proud of myself and Jared because we've made sure her life is as great as we could make it, even if we were struggling. "But, just so you know, nothing is going to change for you for a while. You just might see Ryan around more now that Dad and I are comfortable with that. Is that alright with you?"

She shrugs. "Sure. I don't care," she says, turning to Ryan, "You're pretty cool."

"Is that opinion based on the fact that I bought you ice cream after gymnastics?" he asks playfully.

"Well yeah," she replies in a tone that implies *duh,* "And also you make my mom happy. She smiles and laughs way more now." Leave it to kids to deliver an emotional gut punch right before asking, "Can we have pizza now? I'm hungry." I nod, baffled at how smoothly that conversation went, but choosing not to question it.

Ryan and I stand and lead her inside where the smell of pepperoni pizza wafts in the air. I instruct Emma to go get changed into some dry clothes and Ryan and I go to the kitchen to get everything ready. He picked up the pizza on the way over and my mouth waters in anticipation. Calypso's Pizza is the best local pizza place, and we decided to pull no punches today. Ryan grabs some plates from the cabinet and says, "That went well."

"It did. Better than I was expecting, honestly. I wasn't sure if she was still holding out hope for Jared and me." I pull a few slices off for Emma and get her water ready. Then I remember something and say, "Shoot, I'll be right back. Emma is probably looking for some clean shorts and I think they're all in the dryer." I grab her shorts from the laundry and enter her room with a knock.

As predicted, she's still dripping in her swimsuit and pulling drawers open haphazardly. "I can't find anyy shorts, Mama," she says, throwing me a look over her shoulder.

"I know, sorry. I was washing clothes today." I shut the door behind me and walk across her room to hand them to her.

"Thanks," she replies, peeling out of her wet swimsuit.

When she's in her dry shorts and a tank top, I ask, "So are you really okay with Ryan and me?"

She nods and gives me a little smile, "Yeah. Actually, I have something to tell you." My head tilts in confusion and she says in a rush, "One day a couple of months ago I went in your closet looking for that feather scarf thing that you wore last Halloween because I was playing dress up and wanted to wear it. I saw a man's clothes I knew weren't daddy's, and then when Ryan said he was your friend, I sort of knew he was lying." I sigh and look up at the ceiling, counting to ten in my head. "I know I'm not supposed to go in your room alone, I'm sorry." Her chin wobbles and I pull her into me.

"You're forgiven. Thank you for being honest with me."

She leans back from the hug to look at me, her eyes wet, "I really am happy about Ryan. I can tell you like him, and I think he really likes you."

"You think so?" I ask.

She nods and says, "He looks at you the way Flynn Ryder looks at Rapunzel at the end of the movie." She shrugs and I can see that's about all it takes for her. "And I love Daddy, but he never looked at you like that." I laugh because she's probably right. I don't think Jared has looked at me like that in a long time.

"Well, it must be because I'm a princess," I say, swiping her plastic tiara off her dresser and perching it on my head.

She giggles and says, "Come on, I want pizza." She takes me by the hand and tugs me out of the room.

Ryan sees the tiara on my head when we enter the kitchen and he raises a brow at me, mouthing *I like it*, over Emma's head. "Your majesties," he says with a haughty British accent, bowing low and grabbing my hand to place a kiss on the back of it. Emma laughs at his antics and curtsies before hustling to the pizza awaiting her on the table. We spend the next hour gorging ourselves on pizza, laughing, and chatting. I watch as Ryan makes his crust dance a jig and then bow to Emma's utter delight.

I sit back and feel a pleasant tingle run down my spine as it sinks in: this is my real life. I look from my laughing, pizza-sauced daughter to the man who feels like I tore him from the pages of a book and feel a deep sense of peace. Of home.

Epilogue

I usher an eight-year-old Emma with her overnight bag out the door and wave to Georgia, Vivian's mom who is parked in my driveway. Emma tosses her bag in the car and dives in after it, squealing with her friend. They are so thrilled to be having their first sleepover.

It's a milestone that makes me miss my mom. She always wanted to be the sleepover house so she went above and beyond to make them fun with my friends. We would rent movies, have a giant pillow nest in front of the TV to lounge on, and have as many snacks as our hearts desired. She would have face masks and nail polish at the ready. She knew the perfect blend of hanging out with us to guide the way and giving us space to have fun. If she were here, she would have insisted Emma do it at home and she would have orchestrated some elaborate ordeal to celebrate her first.

I shake away the bittersweet thought as I'm reminded that Ryan and I will have the night to ourselves. We've been wanting to watch the newest Marvel movie and it's finally up on streaming services, so we'll get to. Jared and his new girlfriend, Clarissa, said it was really good when they went to see it in theater a few weeks ago. They recently started dating, and seeing movies has sort of been their thing. I'm happy about it because I always get a review afterward. I really like Rissa and I hope they last.

I walk back inside and heave a large sigh. "You good?" Ryan asks from his position on the couch next to our puppy, Honey. Even if I don't voice what's happening in my head, he always can guess at my feelings. He has a built-in Summer-sensor.

"I'm fine. Excited for her, and a little nervous too. I just hope she doesn't get scared tonight." I plop on the couch and cuddle into his other side. I reach across his lap to give Honey a pat.

"If she does, she'll call and we can pick her up," he says reassuringly. I nod and tuck in closer, not able to get enough contact even after almost two years with the man.

"Hey, do you mind grabbing the snacks while I pull up the movie? I got you a few different options at the store because I didn't know what you'd be feeling tonight. I know we're celebrating your birthday tomorrow with everyone else, but I wanted to spoil you a little tonight, too," He says, kissing me on the temple. I smile because of course he would want to spoil me multiple days in a row. This man.

"Sure," I say, standing to head into the kitchen. I cross the threshold and see a grocery bag on the counter stuffed with all manner of sweet and salty treats. I paw through the bag to see what he bought. He calls my name and it sounds like it's coming from directly behind me. I turn in confusion, "Y-," I start to say, but stop when I see him on one knee behind me, Honey wagging her tail excitedly in the background. I sag against the kitchen counter and clutch my hands to my chest.

He's holding up a ring box and the diamond in the center catches the light. "In the years before I met you, I was constantly searching for my place in this life. I just wanted to belong and feel like I was moving towards something meaningful. I had a gut feeling that I might find that here. The first time I saw you, I knew that I had to get to know you. Of course, I thought you were beautiful, but you had a magnetism that drew me in. Then, when I saw you cradling that giant dog in the pitch black and the pouring rain, I knew I was in trouble because I fell hard for you right away. At the time, I figured it wasn't rational, but now I know. I know that we were meant to find each other. I know that all the hard things that led us here were meant to happen so we could be strong enough to fight for us. I know that I love you with everything I have and everything I am. I know that to be with you is to be home. So, Summer Renee Evans, will you marry me and make an honest man out of me?"

I can't help the laugh that bubbles up through the tears. We've been living together for the last several months, and he's constantly made jokes about me stealing his virtue. I reach a hand out so I can pull him to standing. I look up at this man who will be my husband soon and say, "Yes, absolutely. I love you so much. I never thought I would find someone like you. I never thought I deserved someone like you. But you've helped me see that we deserve each other and all the good things. I am so happy that I get to find little moments of joy with you for the rest of my life."

He places a gentle hand under my chin, tilting it up so our lips can meet. The promise in this kiss is so tangible, I can taste it. He pulls away when Honey rears back on hind legs to join our embrace, takes the ring out of the box, and slides it on the ring finger of my left hand. We both laugh when Honey pads away, seeming to understand that no treats will be had just yet.

He doesn't let go and instead tilts my hand this way and that so the overhead lighting catches on the oval center stone and glitters off the diamonds along the band. We admire it together for a second, heads angled down, basking in the rightness of this moment. He lifts my hand to his lips and presses a kiss to my knuckles. I gently free my hands to wipe the tears that formed along my lashes. I look up to see that he has tears turning his eyes a verdant green. I reach to swipe them away too. "Why are you crying?" I ask thickly.

"I'm just so happy. I can't believe I get to call you my wife soon," he says with a watery grin.

I appraise him teasingly. "How soon are we talking?"

"Tomorrow if possible," he holds up a staying hand when he sees my panic, "But since I know that won't happen, how about as soon as we can reasonably get it together? I think Em would kill me if I took away her opportunity to be the flower girl."

"Did she know what you were planning?" I ask incredulously.

"Oh yeah. Who do you think helped me ferret a ring that would fit out of your jewelry stash so I could get it sized? She knew the exact costume ring that fits on your ring finger." I laugh exasperatedly and he chuckles, "I know. She knows she isn't supposed to go through your things, but I figured this was an exception," He lifts my hand meaningfully, eyeing the beautiful ring.

"I can't even care right now. I'm ridiculously, stupidly happy," I say. I pull him down to me for another long kiss that leaves us both breathless. I break away first and say, "Come on, fiance, let's go watch that movie. I really do want to see it."

"Fiance, huh? I like the sound of that." He grabs the oversized snack bag and leads me back to the living room. Honey curls up on the rug in front of the couch. My heart is still racing when we pull up the movie.

As the opening credits roll, I can't help but look at him and admire the anticipation on his face. I clasp our hands together, expecting the new ring to feel a little odd as I adjust to it's presence. I look down, watching the diamond twinkle, and know why it doesn't seem strange at all. It already nestles into my finger like it's right where it's meant to be. I smile up at Ryan. I know the feeling. I cuddle in closer, resting my head on his shoulder, and we watch as a new story unfolds in front of us.

A Note from the Author

Hello again, dear reader! I hope you loved Like Home. If you did, please consider leaving a review. Like any indie author, word-of-mouth is one of the main ways I reach new readers. Every time you tell someone about my book or share a post online about it, you're helping more than you know!

I read all positive reviews because it gives me so much joy to know that my words took up a little real estate in your heart. I hope that Summer and Ryan gave you a dose of happiness.

If you would like to leave a review and you're on an e-reader, here's a link to do so. If you're reading this via paperback, please consider grabbing your phone or laptop and dropping a review on your favorite sites–Goodreads, StoryGraph, etc. I am endlessly grateful to you for reading this book (presumably to the end) and for leaving a review. Thanks a bunch!

—Megan

Acknowledgments

Okay, so I'm really bad at acknowledgements. Mostly because I get in my head about who, exactly, I'm supposed to thank, and then I start thinking I should thank *everyone*. Which would probably be nuts.

Anywho, my first thank you goes to my wonderful husband, Joe, who has always supported me and encouraged me no matter what harebrained ideas I come up with—like writing a book eleven months postpartum (and finishing it three years later.) And he also deserves a thank you for giving me inspo for my MMCs and being by my side for twelve years now. Love you, babe.

My next biggest thank you goes out to my amazing friend, Mikayla, who read the earliest, roughest draft of Like Home. Thank you for being so encouraging and excited when I told you I was writing a book—you truly gave me the courage to keep going! She was also a beta reader for me (and probably breathed a sigh of relief that the *rough* first draft was going somewhere). All around, one of my best friends and the greatest sounding board any time I got stuck or felt unsure.

I have to thank my parents for always encouraging me to read and write as much as I wanted. I know you both thought my insatiable reading was strange (maybe concerning?), but you supported me anyway. Mom, thanks for always being my biggest cheerleader and believing that I really could do whatever I set my mind to. You've always believed that I would write a book, and here we are! Love you both.

I would like to thank all of my wonderful beta readers for

taking the time to help me make Like Home the best it can be. Your feedback was invaluable, and you helped me catch so much I would have missed. Thank you so much Cassie, Angela, Angie @getlitwithangie, Molly @bookswithmolly_bri, Kellie @sisters_reading, Claire @clairelettersandmore, Sarah @enilydd.reads, Michaela @live.inside.pages, Emily @dremilyreads, and Lizzy @tangerinegem. You all were an integral part of making Like Home what it is. I couldn't have done it without you!

I want to give a special thank you to my friend, Alex @acrochet.esq, for answering all my (not law advice) lawyer questions and being the first to read the mediation chapter. She made me ensure that the mediation process was accurate and that nothing was too outlandish. It was important to me to get it right, and she made that happen. Thanks, Alex!

I have to thank my phenomenal editor, Megan @thornsnroses.co for helping me get Like Home up to snuff. Thank you for your hard work, funny comments, and ability to be both a friend and taskmaster. Your ability to take my vision for Like Home and hone it down to its best parts made the book what it is. Thanks again!

Next I'd like to thank all the people who followed me on Instagram when my page started as a bookish fan account. You folks are the reason I picked Like Home back up and decided to give Ryan and Summer their happy ending. Thank you for the endless encouragement and being so hyped about my book even though I'm sure you were terrified that it was horrible (if it is horrible, please don't tell me lol).

Lastly, dear reader, I want to thank you. Thank you for deciding to pick up my book and reading it through the end. I hope that something about Ryan and Summer's story sticks with you. I hope you know that it's okay to ask for what you need in a partner and to walk away when you aren't being treated right. I hope you know that your body isn't a plot device and you deserve to love and be loved no matter what you look like.

About the Author

Megan Bowen is a romance author who prefers her stories with a lot of heart and a little heat. She lives in a small town with her high school sweetheart, two children, and her pup, Ruby.

Check out her website and sign up for her newsletter for all updates on future projects www.authormeganbowen.com